# Because of Liam

RIGGINS U
Book 2

# BECAUSE OF LIAM

RIGGINS U SERIES - BOOK TWO

ERICA ALEXANDER

This is a work of fiction. Any resemblance to actual persons living or dead, businesses, events or locales is purely coincidental.

**ISBN-13: 978-1-7324215-3-0**


Cover design and formatting by Serendipity Formatting.
Editing by Lawrence Editing.
Proofreading by Carol Tietsworth.

**DISCLAIMER:** The material in this book is for mature audiences only. It is intended only for those aged 18 and older.

*To those who can't remember and*
*those who wish to forget.*

# CHAPTER ONE

## River

The funny thing about life—and I don't mean ha-ha funny—is that those pivotal moments, the moments that change everything in an instant never give you a warning. They hit you with the force of a CAT5 hurricane and most of the time, there's no heads-up. No blaring sirens to alert you to run for cover and bunker down. No pivotal weatherman on TV telling you the life-changing forecast. It always hits you in your blind spot. When you least expect it and think you have everything figured out. Or in my case, nothing figured out yet, just flip-flopping around and trying to fight the current.

The other funny thing about life is that most of the time, when you get hit with that life-changing moment, you don't even know until it's too late.

The morning starts like any other morning as winter begrudgingly gives up its grip to spring. And spring gracefully takes charge, washing the gray away and painting it blue. Hopeful shots of green break through the ground between stubborn spots of dirty snow. It's mid-March, but I've been craving summer and a fresh-made raspberry lemonade, so I make my way to Pat's Cafe to get me some. As I walk outside sipping the sweet and tart drink only Pat can make this perfectly, I see Logan across the street, looking into the open hood of the black SUV parked in his driveway. He's wearing a black beanie, camouflage cargo pants hanging low on his hips, and he's shirtless despite the nip in the air. He's facing away from me as I reach his side of the street. Logan looks . . . bigger. He looks good. Really good, more muscular, and for the first time I notice the huge tattoo on his back. Skye never told me Logan had a tattoo. I don't remember seeing a tattoo that one time I got an eye-full when I caught them in the shower. It must be new.

A beautiful, intricate design of a Bald Eagle and a dragon in battle takes most of his torso. The dragon is on its back, wings spread wide and it's done in shades of gold, black, and green. The eagle has its talons clasped around one of the dragon's paws and its neck. The talons around the neck have red, white, and blue ribbons tied to them. And as Logan moves and flexes the muscles on his back, both the eagle and the dragon seem to come to life.

That nip in the air vanishes. My chest flushes with heat as my eyes run over the flex of muscles on his shoulders and arms, the way his muscular back tapers into a narrow waist. How much do you want to bet there's a six-pack on the other side of him?

*Jesus!* With an inward breath I realize I'm ogling my sister's boyfriend. I shake that thought away and chastise myself for the stray tinkering of my brain.

*Bad River!*

Logan never, ever caught my imagination before. What's wrong with me? I glare at my drink as if it's at fault. I decide right then and there that indeed something is off with the fruity drink, it's evil and is trying to corrupt me.

He hasn't noticed me yet. His back is covered in a thin sheen of sweat despite the chill in the air and a too golden tan for this time of the year. I wonder if his skin tastes as good as it looks. I lick my lips in anticipation of his taste.

*Crap on a cracker! What the hell is wrong with me?*

I swear someone spiked my lemonade. I hold the drink as far away from me as my arm will allow and look daggers at it. An evil thought crosses my mind and with a smirk, I remove the top, take two soft steps closer to him and on my tiptoes with a stretched arm, I dump the evil drink down Logan's neck and back.

Then, I step back and wait with a big mischievous smile on my face as Logan jumps and whirls around with a string of curses under his breath. All of which start with the letter F.

Except that when he spins around lighting fast and looks at me, with his right hand raised in a fist and a furious expression on his face, it's not Logan. It's not Logan at all. I mean, this guy looks like Logan, maybe a younger version of him, but it's not Logan's easy smiling face that looks at me. This man is a different person. There's no softness to him, no warm smile or the calmness Logan always radiates.

Looking at this man's gray eyes, I feel like I've just fallen into a raging storm. And shit, if I'm not the target of all that fury. Yep. I just stepped into a CAT5 hurricane and I had no warning.

My feet take another step back under the intense assault of his stare.

"What the fuck!" It comes out through gritted teeth. His voice is low and dangerous and there's a promise of retribution in it.

"I-I, you're not Logan—" I stammer. I'm fucking stammering! Me! River! Stammering! *Fucking poisoned lemonade!*

"No shit, Sherlock!" His right hand, raised.

I flinch and for the briefest moment there's a flash of regret in his eyes, but it's gone as fast as it came. He lowers his hand to his side, still in a fist.

"River?"

With my heart thundering, I look toward the voice calling my name and see Logan. Relief washes over me, as he gets closer and puts a protective hand over my shoulder, squeezing it lightly.

Logan takes in my startled stance, the empty cup in my hand, the melting ice on the ground and liquid still dripping from the not-Logan guy standing next to us and reaches the right conclusion.

"Let me guess, you thought he was me and dumped your drink on him?"

"Yes, I was wondering when you got the tattoo…"

I glance at not-Logan. His chest is wide and muscular. He has a few faint scars over a pec and shoulder and there's a dusting of light brown hair that disappears into his shorts. And the six-pack is there too. It does not disappoint. *Eyes up, River!* My chest goes tight and a swirl of emotions I can't quite pinpoint flutters about me. *Get a grip girl.*

"I'm really sorry." I hate how he makes me feel. Out of balance, out of sorts. For a moment I thought he'd hit me. A flash of a memory blinks in my mind so fast I can't get a hold of it.

He scared me and I never ever scare. Ever. Except, that one time. *Shut up. So not the time to think about that.*

The Logan look-alike is still on guard, his hands in fists opening and closing like he's trying to gain control. There's something off about him. He looks angry, but the level of anger is more than what the silly prank I played on him warrants.

"Liam, this is River, Skye's sister. River, this is my baby brother, Liam. He's a medic in the marines."

"Corpsman," Liam corrects Logan.

For the first time Liam's murderous eyes leave my face and lock on his brother's. I can tell by the scowl in his expression that Liam hates being referred to as his *baby brother*. He looks back at me then as if taking me in for the first time. His gray eyes look me up and down, taking in the knee-high black boots, black leggings, and loose gray cardigan I'm wearing. His eyes drop to the purple scarf around my neck before meeting my own. His eyes are darker now. The storm still brewing. They soften for a fraction of a second and then harden again.

"What the fuck is wrong with you?"

It's not a question but an accusation. My dislike for him grows.

"Easy there, brother. No harm, no foul. Looks like you needed cooling off, anyway." Logan deflects attention to himself again.

Liam levels his gaze on me one last time and without saying a word stalks off.

"Where are you going?" Logan calls after him.

Liam keeps walking as he answers his brother, anger in his voice. "To shower. I smell like a fucking fruity girly cocktail."

I turn to Logan and say loud enough for Liam to hear me. "Your brother is an asshole!"

Liam's step falters, but he doesn't turn and keeps walking. My eyes track him up the driveway and onto the veranda that takes up the entire front of the blue colonial style house until he disappears behind the closed door. My eyes linger until I can feel Logan studying me with a curious expression on his face.

"I didn't even know you had a brother. Where did he come from?"

Logan scratches his head and presses his lips. He takes a deep breath and exhales. "Afghanistan."

I look at the house and back at Logan. "Afghanistan?"

"Yeah, he showed up late last night."

"Then, is he on a break between tours?"

"I think this is it for him."

Curiosity puts words in my mouth and I can't help asking questions. "How long did he serve?"

"He's been gone over five years."

I notice the odd tone to Logan's voice and the choice of words. *"Gone"* as opposed to served.

"Five years? Your brother doesn't look old enough to have served that long."

"He enlisted at eighteen, on the last day of high school and his birthday."

"Wow, on his birthday?"

"Yeah, we were all surprised."

"We?"

"Our family. My parents and I. Liam never talked about enlisting. He was all set to go to pre-med, or at least that was his plan then. I was away in college and didn't find out until he had already enlisted."

I don't know what to say to that. There's more to the story, I can tell, and I also know whatever it is, Logan won't be shedding any light on it today.

I turn toward the house again where Liam is.

Showering.

Naked.

I can remember all too well what his body looks like and my imagination fills the gaps for the parts I didn't see. I blame the lemonade for my stray thoughts. The ever-present voice in my head says, *Yeah, blame the lemonade all you want. You know you're glad he's not Logan.*

*Shut up!* I mutter under my breath, nod at Logan in lieu of a goodbye, and go to class.

---

I FINALLY MAKE it home after four classes and a study group today. I have classes every Tuesday, Wednesday, and Thursday, and an internship at a behavioral health clinic the rest of the week. Skye and I are going different ways after graduation in May. She'll work at a local newspaper. Skye's pretty excited about landing this job as we can still share the apartment and she can be near Logan. She's taking a combination of on campus and online classes for her master's in English. I decided to go on full-time, getting a master's in psychology with two different tracks. My original track was for guidance counseling and I'm still pursuing it. Can you picture me counseling high school kids? The second track was a last-minute addition after —I shake my head to get rid of the path it's going down.

I'm still thinking about the events of this morning. In hindsight dumping my raspberry lemonade on someone's back may not have been the best idea I've ever had. But I honestly thought it was Logan and he wouldn't have gotten mad at me.

I can't wait for Skye to get home so I can ask her about Liam. Right on cue, the door opens.

She kicks off her shoes and drops her bag on the kitchen island before turning my way.

"Hey, what's up, Sis? Just got home too?"

"Yeah, a few minutes ago."

She looks at me intently. Skye can always tell when something is bugging me—she waits. I say nothing and she comes to the living room and sits on the other end of the sofa, legs crossed under her.

Our apartment is small, just four rooms. Our two bedrooms, the one bathroom we share and the small kitchen and living room are one open area, with the island where we have most of our meals working as a divider between the two spaces. We do have a small dining table that seats four, but we prefer to sit and eat at the kitchen island on most days. Skye could just as easily have talked to me from the kitchen, but she made the effort to come and wait for me to talk. I haven't opened up to Skye in months now. It's a habit that's hard to break after locking myself up for so long.

"Did you know Logan has a brother?"

"Yeah, he mentioned him a few times. Liam is his name, I think."

"It is. I met him today."

"Really?"

"I saw Logan too. He said his brother showed up late last night."

"Logan didn't say he was coming to visit."

"I got the impression Logan wasn't expecting him. Apparently, he came straight from Afghanistan. He's a marine."

"Yeah, I think I remember Logan saying something about him being in the military. What's he like?"

"He looks like Logan, same height but more muscular and his eyes are gray, not blue, but unlike Logan, he's an asshole."

That makes Skye frown at me. "Why would you say that?"

I rehash what happened while Skye looks at me and shakes her head.

"Can you blame him for being upset?"

"It was a little more than upset. He was angry. Angrier than my stupid prank warranted."

"Well, next time you see him, apologize again and it will be fine, I'm sure."

"I don't know, Skye, maybe he's just a real asshole. They do exist, you know."

She gets up and walks to her room. "I find it hard to believe Logan's little brother is as bad as you say. Give the kid a break."

"He's not little, and he's not a kid either," I call after her.

My annoyance has left me and I feel bad for calling him an asshole. The more I think about it, the more certain I am that I'm the asshole in this scenario. I fucking hate that.

# CHAPTER TWO

## River

As luck would have it, I meet Liam again a few days later while getting myself another raspberry lemonade at Pat's. He's getting a cup of coffee. No sugar and black. Like his soul.

He's wearing jeans, combat boots, a gray hoodie, and the same beanie as before. A couple days' worth of scruff on his face tells me he hasn't bothered to shave. Liam does that slight nod guy thing and says nothing. My eyebrows rise on their own and I take a moment to decide if I should be nice or engage the *bitch mode*. Skye's *"be nice"* words come back to remind me the promise I made to be cool. I give it a shot and take a step closer to him. He smells clean, like fresh laundry and soap.

"Good morning. It's Liam, right?"

He looks me up and down, once, twice, three times before his eyes meet mine and he acts like whatever he was looking for is lacking. He says nothing. *What. The. Actual. Fuck! Okay, I can do this.* I try again.

"We started on the wrong foot. I'm sorry for dumping my drink on you. Want to give it another shot?" I give him my best smile and a hand for him to shake.

Liam glares at me with his sugarless, bitter coffee-colored attitude and stone cold gray eyes and ignores my hand.

"Are you going to dump that drink on me again?"

I'm tempted. Oh, I'm so tempted. I look at my cup and back at him again, and I know he can read it on my face how bad I want to dump my drink on him. But it's three bucks and I'm not going to waste another lemonade. I dump words on him instead. Those are free and I got plenty of them. Screw nice. Nice is a two-way road and if he doesn't want to play nice, then neither do I.

"Did it hurt?" I ask with a small sneer.

Liam tenses. His shoulders square. "Did what hurt?"

"Did it hurt when they shoved that big stick up your ass? You know, the stick that keeps you so uptight all the time." My sneer is full-on now.

His right-hand fists and he shifts a fraction of an inch. I catch the almost imperceptible movement. Another person may not have noticed it, but for some unknown reason I'm attuned to him. I see it in the way his eyes narrow for just a moment, and how his body adjusts as if either waiting for impact or preparing to attack. I feel the tension radiating from him and I have to say, I relish in the feeling I'm not alone in this strange game of push and pull I find myself in every time our paths cross. And our paths will cross a lot thanks to my sister Skye and his brother Logan. *All because of Skye.*

"What? Are you going to punch me?" I taunt. "I know you want to do it. I can tell by the way you're moving."

"I didn't move. And I would never hurt a woman." His eyes are fixed on mine.

"Oh, you moved all right. You gave yourself away without even knowing it. And I'm sure if I had balls instead of tits, I'd be on the floor looking for my teeth right now. But as luck would have it, I'm the proud owner of an awesome rack."

His eyes drift to the aforementioned rack and linger for a long time. Long enough for my nipples to harden under his stare. Fucking nipples. It's not even cold. His eyes darken and then a different expression takes over him. I'm about to snap my fingers in his face to get his attention away from my boobs when we're both saved by Skye and Logan stepping next to us.

I know they can pick up on the tension. Heck, a rock could pick the murderous vibes between Liam and me. Skye, always the calm one, defuses it by tugging at my arm and directing me to an empty table.

"Hi, Liam, good to see you again. Come and join us."

When his eyes move to her, he smiles, and it's an honest to God real smile. His face transforms. He looks happy, younger, and carefree. None of the tension he holds around me is there. *Who the fuck is this guy and what happened to the blackened, soulless Liam?*

"Thanks, but I'll pass. I'll catch you later, okay?"

Even his voice is warm and nice. And that pisses me off even more. Why is his disdain directed only at me?

I'm not used to this kind of response from people, especially not from guys. Catty girls' jealousy every so often? Yes, I get that. But I've never been the target of such unveiled dislike. I pissed him off with my juvenile drink-dumping prank. But I apologized. Twice. I tried to be nice. Didn't I?

If he wants to play it like that, I can too. Game on.

# CHAPTER THREE

## Liam

Meeting River again at the café did not go as I expected. I hadn't planned on being an ass yesterday morning—I had every intention of apologizing the next time we met. After our initial encounter four days ago, I had time to think on why I reacted the way I did.

The old me—the me before deployment wouldn't have had that reaction. River is not the reason for my anger, just the target. No idea why, either. Well, maybe I do know a little if I'm to be honest with myself, but I'm not going there. One look at her and my hackles rise. I can blame it on the drink dumping. It really pissed me off. Not so much the getting wet part, but how easily she sneaked up on me like a freaking ninja.

I let my guard down.

Mistakes happen when I let my guard down.

Bad things happen when I let my guard down.

People die when I let my guard down.

I shake my head as if it could also shake away the thoughts inside of it. But they never really go away, do they? No. They just lie low for a while, waiting for a distraction, a weak moment, and then they come back like the sneaky little bastards they are.

Logan invited them both over for dinner. He made his lasagna. I haven't eaten it in years. If I didn't have such a hard-on for that lasagna, I'd go somewhere else, but I've been watching Logan make it for the last couple of hours. I kept trying to dunk chunks of bread in the homemade marinara sauce. The SOB kicked me out of the house and now I'm standing here on the porch steps like a kid in a timeout. The girls will be here any minute now.

I see Skye coming out of her house. Really convenient for Logan to have his girlfriend living right across the street. She's by my side a minute later. Not sure what she's holding in the large brown paper bag in her hands, but it smells fantastic. Something sweet for sure.

"I don't know what that is, but please tell me I can eat it."

She giggles a girlie laugh. There's an air of innocence about her. Maybe it's the clear blue eyes, or maybe it's the fact I've never seen her with any makeup other than lip gloss, or the way she dresses, always casual and comfortable. She's the complete opposite of Logan's ex. That one had bitch written all over her.

"You sure can, but not until after dinner."

I make an exaggerated sad face and pout. She giggles even more and goes inside without knocking. I make sure to stay out here for at least another five minutes. Don't need to witness all the face sucking I know is happening right now. Logan is crazy in love with her and she seems to be crazy in love with him too. I'm glad. Logan needs someone who loves him for who he is and not another nutcase cheating bitch. Thinking about his ex makes me think about my father and the light mood my banter with Skye put me in evaporates. Any time my thoughts stray to my father, I'm overcome with anger. It's such a dark and noxious feeling, I usually have to go for a run or work out the anger through my fists and a punching bag. Can't do either right now. I take deep breaths—once, twice, three times and the anger leaves as I make a conscious effort to let it go.

Just as I start to relax, River shows up. I don't realize it's her at first. The black, sleek Camaro with tinted windows stops right in front of the house and the passenger door opens. She leans into the back seat and grabs something—a backpack, then leans toward the driver again. I can tell it's a guy but can't see his face from this angle. Did she just kiss him? *What the fuck? And why do I care?*

And just like that, I'm pissed all over again.

# CHAPTER FOUR

## River

When I get out of the car, the first thing I see is Liam standing on the steps leading up to the house. And he looks pissed. *Why is he looking at me like I stole the last cookie in the jar?* I just got here. I didn't even open my mouth. I didn't have a chance to piss him off. Yet.

My eyes trail down his body without my consent. Faded jeans hang low on his hips and hug him in all the right places. There's a rip above the right knee and just a little skin showing. It's not those expensive designer kind of jeans with strategic rips already placed in them. I can tell this is a well-worn and well-loved piece of clothing and it has learned the ways of his body to perfection. The faded blue T-shirt is also old and tight on his chest. It grabs at his biceps like it has shrunk from too many washes. He's not wearing a beanie today and his hair is longer than I expected and lighter than Logan's. The dying sunlight makes his skin look even more tanned and golden than before. I try not to look at him too closely. The last thing I need is for Liam to think I'm interested in him. I'd never live that down.

As my steps take me closer to him, I brace myself and hitch

my backpack up on my shoulder. We had a late study group today, and it's heavy with all the books I have to carry around.

His lips are moving and words are coming out of it, but my brain is refusing to understand what he's saying. He sounds . . . *jealous?*

"Nice little walk of shame. Or should I say ride of shame followed by a walk of shame?"

*What. The. Fuck!*

I look over my shoulder trying to understand what he's saying, but the car is long gone. Brian, the guy who always gives me a ride after late study groups, has a girlfriend and zero interest in me. Neither do I have any interest in him, for that matter. She's usually with him when he drops me off at home, but today she had to be somewhere and left earlier.

I hate the height advantage he has on me and being three steps down from him is not making it any easier. I think back on what he could have seen to assume I was coming from a hook-up. Nothing. There was nothing. I reached in the back for my bag and then gave Brian a quick goodbye hug and left. *The hug?* Maybe he thought it was something else? How well could he see into the car from this distance, anyway? It's not a long driveway, just big enough to park a car with a few feet between the bumper and the street. And even if it was true, why would it piss him off? I'm sure he can get some any time he wants. I mean, look at him? If I didn't dislike him so much, I'd go for it.

"What's your problem?"

"Just keep your hook-ups off of my property."

"I wasn't exactly fucking him on your doorstep," I say, not bothering to deny it. That seems to anger him even more.

"Just keep your hook-ups off of my property," he repeats.

"Please, you're acting like a prude or a virgin."

"I'm neither."

"Bullshit, you have to be the most uptight guy I've ever met." I can hear the accusation in my voice. "You know what you need?"

"I'm sure you'll tell me."

"Yes, I will, because no one else does."

Taking another step so we're standing on the same level, I tilt my head up to look him in the eyes.

"You. Just. Need. To. Get. Laid," I say, enunciating each word. "Get it out of your system and then you'll be a lot more relaxed."

"Are you offering?" He smirks, his face inching closer to mine.

*Well, hell. I didn't expect that response.* I look up at him as uninvited and unwelcome images of a naked Liam invade my mind. Liam wrapping his arms around me and—

I stop that train wreck of a thought. "I'm not into angry sex."

Liam's steel gray eyes darken, his voice is lower, huskier. His face so close, his breath mixes with mine and I can almost taste him. His eyes drop to my lips for a few heartbeats before looking back at me.

"No?" he asks. "What kind of sex are you into?" His voice is a whisper and a caress. "I can be very accommodating."

Everything around me seems to slow down in response to my speeding heart. My skin warms under his stare, my stomach clenches, and my nipples strain against my bra. Words escape me for a moment but come rushing back with images of a naked Liam pounding into me. When I respond him, it's with half a lie.

"The kind with multiple orgasms and the kind that *is not* with you."

# CHAPTER FIVE

## Liam

There's a collective moan as we take that first bite of lasagna. A perfect storm of flavors, melting on my tongue. The creaminess of the cheese, the tangy sauce, the freshness of the herbs, all combined into a bite of pure bliss. It's been at least three years since I tasted Mary's lasagna. MREs or military rations come in two flavors: bad and inedible. Some of the guys liked them. But I grew up spoiled with Mary preparing all our meals and she could make anything taste good.

"Bro, this is just as good as Mary's."

Logan has a big smile on his face. I could not have paid him a bigger compliment.

"Nah, you just forgot what real food tastes like."

"Who's Mary?" River asks.

Logan is sitting at the end of the table, Skye to his left, and River next to her. I'm sitting opposite to the girls—it's hard for River not to look my way when she glances over, but she's doing her damn best to avoid me. She's discreet. I don't think anyone else picks up on it. After she threw that little tidbit about multiple orgasms at me, I can think of nothing else but making her come. Multiple times. Add to that the fact I haven't gotten laid in over a year, and my dick is doing somersaults in my pants in anticipation. Maybe she's right. I do need to get laid. Now, how do I get her to be the one to take me up on it?

"Mary is our cook. Or she was when we lived at home still," I answer, my eyes staying on River.

"You had a cook?" River asks, but she directs it to Logan.

"Our mother couldn't boil water." Logan smiles at her the way one would at a little sister. There's fondness in his expression.

"Logan spent a lot of time in the kitchen with Mary and he learned to cook from her."

Skye asks, "How about you, Liam? Can you cook?"

"Liam inherited Mother's ability to cook." Logan laughs, the bastard.

"How did you two meet?" I ask. "I never heard that story."

River groans, while Logan and Skye exchange a look, and Skye's face pinks up.

A huge smile breaks on Logan's face.

"It was all because of River," Skye answers me.

"Yes! Thank you, River." Logan lifts his wine glass.

She rolls her eyes at him.

He goes on. "Well, I was almost at the end of my shift, when I see this car pull through a yellow light and go after it."

"Yep. That was me." Skye points to herself.

"When she pulls over, and I walk up to the car, I can smell alcohol."

That surprises me. I know how much Logan hates people who drink and drive.

"But it wasn't me drinking." Skye picks up where Logan stopped. "See, River was at a party and when her ride bailed on her, she called me to pick her up and she had a couple of drinks."

"It smelled like a brewery in that car," Logan adds.

"Hey, in my defense, someone spilled beer on me. I didn't drink all that much." River glances at me for a few extra seconds now.

"I told Skye to get out of the car to do a sobriety test. Best outfit ever!"

I look at Logan. "Okay, you lost me."

It's Skye's turn to groan and River's to laugh.

"She was wearing these little pajamas and pink bunny slippers. Man, I still think about that."

Skye takes over. "I left the house in a hurry to get River. I was already in bed and got the car keys and ran out, didn't even grab a jacket or my purse, which means I didn't have my driver's license on me and Logan followed me home so he could look at it."

"I'm sure he did." I smirk at him.

"Can you blame me? I mean, those PJs were small and so tight and it was freezing that night—"

Skye slaps him in the arm, but there's no heat behind it. He grabs her hand and kisses her open palm. There's a lot of heat behind that.

"Yeah," River interrupts. "But that was after she offered to give him a blowjob and decided to buy a vibrator."

I choke on my water while Logan is laughing and Skye's face turns five different shades of pink and red.

"That is NOT what happened."

River shrugs, in a very nonchalant way, like a self-satisfied cat. "That's how I remember it."

I look at the three of them and they look like a family. All these stories they share, the words they exchange with just a glance. I feel like an outsider. Like someone looking in through a window. Watching it all, but not really a part of it. It makes me a little sad and a little envious. Don't get me wrong. I couldn't be happier for Logan. I guess, I'm wishing for a bit of the same.

River sneaks looks at me when she thinks I'm not paying attention and I wonder what she sees when she does.

"You cooked, we'll clean up." Skye offers after we're done with dinner.

"Actually, you both did. Logan cooked, and you baked, I can handle the clean- up," I counter.

"I didn't do anything. I guess I should help clean up too." That's River. I'm a little surprised, but I'm not turning her down. I can see in her face that she expects me to.

# CHAPTER SIX

## River

When we finish bringing the dirty dishes to the sink, Liam asks, "Wet or dry?"

I've always enjoyed washing dishes. I find it relaxing, without thinking I say, "Wet."

The big smirk on his face tells me I've walked into a trap. The effort to avoid looking at him during dinner and the two glasses of red wine I had slowed me down. *What did I miss?* I take an extra second to get it. *Wet.* He did not ask me wash or dry. He asked *wet* or dry and I walked right into it. And he's enjoying it immensely. Something twists inside me. There's a change in the way he looks at me, in the way he's talking, and that twisty something inside me likes it entirely too much.

Fuck. Me.

And why is he asking that, anyway? Logan has a dishwasher. No need to dry anything. He's just trying to get under my skin.

I do my best to ignore him and rinse the dishes.

"I can rinse the dishes and put them in the dishwasher, no need to dry anything. You don't have to be here."

"I live here," is his smart-assed answer.

I fight the urge to roll my eyes and try again.

"Listen, it's clear you don't like me and that's fine. I'm not looking for a new best friend. But my sister and your brother are a done deal. And for both their sakes, do you think you can attempt to be civilized around me?"

His eyebrows pop up and disappear under the longish light brown hair falling over his forehead. I have the urge to push the locks off his face so I can see his eyes better.

The two times we met before he had a beanie on. Today is the first time I see Liam without it. I expected his hair to be short, military style. But it's long enough to brush the tops of his shoulders. It lends softness to his otherwise chiseled jaw and steel gray eyes. This is not the trendy haircut popular with so many guys. His hair is long because he hasn't bothered to have it cut in several months. It should look unkept and messy, but it works for him. It makes Liam more masculine somehow.

He evaluates me, trying to read any hidden meaning behind my words. This is the most honest I've been since we met. Yeah, I apologized twice before, but I didn't mean it. Not that I'm actually apologizing right now. This is more like an agreement to stay out of each other's way.

"I don't dislike you," he says. "It's just that you say some things that aren't very socially accepted."

I almost snort at that.

"You don't have to worry about hurting my feelings. Not one drop of my worth depends on your acceptance of me, and I'm not so insecure that I need to gain approval from everyone. I'm fine with you hating my guts, but maybe we can just go on ignoring each other instead of antagonizing each other."

"I don't hate your guts."

"Well, you don't like them either."

The smile that precedes his words is so sexy I have the urge to look over my shoulder and see if someone else is behind me. No way he's directing that smile at me.

"I like parts of you," he says, his eyes trailing suggestively down my body and lazily making their way back to my face until his gaze locks on mine.

Shivers dance on my spine. My skin prickles and my damn nipples get hard. Again.

I need to have a serious talk with my boobs. Either that or buy super padded bras so at least I can disguise the untimely and unwanted reaction of my traitorous body. I'm at a loss for words and his smile grows bigger. I look away from his face and catch a glimpse of something else growing bigger.

I look a moment too long. He catches me and laughs. The sound is . . . beautiful. Light and inviting. I want to wrap myself in the sound of Liam's laugh like a blanket—it warms me and fills a void inside of me.

This is a side of Liam I suspect hasn't come out in a long time. I'm paralyzed by conflicting emotions. My annoyance with him, the need to know more, to get closer, to unburden him from whatever took his joy away and made him the angry person he keeps showing me.

He reads the questioning curiosity in my face and shuts down, putting on the asshole cover again.

I realize there's a lot more to Liam than he's letting out and, like me, he'll go to extremes to protect that side of him.

# CHAPTER SEVEN

## Liam

When I walk into Pat's Cafe, I see River sitting alone at a corner table by the window and after grabbing a coffee, I sit one chair over from her. She's completely absorbed by whatever is going on her phone, and doesn't even glance up at me. I take the chance and let my eyes wander over her. She's tall for a girl, slim, and perfectly proportioned. Long brown hair falls in around her shoulders and frames her face. River is breathtakingly beautiful. Full rosy lips, a perfect nose, big hazel eyes that today are more green than brown, and flawless skin. I can see several guys looking at her with poorly disguised interest, even the ones with girlfriends, and yet she's completely oblivious to them.

"Wow, that's impressive!" She's talking to herself.

River tilts her head to the left and does the same with her iPhone, then pulls her hand back, holding the phone at arm's length, and moves it from left to right and back again.

She glances at me and back at the phone. "It follows you, dude, like one of those weird pictures. It's watching me."

I take a sip of my coffee. "What are you looking at?"

"Dick pics."

The mouthful of hot coffee I took gets stuck in my throat and it's trapped in between swallowing and choking me. I manage to get it down and cough, tears stinging my eyes from the effort.

"What?" Is all I can say, my throat still burning.

"Dick pics. I'm looking at dick pics. See?" She turns the phone toward me and sure enough there it is, some guy's dick in all of its glory looking straight at me.

"What the fuck, River! This is too much, even for you. Why the fuck are you looking at dicks on your phone?" I tried to whisper, but it came out louder than I intended as a couple of heads turn our way. It doesn't faze her at all.

Her eyes meet mine now and an eyebrow rises at my response. Here it comes. I can't wait to hear what she says next.

"Before I address why I'm looking at dick pictures, I have a question for you. What do you mean, 'this is too much even for you?' Is there some rule or expectation I'm supposed to be following I'm not aware of? And should I assume you never looked at a picture of a vagina before? You never went online and typed Vaginas R Us on Google or some other shit like that?"

I blush. I fucking blush. And I don't blush. Ever. The last time anyone made me blush, I had to be twelve. Fuck! I have no answer. I can't deny it and I can't say it's not the same without sounding like a hypocritical ass. I fucking bite my tongue and wait for her to move on.

She gives me a few extra seconds to answer and when I say nothing, she goes on.

"Some ass sent me a dick picture. No idea who, don't know him, don't want to know him, but I figure since he likes sending dick pics so much, he'd like to get some as well. I've been sending them to him all morning."

My mouth drops open. "You mean to tell me that someone you don't know sent you a dick picture and instead of deleting it and blocking the guy, you went online to find more dick pics and send them to him?"

"Yes."

"Why not just block him?"

"What's the fun in that? He'd move to the next random number. Maybe this will make him think twice before doing it again."

I shake my head and laugh. River's moxie seems to have no limits and in an odd sort of way, it's growing on me. She's growing on me.

"Did you send it to him yet?"

"Oh, I sent him about a dozen already."

"What?"

"I'm giving him a taste of his own medicine. Extra strength." She grins a devious grin and her whole face lights up with mischief.

"I have to see this myself, hand it over."

She puts her phone in my hand and I scroll up, past more dicks than I ever imagined seeing until I get to the top.

I see the first picture—the picture the random guy sent her and laugh. It's nothing to write home about.

She scoots her chair next to mine and leans over, her head almost on my shoulder as she peeks into her phone in my hand. "What you laughing at?"

I'm not about to dis another guy's dick, I shake my head and say nothing.

Then I scroll back again, reading the texts between the dick pics and trying not to look at images.

She replied to his dick pic with one of her own.

**Guy: <<dick pic>>**

**River: <<dick pic>>**

**Guy: Sorry bro, I thought you were a girl**

**River: What? You don't want to trade dick pics?**

**Guy: No bro.**

**River: <<dick pic>>**

**Guy: Seriously bro, no dick pics.**

**River: But I have more and mine looks much nicer than yours.**

**River: <<dick pic>>**

**River: <<dick pic>>**

**River: <<dick pic>>**

**River: See? Much nicer, longer, thicker. Maybe you can save them for next time.**

**Guy:** STOP SENDING ME DICK PICS

**River: <<dick pic>>**

**River: <<dick pic>>**

**River: <<dick pic>>**

**River: I especially like the last one. All those piercings...a guy's got to have a lot of balls to stick metal thru his dick, don't you think?**

**River: Balls...get it?** LOL

**River: <<dick pic>>**

**River: <<dick pic>>**

**River: <<dick pic>>**

**Guy: Bro, I'm not gay. It's fine if you are but STOP sending those. I thought you were a girl.**

**River: <<dick pic>>**

**River: <<dick pic>>**

**River: <<dick pic>>**

**Guy: I'm going to kick your ass.**

**River: You're just jealous all my dicks are bigger that yours.**

**River: <<dick pic>>**

**River: <<dick pic>>**

**Guy: Fuck you!**

**River: With that little thing you got? I don't think that's even possible.**

**River: <<dick pic>>**

**Guy: I'm going to find you and kick your ass**

**River: #SorryNotSorry dude, I'm going. Maybe think twice before sending dick pictures to people you don't know who didn't ask for them. Don't bother replying, I'm blocking you now.**

**River: Have fun with the dicks, YOU DICK.**

**River: One more for the road.**

**River: <<dick pic>>**

My whole body is shaking with laughter and she has the biggest grin on her face when I hand her phone back to her.

I raise my hand for a high five and she slaps her hand on mine. My fingers automatically lace with hers and hold on for a few seconds before letting go.

This spontaneous truce we both walked into is not our regular modus operandi. She scoots her chair back away from me and we both grab for our coffees and look away from each other.

Awkward . . .

# CHAPTER EIGHT

## River

It's Saturday and Logan has the weekend off, we all decided to go hang out at a local bar and have a few drinks while watching whatever game is playing on the dozen TVs spread around the room. I like this place. It has an English pub meets a barn feel to it with all the natural wood floors and exposed beams crisscrossing the high ceiling. They have good and inexpensive food and dozens of different beers on draft. The pub caters to locals and students from nearby colleges, including Riggins and the University of Vermont. There's a good mix of twenty somethings and people in their thirties and forties. This is the kind of place that's just loud enough that you have privacy when talking in a group but not so loud you'd have to yell to be heard.

We're all sitting around a table we snagged against a wall in the back—it's not as loud as nearer the bar. And by we, I mean, Skye, her friend Bruno, Logan, Liam, and his date, Barbie. No, that's not her real name, but she has just as much plastic in her as her namesake, so it's fitting. I mean, the girl is platinum blond, her lips have most definitely been enhanced with some kind of filler, she's wearing a ton of makeup. Her boobs could be used as a book shelf and she looks like she hasn't eaten since she was twelve.

And no, I'm not jealous. My boobs are real, thank you very much. Her looks are the least of the things that annoy me about this girl. She's the anti-me. The embodiment of everything I hate in other women. You know the type. Overly done, cunning, and playing dumb and helpless. Normally, I'm not one to rag on other people for their choices. I hate stereotypes and the people who promulgate them. But as soon as she figured I wasn't Bruno's date, her claws came out. And you can bet your ass those are fake too.

When I saw Liam walk into the bar with Barbie on his arm, I started laughing. In my mind I saw this picture of GI Joe and Barbie together and I was half expecting a pissed off Ken to walk in after them. I didn't direct the laugh at them, but somehow Liam picked up on it and knew right away I was laughing at his date choice. We had words while Barbie went to the bathroom to powder her nose. No, I'm not making this up. Those were her exact words. Now Liam is pissed at me because I called him Ken to his face. I don't think he'd mind it too much if I said GI Joe but calling him Ken got his hackles up.

Logan looks at me and then at his brother.

"River?" he calls me to get my attention. I'm a few seats away from him and lucky me, right across from Liam and Barbie. "What did you do now to make Liam so mad?" And then he takes a long pull of his beer.

"Me? I did nothing. He's probably just pissed because he has a tiny dick." I smirk, knowing Liam will pick up on my Ken reference. Everyone knows the Ken doll has no dick.

Logan chokes on his beer and nearly sprays the whole table, turning at the last moment and just getting the floor.

Liam glares at me, Bruno laughs, and Skye just covers her face with her hands. Again.

Liam's date, what's her real name again, Tiff? Tate? Or something like that, who from here on out shall be referred to as the Prissy One, gapes at me in her perfect little pink cashmere sweater set and knee-length black skirt, with her perfect pink nails and perfect peroxided blonde hair. I hated her on sight and it has absolutely nothing to do with the fact Liam invited her to our get-together at the bar tonight.

Absolutely nothing.

She comes to his defense. "That's so rude." She speaks in her perfect upper crust accent. "How could you possible know this? I'm sure Liam's penis is a perfectly normal size." She blushes. I'm sure that's a fake blush too.

"Have you seen it?" I ask.

The Prissy One blushes even more. "No."

"Have you touched it?"

"Of course not!" she says defensively.

"Then how do you know what size his dick is?"

"Well, have you?" The Prissy One counter-attacks.

"Me? Hell no! Never seen it, never touched it."

"Then how would you know?" She smiles her prissy smile, throwing my question back at me.

I lean toward her. "Exactly! I never saw it. You never saw it. How do we even know it exists at all?"

Liam speaks for the first time. "*It*"—he emphasizes the word—"does exist. You'll just have to take my word for it."

"Okay, then." I look back at Liam and there's a dark promise in his eyes. He'll make me pay for this. *Oh well, in the hole for one, in the hole for a thousand.* I continue. "Liam speaks, and he declares he has a dick, albeit a very teeny tiny one." I hold my pinky finger up.

The Prissy One doesn't know when to shut up.

"Even so, I'm sure Liam's penis is perfectly fine," she replies and then looks around the table, trying to gather support. "Penis size does not matter anyway, right?"

I scoff at that as I take a sip of my beer.

"What? You disagree? Everyone says size does not matter."

"And who is everyone?" I ask.

"Everyone!"

"Lies."

"You think everyone else is wrong and you are right? That a penis size matters?"

"I don't think everyone else is wrong. I think they're all delusional." I lean back on my chair, looking the Prissy One over.

"Size matters in everything else. Why wouldn't it matter for a guy's dick size? Have you tried putting on a shoe that is a size too big or too small? Fitting a square peg in a round hole?"

"But that is different!" The Prissy One counters.

"Lies, just lies. Told to appease the ego of guys who are unlucky in the big cock department. You know why?" I ask. "Because there's absolutely nothing a guy can do to increase his dick size, despite all the emails in my junk folder. Women can get bigger boobs." I stare pointedly at her chest before continuing, "Ass implants, and lip injections. What can a guy do about his dick? Nothing, I tell you. So long ago someone created the lie and everyone jumped on it, content to do so and save men's fragile dick egos."

They all look at me uncomfortably. Guys and their dicks. They're so insecure about them.

The Prissy One does not know when to shut up. "Then, you're saying that if a man has a small penis, he cannot please a woman?"

"No, I'm not saying that. I'm saying size matters. But if you're a guy and your tickler doesn't scratch the itch, don't worry, there's still hope for you."

I throw the bait and wait for prissy girl to bite. She doesn't disappoint. Logan's already covering his mouth to stop a laugh. I'm sure he can guess what I'm going to say next since I had a similar conversation with Skye in front of him before. Skye just hangs her head, her face already turning pink. Liam narrows his eyes at me. I can tell he's evenly divided between being amused and offended on behalf of the male species, if not himself.

"So," she asks. "What can a man with a small penis do, according to you?" She's seething.

"With his dick? Not much. But he also has a tongue and he better be damn good with it." I take another sip of my beer.

The Prissy One is as slow as she is—well, prissy. She lets out a little gasp. Her face is burning. Maybe all that blushing isn't fake after all. "You are disgusting!"

"I take it blowjobs are also out of the picture for you?"

"That is so—so vulgar! But I guess coming from you and the language you use and all the experience you seem to have, I should not be surprised." And then she raises her nose at me.

The whole table tenses, waiting for what I'm going to say next. She called me disgusting, vulgar, and a slut, all in the same breath.

I slowly put my beer down and lean closer to the table. I'm about to rip her a new one when Bruno chirps in.

"I like blowjobs."

All eyes are on him.

"What? I do. And there's nothing wrong with oral sex."

I see it when Skye looks at him and mouths *Thank you.*

Bruno saves the Prissy One for now, but the night's still young.

I look around the table like nothing happened and ask, "Who's hungry? All this dick talk has me starving."

When everyone groans at that, I hide my face behind a menu and just smile to myself. My job here is done.

I never saw Tiff slash Tate slash Barbie slash The Prissy One again. Wonder why . . .

# CHAPTER NINE

## Liam

"HEY, PACK SOME STUFF. ENOUGH FOR A LONG WEEKEND. We're spending Easter with Skye's family."

I frown at Logan. "You're going to meet the parents?"

"I already met the parents. Spent Thanksgiving with them. They have a farm a couple of hours away from here. They're very informal, pack everyday clothes and they might make you work, make sure you have something you don't mind getting dirty in."

"I'm not going."

"The hell you aren't." The look he gives me tells me I wouldn't be able to get away with it.

"This is the first holiday we get to spend together in over four years. As far as I'm concerned you are the only family I have and I'd like my family to be with me when I spend Easter with my girl."

"I don't know anyone there."

"You know Skye and you know River."

I snort. "Yeah, River—as if that's a good reason for me to go."

"I've seen you staring at her tits and her ass and her mouth and—"

"Okay! Enough. You caught me checking out the goods. So what? It's been a long time. Pussy didn't come around easily in Afghanistan." I hate the way the words spill out of my mouth. This is not the way I normally talk about a woman.

"You don't seem to be interested in anyone else's goods. If you called any of those girls who were always all over you, they'd be running over here."

"I called one of them, remember? And how well did that end up? I can only imagine what Tate is telling everyone back hom—back in Connecticut. All that was a long time ago. It's not my world anymore."

"You've been back for over a month now, Liam. Did you even tell them you're back?"

I know who he means by them. Our parents. The same parents who manipulated Logan his whole life. The same parents who told me they would not pay for college if I didn't comply and go to law school. The parents who knew that being only seventeen, I couldn't get any student loans, not that I was eligible anyway with all the money they had. Well, seventeen had been too young to get student loans on my own, but as soon as I turned eighteen I enlisted. So, fuck you, Mom and Dad! Fuck you for forcing my hand and making me the angry asshole I am today. I've seen more blood and carnage than any one person should have to. I could be in the middle of medical school right now. They knew it. They'd always known it. As long as I can remember I always, always wanted to go into medicine. But when they shattered my dreams, I went into the navy and became the closest thing I could. I was a corpsman. But all the lives I saved cannot, will not make up for the ones I lost. *Especially, not hers*—I look at my hands and I can still see

Hannah's blood on them. I made her a promise. Told her I'd keep her safe. I failed.

Like always, any time my thoughts drift to Hannah, I'm brought right back to that day, to that moment. The moment I relive in my mind over and over, looking for a different outcome and never finding one. I feel myself folding into the darkness as guilt builds around me.

Logan's voice brings me back to the present.

"Where did you go, man?"

I realize he's been talking to me and calling my name.

"Nowhere. When do we leave?" I don't meet his eyes. I'm sure he'll be able to see the nightmares that follow me even in the light of day.

"We'll head out tonight around seven." He hesitates. "You know you can talk to me, right? You can tell me anything. I don't presume to imagine the shit you saw and went through, but I've had my share of crappy days and I've seen friends go down. I'm here for you, Liam. You know it, right?"

I nod, not sure my throat would work right now. Logan hesitates, trying to read me. He can tell something is off, but he's on the clock and has to leave for work. When the door closes shut behind him and silence fills the room, I close my eyes and descend into darkness as the memories take over, dragging me down a road I've traveled many times before. I don't resist. The pull of despair and guilt is familiar. I'm an observer and a participant, watching a movie in which I'm the main character, and try as I may to think a different plot, to guess at what-ifs, the ending is the same. Like moth to a flame, I let myself burn, welcome the pain, and accept the outcome as I punish myself the only way I can.

*Fragmented images, smells, sounds invade my mind, mixed pieces of different puzzles. Explosions, shots, fire. Screams, words I don't understand. Blood. So much blood. It's hard to breathe. I taste blood and sand. Thirsty. I'm so thirsty. I'm being dragged still holding on to Hannah or what's left of her. Someone tries to take her from me, but my arms hold on to her harder. Pain, so much pain and then darkness again. There's peace in darkness, there's nothingness in darkness.*

*The next time I wake up I'm on a plane. Can't open my eyes, but I hear the hum of an engine. I try to move. I can't. A muffled voice tells me to hang on and I do. The last thought I have before darkness takes me again is Hannah is no longer in my arms.*

*Five days later, I wake up for good. I'm told that after emergency surgery to stabilize me at a military outpost, I was airlifted to the Landstuhl Regional Medical Center next to the U.S. air base at Ramstein, Germany, where I could get a more extensive treatment. There are bandages around my chest, back, and left shoulder. There are bandages around my neck and head as well. Doctors told me I was clipped twice. Chest and left thigh, and the explosion had inflicted dozens of shrapnel wounds. There was impact to my head, causing my brain to swell, and they induced me into a coma. They removed all the shrapnel. I asked about Hannah. I already knew the answer. She didn't make it. Her body had already been sent home. I failed her. I had promised her I would keep her safe and she would see her little girl again. I asked about my unit. Three lives lost, including Hannah's. She was dead before I even got to her, they told me. She hadn't suffered. I don't find comfort in the words even though I know they're meant to comfort me. I still failed her. They tell me that in trying to save her, she had actually saved me. I would have been dead if I hadn't left the cover of that truck trying to get to Hannah. Then she saved me a second time when the explosion went off because her body took most of the impact.*

*On my final day at the hospital after being there for over a week I was granted my discharge papers. I was free to go home.*

*Except I had no idea where home was. I requested permission to stay in Germany, located an old friend of mine in Munich, and stayed with him another two months then spent nearly a year traveling through Europe's countryside aimlessly. I worked odd jobs in farms, in exchange of food and some cash. I needed time to think and for my wounds to completely heal. I hated all the scars on my back. There were dozens and dozens of them over the entire left side. I hated them because they were a reminder of my failure and I hated them because I knew anyone who saw them would ask questions I didn't want to answer. That's when I decided on the tattoo. I wanted it to mean something. To hide the scars, yes, but to mean something as well. I spent weeks looking for the right place and the right person. I had an idea of what I wanted and the right artist would be able to create the image I had in my head. It took hours and hours of work, over a month to complete it. When the tattoo was finished, not a single scar could be seen. I could still feel them under my fingertips, but this guy had used his skills to hide the scars in the design in shades of red and blue and green. In shades of gold and black. The tattoo took up most of my back. It moved with me as if alive. I think the day he finished I smiled for the first time in over a year. I felt free. It was time to go home.*

# CHAPTER TEN

## River

Guess who's sitting next to me in the back of Logan's Escalade? I'll give you a hint, it's not my sister.

Liam has sunglasses on, so I can't see his eyes. His head lies back on the headrest, his long legs fitting awkwardly behind Skye's seat, which is not as far back as Logan's, giving him a few extra inches.

"Stop looking at me," Liam says.

"What are you? Twelve? I'm not looking at you." I totally am.

He faces me now. "You're staring at me. I can feel it."

"Oh, and you're psychic too! Mom's going to love you." I'm fluent in English, sarcasm, and fuck you.

"Mom is going to love him anyway." Skye butts into our conversation if one can call it that.

"Yeah, but she'll always love me more," Logan says, then picks up Skye's hand and kisses it.

She giggles.

I groan, "Can you two save it for later and keep the PDA to a minimum?"

"Haters gonna hate." Logan's eyes meet mine in the rearview mirror and I flip him the bird. He laughs.

Liam's head falls back against the seat again. "It's going to be a long ride."

"You can say that again."

For the next two hours we alternate long moments of frigid silence with heated bickering. It's juvenile. I know. He knows. And yet we can't help ourselves.

Logan and Skye exchange glances every few miles and are having a silent conversation all of their own. A conversation I'm not privy to. My choices are silence or to annoy Liam.

Guess which one I pick?

I glance at him sideways. He's facing away from me and looking at the trees passing by outside his window.

I take the chance to drink him in. He's the same height as Logan, six-foot-two, but more muscular. His shoulders are a little bigger, his chest wider. His biceps strain against the fabric of his dark gray Henley.

I once read that soldiers and marines in Iraq and Afghanistan routinely carry between sixty and one hundred pounds of gear. Every day. For hours at a time. That's like carrying a small person on your back.

I imagine him in a marine uniform, all that gear on his back, sunglasses protecting his gray eyes against the unforgivable desert glare. How strenuous it must have been to be so exposed, not only to the elements in a hostile place but also among hostile people. To be in a place where almost everyone is an enemy who wants you dead and you're responsible for keeping everybody else around you alive.

I know I could never handle a fraction of what Liam must have faced. I have a healthy dose of respect for him and anyone in service. But I'm not telling him that. He still bugs the heck out of me.

Liam may be annoying, but there's no denying he's hot as fuck. It would be a lot easier to ignore him if my insides didn't tingle every time I saw him.

I study his hands now. Beautiful hands, long fingers, nails short and clean, resting on muscular, strong thighs in dark jeans. And a sizable bulge. In my mind, the uniform is gone now, and what's left is a beautiful and muscular man, tan naked skin gleaming in the sun.

I swallow. My imagination is trying to run wild and I have to rein it in.

His chest expands with a deep breath.

I glance up.

He's facing me. I can't see his eyes behind the reflective lenses of his sunglasses, but I know his eyes are on me. His lips tilt in an all too knowing smirk.

"Like what you see?" he asks me.

"A little full of yourself, aren't you?"

"It's hard to be humble when you're among the world's finest."

"And he's modest, too."

Liam's smirk grows. And so do the tingles in parts of my body that shall remain unnamed.

What is it about this irritating man that has me out of sorts? I've dated plenty of hot guys before. Jocks, hot nerds, musicians, sweet next- door types, and yet, none of them got me this hot and bothered.

That's just it—Liam is a man. All those guys before him were boys. Still growing up. They confused cockiness with confidence. But none of them could ever hold up against Liam.

Damn it.
I give him my best cold and dismissing glare and turn away.
It's my turn to look out the window at the passing trees.

# CHAPTER ELEVEN

## Liam

I'VE BEEN AWAKE FOR TWO HOURS NOW. SEVEN A.M. IS IT too early to get up? This is a farm. People wake up early on farms, right? I can't stay in bed anymore. I pull on a pair of jeans and a sweatshirt, then fight with my morning boner so I can take a piss, wash my face, and brush my teeth.

I walk downstairs, the wooden steps surprisingly quiet, and stop at the bottom of the stairs when I hear voices. I take a few more steps toward the sound. It's coming from the kitchen. Last night during dinner, River's dad said the house was over a hundred years old and had been in the family for a couple of generations. It had been gutted and remodeled a few years back. The house has a semi-open concept, with the large kitchen and dining room taking a huge chunk of the first floor. Through the living room archway openings, I can see Skye and her mother sitting at the long wooden table drinking coffee.

"Is River up?" Skye asks her mom.

"If I know that daughter of mine, she was up the crack of dawn and is working up a sweat with Big D. You know she can go at it for hours and hours."

*What the fuck!*

"I don't know how she can handle him. He's a beast," Skye replies to her mother.

Her mom laughs.

Skye continues, "I tried only once. I couldn't go more than five minutes. I thought he'd split me in half. I was limping for two days after."

I can't believe my ears. *What the fuck? And who the fuck is this Big D guy?*

I must have made a sound because her mom looks my way then.

"Good morning, Liam. You're up early. I hope you slept well."

"Yes, thank you, Mrs. Devereux."

"Please call me Serena. I hate formalities. And you are just what I need. A big, strong man."

I know my mouth opened but nothing comes out.

"I need a hand and my man's still sleeping. I tired him out last night." She laughs.

"Mom!"

"Oh, please." She turns to Skye. "Your man is still sleeping too. Your dad's not the only tired one this morning."

Skye has an apologetic look on her face as her mom pushes me out the door.

"I need a pair of strong arms to help me move the hay and then I'll put food in you. You look like you could use coffee and breakfast."

"Yes, ma'am," I tease, tipping an imaginary hat. It's easy to talk to her. She's one of those people who's always happy.

She laughs and brings me to a barn with several stalls. All empty except for one. There's a very pregnant mare in it. I don't know much about horses. I grew up in the suburbs, but

I went riding with friends often, I'm comfortable around them.

"This is Midnight Dreamer and we are keeping her in the stall instead of the pasture because she is about to birth anytime now." She rubs the horse's nose and offers her an apple. "Could you bring me a bale of hay from that pile and put it in her stall?"

"Sure."

As I step closer to the barn opening, I see what looks like a black blur with legs racing down the green pastures with someone low on its back. Both the horse's mane and the rider's long hair are flowing in the wind behind them. River, I realize, and then fear clamps my chest because she's going too fast. If she falls . . . I look at her mother, but she doesn't seem worried at all.

As River gets closer to the barn, she slows the horse to a canter and then to a walk. The animal is restless under her. Picking up his head and shaking it. "Hi, Mom. Do you need help with breakfast?"

"Nope. Take care of Big D. Liam can give you a hand and then you both come in for breakfast." She leaves me with the beast and I'm not sure if I'm referring to River or the horse.

*Fuck! Big D is a horse?* My mind had me going on another direction altogether. I grimace.

I take a few steps closer to River and the horse tries to lunge in my direction, but River reins him in.

"Easy, Big D," she coos to him, scratching behind his ear. She guides him to the barn, comes to a stop by a stall, and dismounts from the biggest horse I've ever seen. His black coat is covered in sweat. The animal looks at me and shows me his teeth. River tethers him and pulls the saddle off him. I bring the bale of hay I've been holding this whole time to the mare and then approach River and the beast. He prances, digging his hooves in the ground. River laughs.

"This is Big D?" I ask.

"His name is Deegan. It's an old Irish name. It means black-haired. But he got so big we started calling him Big Deegan and eventually Big Dee."

I take a step closer and the horse snorts at me.

"He doesn't like you. You should keep your distance. He might kick or bite you."

"Why wouldn't he like me? I did nothing to him." It annoys me that she said the horse doesn't like me. Animals love me.

"He dislikes most males. Big Dee is a little possessive of me. He gets jealous if a guy gets too close."

And right on cue, the horse uses his neck to pull River closer to him and shows me his teeth again. Menacing.

She giggles, grabs a brush, and runs it over his body. "Come on. Give me a hand so we can grab breakfast faster."

I narrow my eyes at her. "I thought you said I should stay clear off him."

"You can come closer. Just make sure not to walk or stand behind him."

I don't move and wonder if she's trying to get me killed. Death by horse would be ruled an accident, right?

River takes my hand and pulls me behind her, stopping just out of reach of the horse. "I'll introduce you to him. Hey, Deegan," she baby-talks to the beast, rubbing his nose. "I have a friend for you to meet. Now be nice to him, okay?"

The beast snorts. And I can almost hear him saying, "Yeah, right."

She looks over her shoulder and pulls me closer to her, then lets my hand go and grabs the brush again. "Put your hand over mine and brush him with me."

I do it, standing just behind her, her body barely touching mine as she moves the brush over the animal with brisk movements. She smells like spring, hay, and wind, making it a heady and sweet combination, and I feel myself getting hard for her. *Fuck!*

"Hold the brush. Keep doing it," she instructs me and then she bends down to pick up another brush from the ground and her ass grazes my groin. When she stands up my free hand goes to her hip and I pull her against me. She freezes.

I nuzzle the back of her head, inhaling her scent. "I like the way you smell."

I pull her harder against my body. I know she can feel me on the small of her back. She sucks in a breath and I watch over her shoulder as her breasts heave. The first few buttons of her blouse are open, giving me a peek into the smooth skin of her cleavage. I let the brush drop to the floor and turn her into my arms, pulling her closer still. He eyes lock on mine. This close I can see flecks of green and gold in her hazel gaze. Her lips part and I lower my head to hers, never losing eye contact until the very last moment, and just as my lips graze hers . . . the beast lunges and bites me.

"Son of a bitch!" I call out as I step back and out of reach, dragging River with me. The horse snorts, whinnies, and kicks his feet on the ground.

I look at River and I can already tell she snapped back to her bitchy mode, but I can't help to be concerned and I want to make sure she isn't hurt. "Are you okay? Did he get you?"

She pulls away from me. "I'm fine!" She spits the words at me. "What was that about? I told you he gets jealous! What were you trying to do?"

"What am I trying to do? I'm trying not to get mauled by that beast!" I look at myself and the shoulder of my sweatshirt is ripped. He got a piece of me!

River looks alarmed for a second as her eyes see the same thing I see—my ripped shirt.

"Did he get you?"

"No, just the shirt."

"Then it serves you right! Provoking him like that!"

"Provoking him? How?"

"By kissing me!"

"I didn't actually get to kiss you, did I?" And before she can reply, I continue, "And I only did it because you so blatantly wanted me to, rubbing your ass on me and grabbing my hand."

"I did not!"

"Did too!"

"Did not!"

"Did too!"

"Did not!" She stomps her foot.

"Did too, but don't worry, I won't do it again. Unless you beg me and beg me you will."

"I will not!"

"You will."

"I will not!"

"You will. One day you'll say the words. You'll beg me to kiss you. And I just might give in."

"Will not!"

"You will."

I smile at her and walk away. I worked up an appetite.

---

I DON'T WALK STRAIGHT BACK to the house. I go around the

barn first and up to the fenced pasture that houses several horses. I have to get my head on straight first and walk off the raging hard-on in my pants.

What the fuck is wrong with me? Why did I try to kiss her? I don't even like her. She has a foul mouth, and she's too cocky for her own good.

*Okay*, I reason. She's beautiful. And hot. *And* she was rubbing her ass on me. Had I read it all wrong? No. I don't think so. I saw it in her eyes. She was surprised at first, yes, but I saw how her gaze dropped to my mouth and how she licked her lips in anticipation. She may not even know she was doing it. It was not the studied seductive move I've seen so many times from the girls I knew in school and the preppy neighborhood I grew up in.

As free as River voices her opinions about everything and as much as she talks the talk, there's a certain innocence about her that's at odds with her words and her behavior. It's . . . intriguing.

I've been an ass, too. I admit. I've been an ass from day one if I'm to be honest about it. I didn't set out to be an asshole. It wasn't my default mode, but that first meeting set the tone for all our meetings afterward. In the beginning, I was just angry. Not at her, but that day she dumped her drink on me, she became the target of my anger. Had it been a guy, I'm sure I would've knocked him out cold. I haven't been back home long and adjusting to a normal life seems impossible for now. But each day I push myself to move forward and leave all that happened in the past. They say the hardest part of coming back home is leaving the war behind. It follows you. In your thoughts and your dreams. I've been back stateside for five weeks. Sometimes it feels like seconds, sometimes it feels like years. It'll change. I'll change. I have to go back to being me again. I'm tired of the man I've become and I don't like him very much.

# CHAPTER TWELVE

## River

WHAT HAPPENED? I'M STILL DAZED BY THE LAST COUPLE OF minutes. How could so much happen in such a short amount of time?

Deegan's whinny reminds me I didn't finish brushing him. I pick up the wire brush again and resume grooming his ebony coat with firm strokes.

Liam had been charming and not at all his usual jerk self, and I'd been drawn to him. I would have kissed him. I want to kiss him still.

Fuck! That's not good. Not good at all. I have to cool off. I have to calm down.

I can't—I won't hook up with him.

Yes, he's hot. Hell, he's hot as fuck. Yeah, I have noticed. More than once.

One would have to be dead not to notice how hot he is. And more than that. Liam has a certain air of confidence about him. Like he knows who he is and makes no apologies for it. Maybe he was always like this. Maybe it's a marine thing. Guys in the military are sexy.

Whatever this is, it's not good for me to get any ideas about him and I can't avoid him altogether.

I mean, his brother and my sister are madly in love with each other. Skye fell hard and fast for Logan, and he's just the same. Skye's a different person since meeting him—different in a good way. She has always been quiet and reserved. She's such an introvert. Logan's love for her makes her more self-assured, confident, and even more adventurous.

I'm the opposite. And I don't want to change or be changed by a guy. No matter how hot said guy is.

I think of his hands on my hips, the feel of his hard body and his lips almost on mine—a shiver runs down my skin and I rub my arms to shake it off.

I like my snarky, in your face personality. I don't want to change.

If falling in love with someone does that—changes people—I want nothing to do with it. What would love do to me? Make me coy and insecure?

Fuck that noise! And then that little voice in my head speaks, *'Love makes you a better version of yourself.'*

Does it? I'm not so sure.

# CHAPTER THIRTEEN

## Liam

It's Saturday and we have two more days here. We're leaving on Monday morning. What the heck am I supposed to do? I have no problem being an ass when it's just the two of us together, but I don't want to come off as a jerk in her home and in front of her family. The thing is, biting my tongue has never been a skill I mastered. It's going to be a very long weekend.

Once I get back into the house, I find everyone gathered in the kitchen and just about to sit down. I'm instructed to wash my hands by Serena and comply before taking my place at the table, the only free spot between River and her mom.

Long weekend indeed.

I really like her parents, Serena and David. They are the complete opposite of mine. They make me feel at ease and as if I belong. As if I have as much right to be in their home and eating their food as they do. It's a welcoming feeling and a troubling one too. I've been adrift too long, without a real home or a place to belong to.

Up until this moment, I had no idea this was something I was missing. That I needed this. The thought scares me. It tugs deep into my chest. This unnamed thing that has always been there but I didn't have a name for. But now I do—longing.

Longing for a life I've never had, longing for what I see around me at this table. I glance over at River. Maybe I can have it too.

When I look up, Serena's eyes are on me and a small, sad smile graces her face. I can almost swear she knows what I'm thinking.

Logan's voice gets my attention back to the conversation.

"You've been married for twenty-five years? That's great! Not a lot of people make it that long."

"True," River says. "Most of our friends have divorced parents."

Skye nods in agreement as takes a bite of her omelet.

"What's your secret?" Logan asks Serena.

Serena grins. "Men are simple to please. You keep their bellies full and their balls empty and they're happy."

"Mom!" Both Skye and River protest while I choke on my orange juice and Logan's face turns red.

David, their dad, jumps in.

"Agree one hundred percent. Already worked on the latter, now I'm working on the former," he says, pointing to his almost empty plate.

Breakfast is interesting to say the least.

# CHAPTER FOURTEEN

## River

The last forty-eight hours have been the most exasperating and intense of my entire life. Having Liam around and being on my best behavior in front of my parents has been a challenge. Every time Liam and I occupy the same space, which happens quite often since Mom has us working together and we are sharing all meals, not to mention our Saturday movie night, a tradition in my family for as long as I can remember.

We had to share a love seat. His thigh pressed against mine for the entire two hours and thirty-three minutes of *Armageddon*. Plus, the trailers of six other movies on the DVD. At five-foot-seven and one hundred and twenty pounds, I'm not exactly tiny, and he's a big guy, six-foot-two and two hundred and twenty pounds easily. We were nearly glued to each other's sides. Add to that the fact he's sleeping in the room right next to mine and I can hear him moving about and can smell his scent every time I step into the shared bathroom across the hall. Yeah, I'm batshit crazy with pent-up anger.

Yes! That's what I'm calling it. Anger. Deal with it!

He's not making it easy on me either, the bastard. I swear last night while we were watching the movie, and he put his arm around the back of the seat, he was playing with the ends of my hair. And earlier today when we were loading bales of hay onto the back of the truck to feed the horses out in the back pasture, he kept brushing against me on purpose and every time he took a bale out of my hands, his finger grazed mine. The fucker is teasing me and I caught him staring at my ass more than once.

I don't know what his game is, but I'm not playing it.

No way.

No how.

Fucker!

---

LIAM

I'VE NURSED either a semi or a hard-on for nearly three days. Three fucking days of discreetly trying to adjust myself. I think River's mom caught me at least twice. I can't even look at her straight anymore. That woman sees and knows everything, I swear.

Logan and Skye are working with her dad. They have it pretty well-organized. I enjoy the work. It's not hard. I relish the physical exertion. After so many years in the marines and the last year backpacking through Europe and working on small farms much like this one before I decided to come back home, I kind of miss the physical demands of daily workouts.

I've been running and sparring with the punching bag

Logan has hanging in the garage, but I think I'll join a gym when we get back home.

That's a bittersweet word for me, *home.* I haven't had a home for so long and I'm starting to think of Logan's place as my own. Well, it has always been ours, Grandma made sure of it. She made sure neither of our parents would ever have any stake in the house she grew up in and she transferred ownership of it to us years back. My thoughts go back to River.

She's been around me for most of our waking hours. We're either helping her mom with some of the chores that are normally done by employees—they got Sunday off to spend with their families—or eating every meal together. We even have to share a bathroom. And I may or may not have jerked off with River's conditioner. What the fuck is wrong with me?

---

RIVER

DAD IS MAKING burgers for lunch while the boys clean up. They worked up a sweat and said some cooling off is needed. I'm in the kitchen with Skye gathering chips and drinks. This will be a light lunch. Just enough to hold us off until five-thirty when we have our traditional Easter dinner. Pies have been baked, veggies are cleaned, cut-up, and ready to go. And Dad has a slow cooking roast in the smoker outside on the kitchen porch.

I bring the pitcher of lemony ice tea I just made to the table while Skye gets the rest of it set for lunch.

"Skye, I'm checking to see if Dad needs help with anything," I call out to her before leaving the kitchen through the backdoor. I take two steps down the stairs when I hear a sound to my right and I see Liam less than six feet away.

A shirtless Liam with the water hose and he's washing himself. He's bent at the waist and has the water over his neck and head. It's running down his back, arms and chest. That water has to be freezing. It's no more than fifty degrees out. He doesn't seem to mind it at all.

He finally notices me standing here when he rights himself and turns off the faucet. I'm stuck in place, my eyes glued to the tiny drops running down his chest and getting caught in the hard ridges of his stomach. The first thought that pops in my mind is that I want to lick those little drops.

Lazily, he reaches over to a bush and picks up the blue and gray flannel shirt he was wearing and pulls a white T-shirt from the inside of it. He must have been wearing both before. I tried really hard not to look at him all morning.

So much for that because I can't stop staring at him now.

He's drying himself, very poorly I may add, with the white T-shirt. He tosses it back on top of the bushes along the porch and puts his flannel shirt on, buttoning only the three middle buttons, leaving the top and bottom open. I'm staring and I've forgotten my words. All of them are gone. If I thought he was hot that first day we met when he was also shirtless, now, shirtless, wet, and smirking at me instead of glaring Liam is even hotter.

Yeah, I'm so screwed.

---

Liam

The way River is looking at me right now is not helping

matters one bit. Matters being the bulge in my pants. So much for the attempt to cool off with the freezing cold water I dumped over my head. I guess it was the wrong head. Should have doused my other head in the freezing water, the one farther south and currently holding hostage all my blood supply.

She's looking at me like I'm a tasty meal and she's been starved for months and my dick loves it. If I'm to be honest, I love it too. We are at a stalemate. Neither saying a word, neither able to move. I should say something, do something, but if I make a move right now, it will be to push her against something solid and kiss her until I can't feel my lips anymore. I don't think that would make for good family lunch entertainment.

My feet start moving toward her I realize, but I'm saved from doing something really stupid by the voice of her mother calling River to help bring the burgers inside the house.

---

## River

Holy crap! Saved by burgers and a call for help. I'm not sure what's going on, but whatever it is, I would have been down with it. I would have been one hundred percent into whatever Liam was offering and I'd be doing it right here on the back porch.

My mother's voice and her imminent approach has me crashing back into reality, gathering my wits and rushing to meet her before she can take one look at us and figure out just what was happening.

Mom is one of those people who can read a person or a situation in .000003 seconds flat. Skye can attest to that. And

Mom has been keeping a sharp eye on me for months now. Living far from home may have bought me some time and cover, but I know eventually she'll figure me out. The only reason she hasn't yet is because I, myself, don't actually know what happened.

# CHAPTER FIFTEEN

## Liam

THE REST OF YESTERDAY WAS SURPRISINGLY UNEVENTFUL. Lunch was fine, and dinner was great. I felt comfortable for the first time in over a year. Logan is right about his girl's family. He's one lucky SOB for finding not only the girl of his dreams but also the family we never had.

The entire meal, my eyes kept straying to River sitting across the table from me. Serena had rearranged the seating, I was sitting directly across from River and her mom was at one end of the table. Skye, Logan, and David filled the other spots around us. I swear she did it so she could watch us and gather intel.

I'm not entirely sure she's not secret service, FBI, or something like that. I'd like to introduce her to my commander. She'd have everyone pegged in seconds. I wouldn't be surprised if she announced she can read thoughts and proceeded to tell me all of mine. Of course, they would be extremely embarrassing since eighty percent of it involves all the things I'd like to do to River. The other twenty percent is what I want River to do to me.

We're on our way home now, loaded with leftovers, enough for days. Logan is driving and Skye is shotgun. River and I are in the back as before.

She's not sitting as far away from me as possible this time. She's closer to the center of the seat, a leg curled under her. She's wearing leggings and a big hoodie. A guy's hoodie based on the size, perhaps stolen from an ex. I haven't seen her with anyone or heard anything about her going on a date. The thought of her with someone other than me pisses me off. I glare at the hoodie. It should hide her slim body, but instead, it makes her look sexier.

River leans around Skye's seat and her hair brushes my knee. Knowing the long hours of drive ahead, I'm wearing track pants, which are more comfortable than jeans but way more difficult to hide a hard-on in. Day four and counting.

"Skye?"

"Yeah?"

"Did you borrow my conditioner?"

"No, I brought my own, why?"

"Weird . . . I could swear the bottle was a lot fuller when I packed it."

Logan's all too knowing eyes meet mine in the rearview mirror and I look out the window. I'm so fucking busted.

# CHAPTER SIXTEEN

## River

I have a few minutes before I have to leave, so I call Mom. I talk to her a few times a week, but I haven't called her in a couple of days. Skye talked to her yesterday and I know she's expecting me to call.

"Hi, Mom, do you have a few minutes to talk?"

"Hi, sweetie, sure do. How's everything?"

"Same old stuff, classes and the job at the clinic."

"Are you dating that boy yet?"

That's my mom. She never beats around the proverbial bush. She gets straight to the point. I bet she already asked Skye about it and my sister set me up by not saying anything to me.

"Which boy, Mom? I'm not dating anyone."

"River, why do you do this? You know exactly who I'm talking about. Liam, that gorgeous specimen of a man. You know, the tall, dark, and handsome guy you brought home with you and couldn't keep your eyes off the entire time."

"First, I didn't bring him home with me. Skye invited him because otherwise, he would've been spending Easter alone. I was very much against it, let the record show. And second, I didn't keep my eyes on him at all. I can't stand him. He's an arrogant ass."

"Hmm, you're perfect for each other, then."

"Mom!"

"What?"

"Did you just call me an arrogant ass?"

"You have been known to be both and proud of it."

I'm at a loss for words, betrayed by my own mother. I sputter my disbelief with a few sounds that roughly translate to, "Pfff."

"What are you waiting for? That boy couldn't keep his eyes off you either. I know you're not a prude or shy like Skye, why deny it?"

"Didn't you just hear me say he's an ass?"

"I did notice his ass. It was a fine ass, I might add."

"Mom! Seriously, you have no idea what you're talking about. Liam is not the nice, sweet guy you think he is. All that nice behavior during meals and when he was helping out is not how he acts around me."

"I sure hope not. That would be a waste of man candy if he were nice and proper all the time."

"Oh my God, of all the mothers in the world, why did I have to get one with no filters?"

"River, it's obvious you're attracted to each other. Why fight it? You're young, have fun, enjoy life. I'm not telling you to marry the guy. Just be open to the possibility that maybe the two of you together is a good thing."

"There's no two of us, Mom. The only reason we're even around each other is because Skye and Logan are in each other's pants every day."

"I never thought I'd say this to you, being that I've said it to your sister for years, but maybe you should be a little more like

Skye now. Just go for it."

"Mom, there's nothing to go for." The words sound like a lie even to my ears and I want to believe them so badly.

"Okay, sweetie, deny all you want. It won't make a difference."

"What do you mean?"

"The cards have spoken. It will happen. All you're doing is wasting some good fun time."

Oh yeah, how could I have forgotten my hippy mom's love for Tarot cards, crystals, and all woo-woo things. It's time to go.

"I gotta go, Mom. Have work starting in a few. I love you. Talk to you soon."

"I love you more. Just follow your heart. If you risk nothing, you win nothing. Then one day you'll be on your deathbed wondering about all the 'could have been's and all the risks you didn't take because of the potential of failure. One broken heart is worth a thousand unloved ones."

I think over her words—*One broken heart is worth a thousand unloved ones.*

"River? Remember your name and go with the flow. You can fight the current, but in the end the current always wins."

I hold the phone to my ear long after she hangs up, her parting words still bouncing in my mind. The current always wins. I've been swimming upstream for months now. Liam is just one more thing I'm fighting against and I'm so tired of trying to keep my head above water. So tired of going at it alone. It would be easy to break down and let go, to let Liam take me and erase all the non-memories in my head. But I'd be using him and something tells me he'd not be too keen on being used that way. Something tells me he would want to know and he would want to fix me. But I can't be fixed. I can't go back in time and make a different choice. I don't even know what different choice it would be. I don't even know what or who to blame. If I can't blame anyone else, then the guilty party must be me. My choices are my punishment, my problem to deal with. I don't want to share the burden with anyone else. I don't want Skye or my parents looking at me with pity and wondering if I'm okay. I'm not okay. I haven't been okay in over six months now. And above all, I don't want Liam to look at me and see what I see when I look in the mirror.

My brain tells me I need help. I need to speak with someone. I know it to be true. I'm a Psychology major. I know what the text books say. I know I fit perfectly into their description. I know all that and yet, I deny it all. It's not real. If I don't speak about it, if I don't think about it, it won't be real.

# CHAPTER SEVENTEEN

## Liam

It's been three days since we dropped off the girls at home and I last saw River. I'm still thinking about our almost kiss in the barn and what would have happened if it wasn't for that crazy horse. It's still spring break. The girls won't be back to classes until next week and I've been watching out the window on and off to see if she walks into Pat's Cafe. Yeah, I'm a stalker now. My stalking is rewarded when I see River walking into Pat's just fifteen minutes later.

I wait a bit and walk out of the house and cross the street just as she's walking back out. She hesitates a few steps away from the front door, that fruit thing she's addicted to in her hand.

Dark skinny jeans hug her hips, a black tank top under an open blue Riggins University zip hoodie. The hoodie does absolutely nothing to hide her curves and the cleavage popping out of her shirt. The strap of her black bra peeks from under her tank top where the hoodie slides off her shoulder a couple of inches.

I stop right in front of her, so close our booted toes nearly touch. I'm invading her space, I know. I want to do a lot more.

Her expression is one of caution and she hasn't said a word yet.

"You really love this thing." I nod in the direction of the large plastic cup filled with the pink liquid. "What is it anyway?"

"Raspberry lemonade."

I guess that explains all the fruity bits floating in it. Without taking my eyes off her, I grab the cup with her hand under my own and bring the straw to my lips, taking a long slow drink. The hand below mine squeezes the cup harder and her lips part in a little gasp. My mouth breaks into a smile around the straw and I realize this is the first time I've truly smiled at her. Her eyes dilate and I can tell she's trying to gather her thoughts and figure what I'm up to.

"Tasty. No wonder you're addicted to it," I say, still holding the cup, her hand still under mine.

She pulls the cup away. I let it go.

"Why are you being nice to me?" Direct to the point. I like that and follow her lead.

"I've been thinking about you."

She narrows her eyes at me.

"You were right the other day. We did start on the wrong foot. Maybe we can give this another try and be . . . friendly?" I end it like a question. She's really suspicious now.

"How friendly are we talking about?" Still direct and to the point. I'm really enjoying myself.

"As friendly as you want."

"Not gonna happen, buddy."

"Aw, you already have a pet name for me."

"I do. It starts with an A and ends with an E and in case you can't spell, it's assho—"

I stop the word by placing a finger on her lips. They're full and warm on my skin. She pulls away and my hand drops.

"Such a firecracker, aren't you? We both know I can have you begging me to kiss you, just like you did back in the barn."

"I didn't beg! You're delusional."

"I have an idea. How about a bet?" I say.

"A bet?"

"Yes, just a friendly wager between you and me."

"What are we betting?"

"Sex."

"Sex?" River repeats as if doubting what she heard.

"Yes, sex. I bet I can have you begging me. I can have you saying *Liam, please*," I say as seriously as I can.

She scoffs. "And just out of curiosity"—she narrows her eyes at me—"how exactly would that work?"

"Well, if you lose, you have sex with me and if I lose, I have sex with you."

She raises one perfect eyebrow. "And that's different how?"

I shrug. "It's a win-win any way I look at it."

"For you!" she accuses.

"For you too. You'll get those multiple orgasms you keep talking about."

"Once! I said it once!"

"Yes, I accept the challenge."

"What challenge? I did not challenge you to do anything! And what will keep *you* from begging?"

"I never beg, and I'm not depriving myself of you begging me."

She's getting a little flustered. I love it when her cheeks are flushed and I get her off balance. She's always so sure of herself, so firmly planted on her own two feet. I really, really want to affect her in the same way she affects me.

"It's very unfair really if you think about it. Guys don't get to have multiple orgasms. We've got one shot, and that's it."

"I'm not having sex with you!"

"Okay, we can do it the Clinton way then."

"What the fuck is the Clinton way?"

"I lose, I go down on you. If you lose, you go down on me. Don't worry. I won't get anything on your dress."

Her mouth drops, and she stares at me for a very long moment, and I worry I pushed her too far. With River I have no idea what her limits are. She never censors herself and is always in everyone's face.

I would never, ever say anything like this to another girl, ever. It's completely inappropriate and probably offensive as hell, but there's something about River that pushes all my buttons at the same time—that makes me want to push back just to see what will happen.

I know deep down that someday I'll go too far and maybe this is it. There will be a day I'll say or do something so fucked up it'll be the end of whatever this thing between us is. I love making her angry, love tipping her scales and pushing just to see what she'll do or say next and every time I see her—which is often enough being that our siblings are in each other's pants 24/7—I have the need to poke at her with a very short stick and watch mayhem unfold.

At night I relive those moments and laugh myself to sleep.

But right now, I'm a bit worried as I wait for her answer. It's the longest I've ever seen her take with a comeback.

And then the thing I least expect happens. She starts to laugh. And she's laughing so hard, she's holding her sides, nearly dropping her drink, and she has tears coming down her face. It takes me a moment to figure she's not mad. She's amused. Then I start laughing too because when someone is laughing that hard you can't help but join in.

She's wiping her tears away and trying to catch her breath. "Oh, oh my God—oh my God." Then she lifts her left hand to high five me. "Good one," she says, but as I slap her hand, I grab it and shake it.

"Okay, we got a deal then," I say.

Her small hand in mine stills. "What?" She sobers fast. "I did not agree with anything. There's no deal."

"Yes, there is, we just shook on it. In fact, we're still shaking on it. That's a deal and if you try to get out, you forfeit and lose."

She looks from my face to our hands still joined and tries to pull away, but I easily pull her closer to me so our bodies are touching.

"There's no deal. There's no bet."

I grin at her. "The way I see it, you can forfeit and lose now, or give it a shot and lose later. Either way, this bet is on. We shook on it. So, what's it gonna be?"

# CHAPTER EIGHTEEN

## River

"Arrogant son of a bitch!" He has me and he knows it. I'm too much of a hard-ass to back up from anything and I do love a challenge. Especially one that'll leave Liam on his knees. An image of him kneeling, his head between my legs takes over my mind and try as I might to shake it off, it just won't go away. *Bad River, bad—bad River!* I tell myself as if admonishing a puppy.

---

The stupid bet has been haunting me for three days. Three days I haven't seen him but can't stop thinking about it. Can't stop thinking about his hand holding mine, his chest brushing my boobs, his smell, clean and minty and something entirely Liam.

I have to put an end to this and I have to do it now. I know Logan is at work, doing whatever it is cops do driving around in their cars. This is the perfect time to corner Liam into backing out of this stupid bet so I can stop thinking about it and all the things I'd like him to do to me.

*River! Stop it! You are not helping! Stupid hormones.*

I walk to his house and the garage door is open. The SUV is parked on the driveway. And he is shirtless. Shirtless and doing pull-ups on a bar hanging from the ceiling. He's facing the wall and hasn't seen me here yet—the black track pants he's wearing hug his ass in the most delicious way—and I take a few seconds to admire his back and his arms, the way his muscles bulge and contract.

His hair is even longer now and brushing the top of his back. Long enough to grab on and hold on to when he lowers his head between my legs. *Oh fuck! Fucking fuckery fuck!* No, no, no, no, no. We are not going down that road. Again. *Jesus!* I need to stop thinking about him like that. He put all these dirty thoughts in my head. And they need out. Out. Out right now!

He drops to the floor, landing with more grace than I'd expect from a guy his size. He walks to a bench, picks up a towel, and rubs his face, neck, and chest before turning to face me, a smirk already on his face. "Did you enjoy watching me? I'm here every morning around this time."

He drops the towel and grabs a water bottle from that same bench and I notice for the first time, the mirror attached to the wall and the rest of the workout equipment around it. Busted! I don't bother with a denial and go straight to what I came here to do.

"We have to talk about this bet. It's ridiculous. We don't even like each other!"

He looks hurt for the briefest moment. I must be imagining things. I *know* he doesn't like me. Something tightens in my chest at the thought of Liam not liking me.

*Whatever. Barking up the wrong tree, River.*

"The bet stays."

"Why?"

"Because."

"Because is not a reason. I'm trying to be reasonable here. We have to be around each other because of our siblings. Maybe we can make this less annoying and weird and just act like polite strangers for a change."

"But we're not strangers, are we?"

"Well, yes, we kind of are. It's not like we know each other well."

He takes a step closer to me. "We will. As soon as you say that little six-letter word, we'll get to know each other very well."

"I'm never saying it. You must know that."

"I know a few things. Your breath catches when I'm within touching distance and your nipples get hard when I touch you. I know your hazel eyes go deep brown when I talk dirty to you. I know you watch me when you think no one is looking. And I know you press your thighs together when I lower my voice, like this"—he lowers his voice and takes another step closer and points at my thighs—"and like that." He smiles, not a smirk. A hungry, predatory smile. The smile of a hunter, just before he sinks his teeth in the prey.

I take a step back, engaging into a prey and predator dance when he circles closer to me. I stop. He stops, no more than three or four feet from me. I deny none of his words. I don't confirm them either. I'm so taking the fifth on this one. He waits for my move and I have no moves right now.

"Can we please be serious about this? And act like adults?"

"I'm very serious about fucking you and thank goodness we

are adults because the things I want to do to you are illegal in several countries."

The smirk comes out now. The left side of his mouth a little higher, a dimple almost makes him look like an innocent little kid, but the look in his eyes betrays him. There is absolutely nothing innocent about it. And damn it if I don't like it. I like the way he's looking at me and that's the very reason I have to put a stop to this. Because I know, I just know he could have me begging and I won't do it.

I will never beg again.

*But this is different.* The voice tells me. *I won't beg ever again,* I reply to myself.

"It will never happen, Liam. Give it up."

"Never." His reply is soft and even more intense because of it.

"Oh my God! You're so stubborn! You don't give an inch, do you, Liam?"

"I can give you eight."

"As if—"

"Would you like to check it out?"

"Please don't flatter yourself. Let me put things in perspective for you. Vaginas were designed to deliver a seven-pound-plus, twenty-one-inch-long baby. So there!" That gotta shut him up. *Fuck! Now my favorite number is eight.*

He looks at me and winces. "Yeah, that's gotta hurt. I wasn't going for pain, but hey, if that's your thing—"

"Ughbragh!" I growl. I actually growl. Then I walk way. Okay. I stomp my feet away. Why is every word out of his mouth about sex?

That little voice tells me he sounds just like me, but I tell it to shut the fuck up. I get as far as the garage door and turn back around. In hindsight, it was a big fucking mistake. I should've keep on going.

"You know what I hear, Liam? A whole lot of bark and no bite!" I walk back to him until I'm so close I have to look up to meet his eyes and then I jab my finger on his bare chest after each word. "Every time I see you, you tell me you'll fuck me five different ways from Sunday and yet here we are and it's just blah, blah, blah and you think all this talk about fucking will get me to come after you and beg for a lay? It will never happen!"

He grabs my jabbing finger and then flattens my hand on his chest. I can feel his heart's furious beat under the palm of my hand.

"Say the word, River," he orders me.

"No."

"Say the word, River. Say please."

I laugh. "You think you have a magical dick and I'm enthralled by it? Do rainbows and unicorns jump out of it when you come?"

His lips hitch up a bit at the mental image I painted for him. But he fights the smile, then moves my hand down his chest and over his abs and holy shit, I've seen his abs before but damn, touching them is something else altogether. I'm distracted and I should know what he's up to, but can you blame me? I didn't catch on until it was too late and there's a full smirk on his face and it's not the only thing that's full.

So is my hand. Yep. My hand is full of dick. His dick and it's hard and long and my freaking hand is actually groping him. Or it's trying to because I can't close my fingers around his dick. Fucking traitorous hand. I hate his track pants. I love his track pants.

He closes his hand around mine, tightening it around his

dick. Nope, still not able to close my fingers around him. "Why don't you give it a try and find out, River? I do like to bite. I like it a lot."

---

It's been two hours and I'm sitting on the couch staring at my hand when Skye comes in loaded with grocery bags.

"What are you doing?" she asks me.

"Do you think I have small hands?" I hold my hand up for her to see.

She puts her hand on mine. "No, not really. Our hands are the same size. Why?"

"Have you ever held a dick your hands could not wrap around?"

She blushes. The curse of pale skin. Every thought shows in her face.

"Logan?" I ask.

She nods.

"I guess it runs in the family," I mumble.

Her eyes go round. "You and Liam—"

"No. Nothing happened. Well, one thing happened. He grabbed my hand and put it on his dick."

"What did you do?"

"I didn't do anything. My hand did it all by itself." I hold my hand in front of me again as if it's an alien object. "This freaking traitorous hand has a mind of its own."

"But how? What—"

I cut her off before she has a chance to ask anything else. "I don't want to talk about it right now. It's weird. You're dating his brother. Come on, I'll help get the rest of the stuff from the car."

She lets it go, but I can feel her worried eyes on my back. She's been looking at me like that often in the last few months. If she only knew why I've been so evasive, but I can't. I can't talk about it. If I don't think about it, if I don't talk about it, it's not real. My rational brain recognizes what I'm doing. Denial is the first of the five stages of grief. I tell my rational brain to shut the fuck up. I've been saying it a lot lately.

# CHAPTER NINETEEN

## River

I HAD NO INTENTION OF GOING OUT TONIGHT, BUT WHEN Skye mentioned the boys were coming over to watch a movie and hang out, I knew I had to get out of the house before Liam showed up. I ran into him a couple times after the track pants incident and managed to be polite and stay cool. I made sure there was always someone else around when we met. Liam behaves himself when other people are around. He saves his special kind of pervert just for me. His words may be polite and casual when other people are around, but his eyes—they speak a language of their own. Those eyes tell me things that keep me awake at night. He'll be nice and casually touch me, his fingers trailing down my back or arms. It all looks so innocent from the outside. It's anything but. He knows what he's doing, and it's driving me crazy. Hence the need to flee my own home tonight and be at this party. It's been three hours now and I've had enough of the loud music, the mixed smells of perfume and cheap beer, and too many bodies bumping into me in the cramped space. Three hours should have been enough to watch a movie. I texted Skye fifteen minutes ago and asked her to pick me up, yet again.

The party is getting out of control. Two girls are making out with each other much to the delight of the hockey team. I try to get away from the girls, but I'm trapped in the corner by the half open window where I stand trying to get a breath of fresh air. I check my phone again. Skye said she'd text me when she gets here to pick me up. Nothing. I will never ride with Becca again. This is the third time she left me to fend for myself this semester alone. *Yeah, right.* I snort at myself. I know I will, if for no other reason than knowing that Becca doesn't have many friends and I need to watch her back.

The girl-kissing duo tries to pull me between them.

"Err—thank you, girls. But I will not be the third one on your ménage à twats. I kind of like dick."

I'm trying to pull away from them when a big muscular arm wraps around my waist and picks me up, pulling my back against an equally big and muscular chest. My feet are no longer touching the floor. Lips touch my left ear.

"You seem to be obsessed with dick. Every time you open your mouth, the word comes out. Or does this only happen when I'm around you?"

*Liam.* My arms instinctively grasp his, holding on as he easily gets past the girls and through the throngs of people. They part for him like the Red Sea.

"Put me down! Liam! Put me down right now!"

He stops, still holding me tight against his chest, and my body is all too happy about it. "Did you leave anything behind?"

"No, I have my phone and my purse."

"Then there's no reason to let you go."

He ignores my trying to pry myself from him and continues

to hold on to me. We're outside and he keeps on going, cutting across several lawns until he comes to Logan's truck. I can feel him, all of him through the fabric of my dress and his jeans. Then my brain registers it. I CAN FEEL HIM! And he's hard. Really hard against my ass. Fuck! I've been struggling this whole time, trying to get him to let me go, and all I did was rub myself on him. I stiffen. And his chest rumbles with contained laughter. He's enjoying this.

Then he opens the passenger door while still holding me, my feet still dangling, and slowly, very, very slowly, Liam slides my body down his. I feel his warm breath on my neck and his lips move into my hair, but he says nothing.

My dress of course rides up in the friction between our bodies and I'm so aware of him, of his smell, of his heat and the way his arm pushes into me and how my hands can trace and feel the muscles and the veins beneath it.

When he finally lets me go, I wobble a little and both his hands go into my hips, steadying me. I turn to face him, pulling my dress down my thighs, but it's too late. Thanks to the lights coming from inside the truck, he got a good view of my bare ass.

He smirks. "Now tell me please because I can't quite tell. Are you wearing a thong or are you panty-less?"

"I have underwear on! Not that it's any of your business!"

He pouts. He freaking pouts! *And fuck me! Fuck me hard if I don't want to suck on that lip and bite it. What's wrong with me? Bad River! Bad, bad River!*

"What are you doing here?"

"Skye was busy with Logan. I saw the message on her phone. I volunteered to come get you in her place."

"You volunteered? Is this the *Hunger Games* now?"

He looks me up and down slow, taking in the red dress I'm

wearing, the four-inch fuck-me red sandals that lace up my calves. He licks his lips. "Yeah, I'm really, really hungry right now."

My body tightens. There's so much lust in his eyes and so much promise in his words. I suck in a breath and mutter under my breath.

"What did you say?"

"Nothing."

"Oh, but I heard you, River. You said, *'fuck me, fuck me hard.'* I can do that. I can fuck you hard and I can fuck you slow. I can fuck you any way you want. Just say the word, River."

I scoff. "In your dreams!"

"Oh, River, in my dreams you have already been thoroughly fucked. In every way possible. You have no idea. But I can show you. Just say the word."

I bite my tongue, get in the truck, close the door, and look straight ahead. I can feel him looking at me through the window and then again while he drives us back to the house. I don't say another word until we get home. In fact, I just walk right into the house, past Skye and Logan entwined with each other on the couch watching TV and go straight to my room and lock the door. I don't say another word until the next morning when I first open my eyes, and when I do, the only thing I can say is, "Fuck me! I'm so fucked!"

# CHAPTER TWENTY

## River

Rolling out of bed, I drag my ass to the kitchen. Skye is sitting at the counter holding a cup of coffee and blowing on it before she takes a sip. When she sees me, she puts it down and walks to the coffeemaker and pours a cup for me.

"Thanks, sis." I feel like I have a hangover even though I didn't drink yesterday. I didn't sleep much. Liam's words are seared into my mind. *He dreams about fucking me? In every way possible?* When I did finally fall sleep, I dreamed of him and the way his body pressed into mine.

I look back toward her bedroom. "Logan didn't sleep over?"

"No, he has an early shift today. He left with Liam right after he brought you home."

She waited for me to say something, but I said nothing.

"How was the hockey party?"

I snorted. "It was a testosterone slash slut fest. These two girls tried to get me into a threesome with them."

Skye laughs at that. "Only you, River."

"If I ever tell you I'm going to a party with Becca again, please lock me in my room and throw away the key."

"I can't believe she left you hanging without a ride again. And why can't she find guys who have cars so she can let you drive?"

Becca has two rules. She only dates guys younger than her, and she never drinks if she's with a guy. Ever. If she's on the prowl for a hookup, she's sober and in control. There's a pattern to how Becca behaves. It didn't register at first, but of late and the longer I know her, there's more to Becca than meets the eye. I don't really know all the details about her life, but I know enough and what I know isn't good. Despite all appearance to the contrary, Becca is a good friend, but she keeps her past under lock and key. She has allowed little bits and pieces to escape here and there, but as soon as I try to get her to open up, she shuts me down. I can respect that. *I so* can respect that.

"Becca is a cougar in training. She only goes after freshmen and most of them don't have a car on campus. And she knows I have you to bail me out."

Skye looks at me over her cup and I know she'll ask me something I don't want to talk about.

"What's going on with you and Liam?"

"Nothing, there's nothing going on."

She narrows her eyes at me. "There is a *lot* going on. Maybe you two haven't acted on it yet, but you can't say there's nothing going on because it's clear for anyone with eyes that as soon as the both of you enter the same zip code there's a whole lot happening."

"There's nothing—"

"Why are you denying it? It's not like you to see something you want and run from it. If it were anyone else, you'd be all over him. Is it because he's Logan's brother? If so, you don't have to worry about it. We're good with it."

"First of all, I don't want Liam. Second, why are you and Logan talking about me?"

"You want him just as much as he wants you."

"No and no!"

"As soon as you come into the room, his eyes are all over you. He tracks you around like a heat-seeking missile and he always asks about you."

"He asks about me?" I'm surprised.

"He asks about you in very indirect ways."

"Like what?"

"Like he's asking me questions about me, but they really are about you."

"Can you be a little more specific?" I say, irritated.

"Like, 'What are the Devereux girls up to today?' or he'll make a comment about whatever we're talking about, but he's really fishing for info on you."

"Where's all this talking taking place?"

"Every time I go over at Logan's and he's there. We talk sometimes."

"And you're just telling me this now!" My irritation is rapidly approaching bitch levels.

"I thought you weren't interested." She smirks at me. She's got me.

"River, you know you can tell me anything, right? We haven't really talked in months. You used to tell me all about your dates. If Liam is anything like Logan, he'll be a solid ten."

Yeah, I used to talk to Skye about everything. I have certainly overshared, even when she did not want to hear it. But I can't anymore. I just can't. To say it out loud. To actually say the words—it will make everything real and I can't. I can't make it real. I want to forget it. I want to forget it ever happened and then the irony of it hits me so hard, I don't know if I want to laugh or cry. I want to forget something I can't remember. I cried enough, so I choose to laugh.

"Well, you haven't shared much either, Skye. Why don't you tell me about Logan?"

She blushes and I successfully deflect the conversation to her.

# CHAPTER TWENTY-ONE

## River

We're about to clean up after dinner when my cell phone starts to ring.

I look down and see it's Mom. I cringe a little because I haven't talked to her at all in nearly two weeks and I know she will not stop calling until I answer.

I accept the call and put it on speaker, placing the phone on the table between us so Skye can talk to her and take some of the heat off me.

"Hi, Mom. How are you?"

"She lives!" Is Mom's sarcastic reply.

"Sorry, Mom. I've been busy. Hey, I have you on speaker. I'm here with Skye, Logan, and Liam. We just finished dinner."

"Even E.T. found a way to phone home, and he had to use an umbrella. Being that you have a cell phone at your disposal, you'd think it would be easy enough for you," she says, but there's no anger in her voice. Mom never gets angry.

I've been avoiding calling her since our last talk. Mom always knows when something isn't right and I really don't want to get into a Liam discussion with her again.

"I'm really sorry, Mom. Just busy with school and all."

"You've been busy with school for the last three years and that never stopped you."

"Hi, Mom," Skye jumps it, trying to deflect Mom's attention. That never worked. "How's dad?"

"Skye, I spoke with you this morning already. You know your dad is fine. River, there are only two acceptable reasons for why you haven't called me all week."

There's a pause before she continues.

"One, you're so sexually frustrated because that boy has not taken you to bed yet, and your hands have been too busy trying to get yourself off for you to reach for your phone, or two, that boy has taken you to bed and you have not left it yet and are too tired to reach for the phone—"

"MOM!" Skye and I say at the same time.

I'm blushing, Skye is blushing. I look over at Logan and Liam and they're both blushing. *Holy shit!* How could I have forgotten how my mother gets when she wants to make a point?

She goes on as if we haven't just called her name.

"So, Liam, which one is it? Frustrated or satisfied?"

Liam's mouth opens and closes a few times and he looks at me like I can stop my mother.

"I'm sorry?" he finally says.

Thankfully she lets him off the hook. "Well, I just want to make sure everyone is alive. Don't make me drive all the way over there, River. Call me. Got to go now. Love you all!"

"Okay, bye, Mom."

"River?"

"Yes, Mom."

"You should know better than put me on speaker." And with that she hangs up.

We all look at each other in silence for maybe ten seconds

until Logan bursts out laughing and then Liam and Skye. I'm not laughing.

Skye looks at me. "Ah, come on, it's funny."

"Holy shit," Liam says. "Now I know where you get it from."

I scoff. "And you think I'm inappropriate? Try growing up with her."

# CHAPTER TWENTY-TWO

## River

No school today because it's the last week of classes and we're pretty much done. The next two weeks are finals and project presentations and then, that's it—graduation. My only plan is to sleep in and maybe move from the bed to the couch, Netflix and chill. The alone kind of Netflix and chill. Tomorrow I can start cramming for exams. But like all the best laid plans, someone or something always derails it. This someone being Skye when she walks into my room, opens the shades, then plops herself next to me on the bed. I squint against the invasion of light into my previously darkened room, pulling the covers over my head and trying to avoid the conversation I know is coming since Mom's call last night.

Skye pulls the blanket back down and off my face.

"Fess up, what exactly is going on between the two of you?"

"It's complicated."

"I have time."

Stretching my arms over my head, I arch my back and settle into the pillow, finding a more comfortable position. "Well, you may as well sit down. Oh, wait, you already are." Is it too early for sarcasm? Nah . . . never too early or too late for sarcasm.

Skye seems annoyed as she grabs a pillow of her own and props her head on a hand to look at me.

"Okay, I'm ready. Just dump it on me."

"We have a bet. A bet he coerced me into."

"A bet? What kind of bet?"

"A sex bet."

"Come again?"

I narrow my eyes at Skye. "Is that your idea of a pun?"

"What do you mean?"

"You said, 'come again'—is that a double entendre?"

"No! Oh—I get it. No, I did not mean it like that. Although now that you bring that up it *is* funny."

"So anyway, as I was saying. He trapped me into a sex bet. He thinks he can make me beg for sex or a kiss. Whichever comes first."

She's trying really hard not to laugh. "How did you get sucked into this bet?"

"I have no idea. But I think it started back home over Easter."

"I thought you two hated each other back then, but now thinking about it, it's not hate at all. It's sexual tension. Enough tension to send a rocket to the moon."

"Tell me about it. He taunts me and takes every opportunity to tease me. I might have to take back that vibrator I bought for you. Did you open it yet?"

"Err . . . so not going there with you."

"I will take that as a yes. So, eeew, no. Not sharing it." I smirk at her. "Come on, you can tell me."

"Yeah, so you can bring it up next time we're having a family dinner? No, thank you."

"I won't. Pinky swear." I lift my pinky to her and she knows I won't say a word. Pinky swear is law.

"I had it in my nightstand and Logan opened the drawer to stash condoms in there and found it."

"And?" I encourage her.

"After I nearly died of embarrassment. He opened the box and plugged it in to charge."

Skye does her best impersonation of a tomato and presses her fingers to her cheeks as if that could contain the redness spreading on her skin.

"I'd still rather have Logan and the real thing, but it's a nice addition to our—"

"Fuck fest? Told you you'd have fun with it."

"I was going to say lovemaking." Skye still blushes often, but she's holding her own more and more. I love the new confidence with which my sister carries herself.

"Yes," she continues, "but back to your issue. What are you going to do about it?"

"I don't know. All my insults and efforts to stay away from him are not doing anything. He just comes back at me harder. Double entendre intentional. If it weren't for that stupid bet, I'd be all over him. I'm afraid I've fallen in lust with him."

Skye bites her lip, which tells me she's thinking. She smiles a devious smile and it's all kinds of wrong on her usually angelic face. Logan is doing her good. In more ways than I think she realizes.

"What?" I ask, eager to know what she's thinking.

"What are the exact terms of this bet?"

"Whoever gives in first and asks, A.K.A. begs the other for a kiss or anything sexual wins."

"And what exactly do you win?"

My face blushes at this. "Head. Or sex."

"Come again?"

"Whoever loses has to give the other head—oral sex—cunnilingus, blowjob, or have sex."

"Okay, okay, I get it. That is the weirdest bet ever. You have to ask for sex to win sex?"

"Yep. That's all him. He came up with this."

"You know, River, two can play this game. He's obviously attracted to you. You can use it in your favor. I think it's time for you to be the cat instead of the mouse."

I look at Skye and I can't believe I haven't thought of this before. "Turn the table on him? Make him run for a change? I love it!"

"Time to put on your big girl panties, River."

"Fuck the panties! I'm going commando."

"Does that mean you're actually flashing him?" Skye asks me, concern in her voice.

"I'm going Basic Instinct on his ass."

"Oh shit. What have I done?"

"I love you, sis. Always have. But Skye 2.0 is so much cooler than original Skye. Logan is good for you."

## CHAPTER TWENTY-THREE

# River

Liam and Logan are coming over for dinner. I'm standing behind the shades watching through the window when Skye comes into the living room.

"What are you doing?"

"Watching the window?"

"Why?"

I give her my most devilish smile. "*Operation Knock Liam On His Ass* has been activated."

She looks me up and down. "Is that what you're wearing?"

I look down at my ripped denim daisy dukes and baby blue tank top. "Too much?"

"No, not enough. Everything is hanging out."

"That's the point, Skye. It's not like I'm going out dressed like this. Just hanging out at home in casual clothing like I'm not expecting anyone to show up."

"But you do know they're coming—wait, are you wearing a bra?"

"Yes and no," I answer both her questions.

"My boyfriend is coming too and those boobs of yours could eclipse the sun on a bright day."

"Logan only has eyes for you. I could parade around here naked and he wouldn't even notice." She looks alarmed. "But don't worry. I won't."

I look out the window again. "Oh, here they come!" I run to the kitchen, open the freezer, and grab a grape ice pop and run back to the living room. I lie down on the couch, casually propping my legs on the back of it, and grab a book. Sucking on the ice pop. I smirk at Skye.

"You're going to kill Liam."

"That's the idea."

"Flip the book, it's upside down."

No sooner does Skye tell me that, than there's a knock on the door. She lets them in and I wait for a few seconds until I'm sure Liam's eyes are on me. Then I look over my shoulder at the door and let my head drop over the side of the couch so my hair is falling to the floor. My girls are popping over the edge of my tank top and I'm looking at Liam upside down. Then I suck the ice pop almost all the way down and pull it out slow, never breaking eye contact with him. I lick the top then my lips and smile. "Hi, guys."

# CHAPTER TWENTY-FOUR

## Liam

*Ahh fuck!*

What's she doing?

And what's she wearing?

And why the fuck is she upside down on the couch looking at me while sucking on a popsicle?

Her lips are tinted a wine color from the ice pop and her eyes are locked on mine. And did I mention she's sucking on the damn thing, sucking it all the way down and—shit! Now she's licking it.

I think she said something and Logan behind me laughed and said something in reply before following Skye to the kitchen. I don't have a clue what either of them said. Because I have no fucking blood left in my brain and I probably need that shit to make my ears work.

My dick, however, is working just fine right now. And so are my feet because somehow, I end up right by her. She turns her head to look at me better, then rights herself, wiggling her ass into the couch to get comfortable. Half of her ass is peeking out of the cutoffs she's wearing. That damn ice pop is still in her mouth and she's moving it up and down, up and down, sucking and licking.

"What're you doing?" I hear myself ask. It's more of a growl.

"What does it look like?" she asks me back. The tip of the ice pop rests on her plump bottom lip and her tongue comes out to lick it. She looks at me all innocent, but my dick and I know River just amped up the game.

"You reading?" I ask and I'm dumbstruck by my own words because I really have nothing right now. I'm used to being in charge. To being in control. I attack and she retreats. That's how we play this game and River just changed it up on me.

"Not really, just looking for the good parts." Her lips form an O around the ice pop and she sucks it a little harder.

"Why do girls like to read smut? Doesn't it leave you high and dry?"

"Who says I'm dry?"

*Fuck. Me.*

Skye's voice floats to us across the kitchen island that separates the two spaces in the open concept living room. "Try chapter three and oh, chapter seven gets a lot better." Then Skye squeals. When I glance over, Logan has his arms around her and his face in her neck.

River moves and I watch as two melting drops slide down the ice pop and fall to her chest, running down into her cleavage. My eyes follow.

"Oops," she says as she dips two fingers between her tits, catches the drops, and brings them to her mouth, sucking on them. Book abandoned on the couch, she gets up and stands inches away from me. Her cinnamon and sugar scent envelopes me. She gives the ice pop one more suck and lick.

"Better go clean up. I'm all wet and sticky now." Then she takes a bite of the ice pop tip, hands it to me, and walks away toward the hall. I stand there with her melting ice pop, wondering what the fuck just happened.

# CHAPTER TWENTY-FIVE

## Liam

We're done with our late lunch and just waiting for the check when we hear voices from the booth just on the other side of us. At this time of the afternoon, between lunch and dinner crowds, King's Pub is empty and the voices carry easily over the thin dark wooden panel that divides the sections of booths. The wall is about six feet tall and runs the length of this section, giving people on both sides privacy. Normally we wouldn't be able to hear the people on the other side of the panel, but in the quiet afternoon their voices are clear. Both Logan and I notice when Skye freezes and tenses. She looks at him and mouths one word: *Jon.*

I have no idea who this person is, but Logan seems to recognize the name. He nods once and stays quiet, so I follow his lead and tilt my head to better hear what the two men on the other side of the wall are saying.

"You're not going to believe who I saw yesterday," one of the men says.

"Who?"

Skye flinches when she hears his voice.

The other guy replies, "Your ex."

"Which one?" The asshole snorts. I don't even know him and I already hate his guts.

"The one who got away," the other guy says.

"Skye?" Jon asks him back.

"The one and only. You never tapped that, did you?" The other guy laughs.

"The little bitch put up a fight every time I tried. Cold as a dead fish."

Logan fists his hands on the table and Skye covers them with hers. My lips press in anger.

"She wasn't putting up a fight with the guy I saw her with yesterday, right outside Pat's Cafe. In fact, it looked like she was really enjoying all the mauling and groping that was going on."

Logan smirks at this and Skye blushes.

"Who's the guy?" Jon sounds pissed.

"Don't know. He looked older. I don't think he's an RU student. Big dude too. Maybe you're just not big enough for her," the other guy teases.

"Well, her sister didn't complain about it," Jon retorts, venom dripping from his words.

Skye's mouth opens in a small gasp. I shift in my seat, ready to take the wall down and beat the living shit out of this Jon guy. It's Logan's turn to grab my arm and still me. The two on the other side of the partition continue talking, ignorant of our presence and how close they are to a beatdown.

"River? No way you tapped that. She hates your guts."

"Maybe she didn't. Maybe it was all a front because she wanted me but couldn't have me thanks to her sister. I wouldn't have minded double-dipping into the twins." He laughs.

"No way, man. I don't believe you. River hates your guts. When did this happen?"

"About a year ago."

"No, it didn't happen. If you had said last week, I might have believed you. But a year ago, there's no way. Those two are tight and—"

"It did and I have proof."

"Proof? What kind of proof? Did you get a video or something?"

"No, nothing like that. But she has a birthmark shaped like a heart in a place no one would be able to see. And I saw it."

I look at Skye, hoping for denial and finding confirmation. The shock in her face is enough for me to know it's true. The asshole had, at the very least, seen River naked and her heart-shaped birthmark, wherever it is.

"Dude, where's this birthmark?"

"Not telling you and if you say anything about it to anyone I'll kick your ass."

"Why are you keeping this on the down low, man? I know you like to brag about all the ass you get."

"River doesn't want anyone to know and if anyone says anything and it gets back to her, she'll know it was me. If it comes back to me, I'll point her in your direction. Do you want to be on her shit list?"

"Hell no, that bitch is crazy."

Skye gets up and walks out, making sure the two guys don't see her. Logan goes after her but not before giving me a look that says, *don't do anything stupid.* I get up and intercept the waiter before he can get to our table and hand him a fifty. It should be enough to cover lunch and tip. Stepping outside, I meet Skye and Logan by the car. The day is warm, but I feel chilled inside.

"Can someone tell me what's going on? And while you're at

it give me a good reason not to go back in there and kick that guy's ass."

Logan looks at Skye and she nods. He turns back to me. "Jon is a guy Skye dated back a couple of years ago."

Skye takes over. "We only dated for a few weeks. Not even a month. He was nice and sweet at first but then turned out to be a jerk, and River hated his guts. From day one she made it very clear she thought he was an ass, and she told him every opportunity she had. I can't imagine she'd ever hook up with him."

"You think he was lying?"

"I would, except for—"

"Except for what?"

"He knows about the birthmark. How can he know about it? It would be impossible for him to know unless he—" Skye's gaze drops to her feet. She can't even say the word.

"It makes no sense at all. River hates him. She called him, '*you know nothing Jon asshole,*' to his face every time she saw him," Skye says.

She looks at Logan. "Can you take me home? I have to talk to River. Whether or not this is true, she needs to know Jon is talking about it."

"Sure, babe."

I open the back door of the car and settle in. "I'm coming too."

Logan looks at me. "Liam, this has nothing to do with you."

"The hell it hasn't. Try stopping me." I glare at him.

Logan's shoulders drop in resignation. "Okay, I guess we're all talking to River."

# CHAPTER TWENTY-SIX

## River

Skye and the guys walk in and when I glance at them, I can tell something is wrong. There's apprehension in Skye's face. Logan looks resigned and Liam seems mad as hell. I put my notebook on the coffee table and get up, my eyes darting from face to face. They're acting like they're ganging on me for some unknown reason.

When I stayed home to study for a final instead of going to lunch with Skye and the boys, the last thing I expected was for them to come home planning a fucking intervention. Especially when it's for something I have no fucking clue about.

"What's going on?"

"River, I—" Skye looks around, and I can tell she hates whatever she's going to say next. She's clearly upset. "We have to talk to you about something you probably won't like." She looks at Logan as if searching for reassurance.

"Maybe you two should discuss this alone," he says.

"What's going on?" I ask again.

Skye lets out a heavy sigh. Logan leans on the wall by the door, his hands in his jeans pockets, and Liam has his arms crossed, his legs apart as if standing at attention, an odd look on his face.

"I'm not going anywhere," Liam replies to both of them and if possible stands even taller and stiffer.

"What's going on?" I ask for the third time.

"When we were at the restaurant, we ran into Jon." She looks nervous and intently at me. As if I should have some kind of reaction to her words. "Well, he didn't see us, but we overheard his conversation."

"You know nothing Jon asshole?" I frown. I hate the guy.

"Yes."

"What about him?"

"He said he slept with you."

"Come again?"

"He said he had sex with you, River—"

My body tenses. I'm getting angry now. I don't like feeling like they're backing me against a wall.

"I know what slept with someone means. What I don't know is why you're telling me this as if you believe him."

I cross my arms defensively, much like Liam, I realize. Mrs. Spencer, my behavioral psychology professor, could have used me as a text book example in class. My body language says: *Back the fuck off because I don't like where this shit is going one bit.*

Skye wrings her hands. She hates confrontation. She's always the peacemaker and I can tell it's hurting her to ask me this.

"Because of what he said."

"What did he say? And when, please enlighten me"—my sarcasm is full-on now—"did Jon and I have this love affair?"

"He said about a year ago—"

I cut her off, "You do know I hate his guts, right? More

than hate, I despise him. He's a piece of shit and I wanted to throw up every time I saw him with you."

Right then what Skye said hits me. *About a year ago.* Could it be? *No, God no. Anyone but him. Not Jon. Not Jon. Not Jon. I can't take it if it was Jon.* There's a mantra in my head and it keeps repeating, *not Jon, not Jon, not Jon.*

"I still don't understand why you think I'd ever have sex with him. I'd rather fuck a hanger in my closet."

"Because he knows, River."

"He knows what?"

"He knows about the birthmark. He described what it looks like and he said it was in a place no one could see unless . . ." she trails off.

My arms drop. My defensive posture, gone. I feel myself go limp. The mantra inside my head turns to screams, but I don't say anything. I need out. I need to run and hide. I almost collapse right then and there and it takes everything I have to hold on. I don't say a word, don't deny, and as the first sting of tears burns my eyes, I turn and walk to my bedroom, closing the door as Skye's voice reaches me, calling my name. I try to make it to my bed, but three steps into my room, I fall to my knees and the tears follow.

*Not Jon.*

*Not Jon.*

*Please God.*

*Not Jon.*

*Not Jon.*

*Not Jon.*

## CHAPTER TWENTY-SEVEN

# Liam

I SEE IT IN HER EYES. THE MOMENT RIVER KNOWS WHAT Skye is saying is true. And I see something else too. Something I've seen all too often in my own reflection. Something I hoped to never see again. The look in her eyes, the hurt, the pain, the shame, it's all there, and in this moment, I know what happened and I know River just found out herself.

It took every fiber of her being to walk away. She's crumbling inside. I recognize that too.

The same despair I've seen in my own eyes. The powerlessness of what-ifs, the pain of regret and wishing for a different outcome. It's all there in her eyes, and I'm frozen in place as I watch it unfold.

Skye calls after River and enters my line of vision. I snap out of it and stop her.

"No, I'll go. You stay here with Logan."

Logan turns to me then. "I don't think that's a good idea, Liam. Let Skye talk to her—"

I get in his face, years of marine training kicking in, and through gritted teeth I say, "I'll go. You both stay here. Do not follow me. I'm going to talk to her alone. Do I make myself clear?"

Logan flinches but doesn't say anything. He looks at Skye and she nods.

Knocking softly, I open her door and step into her room, closing it behind me. She's on her knees, her body bent on itself as if trying to be as small as possible, her shoulders racking with silent sobs. I kneel next to her and pick her up, curl her to me like a baby and walk to her bed. Sitting down, I lean against the headboard with River on my lap.

She doesn't fight me or say a word. She just cries and every so often her head shakes slightly, as if saying 'no.' I take a deep breath, my chest expanding under her, and let her pain wash over me and mingle with mine. And for the first time since I was seventeen, since my parents turned their backs on me, I cry. I cry silent tears like River's.

I feel her pain as mine and I feel my own pain breaking free again, remembering the day of my own attack. I hold on to River and cry. Cry for myself and all that I lost and I cry for River because I know what happened even if she hasn't said a word about it.

I know what this guy Jon did to her and I know I'm going to kill him and enjoy doing it. I'll do it with my bare hands. I look at my hands then, the hands that so gently hold her trembling body against mine, the hands that have patched and stitched and saved hundreds of lives. These hands will see blood again, but it won't be from a bullet wound, an explosion, or shrapnel. These hands, my hands will see Jon's blood on them. They will take a life instead of saving it. I want him to look into my eyes when the light goes off in his own, knowing I did it for River. The bastard will never hurt anyone again. It's a promise I make to myself. A promise I make to River even if she'll never know it.

After a long while her sobs diminish, her shoulders no longer trembling. I reach over to her nightstand and grab a few tissues, dabbing her eyes and drying her face. Her eyes are red and swollen, her skin is blotchy, and her nose is running, but when I look at her, at the wet lashes that frame her hazel eyes, now green from all the crying, I can't help but to think she's beautiful. Then I grab more tissues and dry my own eyes. She looks at me confused because of my tears, her eyes searching mine, searching my face, and I let the walls drop. I let my shields down and I let her see me. I let her see the boy inside the man. I let her see the pain behind the sarcasm. I let her see all the broken pieces that make me what I am today and how I long for the carefree and happy kid I once was. I let River see all of it and she understands, even though she doesn't know what caused my scars. She sees them and she doesn't pull away. She touches my face with her fingertips and then palms my cheek—I lean into her hand and close my eyes. When I open them again, there's a small smile on her lips. Her walls are down. She dropped them for me and the openness in her eyes nearly undoes me. Then I tell her. I tell her everything.

# CHAPTER TWENTY-EIGHT

## Liam

SHE ASKS NO QUESTIONS. SHE DOESN'T SAY A WORD AND yet there's so much being shared right now. So much happening between us. The last three months of fighting and getting on each other's nerves is coming to an end and we find ourselves in an odd and yet comforting place. We both share a secret, a part of our lives we've never shared with anyone else. We both have pain and scars we go to extreme lengths to hide. I bear some of those scars on my skin, hidden under the color and designs of a tattoo, but they're still there. The other scars, the ones we carry in our souls, are far deeper and harder to hide from.

She moves from my lap but sits in front of me. Her legs curl under her. I bring my left leg up, bent at the knee, and she leans on it. My hand finds her hair and plays with it.

"Logan thinks I was discharged three months ago, when I first showed up at the house. But the truth is, I was discharged over a year ago. I spent all that time backpacking through Europe, crashing with some friends, in hostels, and more often than not, working on small farms and sleeping in barns."

Her eyes remain on mine, the tears gone but her long lashes

still damp. I brush a lock of hair behind her ear and her eyes flutter closed for a moment before meeting mine again. She stays silent and I continue to speak.

"I should be dead."

Her eyes widen and she flinches. I squeeze her shoulder, letting her know I'm okay.

"I was in an explosion, within the kill zone. My back was covered in shrapnel and I was in an induced coma because of swelling in my brain, a result of the explosion impact."

I close my eyes to the haunting images swimming right in front of me as if it's happening now, but I can't escape the memories inside of my mind. I can smell the gun powder, taste the dust that coats my throat and the blood on my tongue. The sounds of destruction and death sting my ears. I can still feel the impact of metal shards as they entered my body and the deep burn of each piece as they cut through my flesh.

Thankfully, I don't feel the pain. I was once told the brain has a defense mechanism that keeps the body from reliving pain. So while one can still remember the tastes, smells and how it felt, the physical pain itself is blocked. I wish the brain could also block the pain of loss, the despair of dying, the impotency of not being able to save a life you swore to protect.

When I open my eyes again, she's watching me intently. Her breath is even, and it calms me. I take her hand, press my fingertips to her wrist, counting the beats of her heart. I match my breathing to hers, our hearts in sync. It gives me strength to speak out loud the words that never left my lips before.

I give her the short version of my story. "As far back as I can remember, all I wanted to do when I grew up was to be a doctor. I used to read medical books for fun. I was such a nerd, I know."

She smiles at that.

"Logan was always a jock. He loved sports, he loved the competition, the adrenalin that came with it. Hockey, football, running—it's how he felt alive, how he could be himself and do what he wanted without our father being up his ass." I pause, letting the memories wash over me.

Her hand squeezes mine in a show of support.

"I loved playing sports too but for a different reason. I didn't play to win. I just liked the way being active made me feel. For me it was a study in anatomy. The way the muscles moved and worked together to accomplish a goal. Nerd, remember?"

"If the nerds in my high school looked like you, I so would have been in the math and science clubs." She makes me laugh despite the heaviness in my heart right now.

"Our parents, my father specifically, had strict ideas of what we should be and do. Our future was mapped out for us. We were to go to law school and join him in his company. Neither one of us was too keen on it, but we knew better than to say anything. We tried to keep our heads down and stay out of his way as much as possible. When Logan went to college and showed some resistance to our father's plans, his focus turned to me—he was going to make sure I didn't stray."

I take a deep breath before going on.

"I applied to several schools where I could take pre-med classes and as the school year rushed into the end, I didn't get a single letter back. No acceptances or refusals. I was getting worried. My grades were perfect, and I had no idea what was happening. Then I found out my father was intercepting and hiding all the replies I got back from the universities. I confronted him. He showed me an acceptance for pre-law at Harvard, my father's alma-matter and a school I didn't apply to. I told him I wouldn't go into law school and he told me I would. We had a huge fight. It was the first time I ever raised my voice to him. He didn't take it well. He told me he would never pay for any college other than pre-law at Harvard and until I decided to comply, I wasn't welcome at home any longer. He kicked me out."

"Oh my God! What did your mom do?"

"She tried to reason with him and with me, but neither of us would listen to her. In the end, I crashed with a friend for a couple of nights, trying to figure out what I would do. I was seventeen, weeks away from graduation. My birthday's in June and because I was a minor and my parents made too much money, I wasn't eligible for any kind of student loans. I went home when I was sure neither of them would be there and packed my things. I had no idea where I was going. Mary, our cook, gave me the keys to her apartment, and I stayed with her. My parents had no idea. Still don't. Mary had always been more of a mom to me and Logan than our own mother. She even offered to loan me her life savings to pay for the first semester of college. I couldn't take it, of course. I finished high school six weeks later and enlisted in the navy. On my eighteenth birthday."

"Did your parents try finding you?"

"No. They didn't even show up for my graduation. Only Logan and Mary were there. Mary said Mom wanted to go, but my father forbade her. He was sure I would come home with my tail between my legs and do his bidding. When I was researching a way to pay for college, I stumbled onto a website and found I could train to be a medic with the army or a corpsman with the navy and eventually, once I finished my tours, I could enroll in college. So that was my plan."

"You were so young. Your parents didn't try to stop you?"

"They had no idea. I didn't tell them. They never bothered

trying to find out where I was. The last time I saw or spoke with either of my parents was the day I left home."

"But what about Logan? Didn't you try to talk to him?"

"I didn't tell Logan either. Not until I was already enlisted, and it was too late for him to do anything about it. He was furious with me for not reaching out to him. He went back to Connecticut to confront our parents. It was the first time he'd gone back since what happened with his ex."

Her hand covers her mouth and I tug it back down, lacing my fingers with hers.

"But why? Why didn't you tell Logan what happened? Didn't you have anyone else you could reach out to?"

"I was young, stupid, and angry at the world. Not a good combination. I could have gone to Logan. Or my grandmother. I know, either one of them would have helped. Would have loaned me the money for school, but I needed to do it on my own. I needed to prove to my father I was not dependent on anyone."

Understanding flashes in her eyes.

"Fast forward a year and I'm a corpsman with the marines on my first tour in Afghanistan. Dr. Foster, Hannah, was the head medic and took me under her wing. She had a daughter not much younger than me and I think somehow, I filled the void from not having her daughter with her. I learned a lot from her and we watched each other's backs. On my second tour, we worked together again with an entirely new platoon. There was this one soldier who came to the medic barracks for help. He was high on something. We have to report everything, but we especially have to report anything that could put the lives of other marines at risk. His friends tried to pressure me into lying. I didn't. The next night, I was staying overnight at the medical unit so I could keep an eye on the guy who nearly

O.D.'d. It was late, maybe two or three in the morning, and I was sleeping. There were five of them. I tried to fight back, but they overpowered me. One of them shoved a T-shirt in my mouth and put duct tape over it so I couldn't scream. They carried me into the dunes, under the cover of darkness, and started to taunt me. They said I had to learn a lesson in loyalty and how not to turn my peers in. They tied my hands behind my back. In the beginning, it was just shoving and pushing. Then the punches started. They made sure not to hit me in the face or any place marks would show. They told me if I talked, they'd come back and kill me. It would be easy. Friendly fire in the chaos of battle. It would come, I'd just never know when. I tried to fight back and the more I kicked at them or shoved back, the angrier one of them got. He said the beating was not breaking me down. He said there's a sure way to break a man and I would soon learn how."

I let go of River's hand and fist my own. The rage and fear come back to me. I breathe through it, willing the anger away before I speak again.

"This one guy told the others to hold me down. Then he told me he was going to rape me. It would be my punishment for not keeping my mouth shut. Two of the marines holding me tried to talk him out of it. He threatened them as well. They shut up and held me down. I fought them even harder, but they were marines. They had the same training I did. One of them put me on a headlock—while the others held me still—applying just enough pressure so I wouldn't be able to fight but not pass out either."

New tears pool in River's eyes, and she's shaking.

"Hannah saved me. She came to the barracks to check on me and she heard sounds coming from the dunes. She saw the lights from their flashlights and followed it. She walked up to them and pointed her rifle directly at the head of their ringleader."

"They didn't . . ." she whispers.

"They didn't. Hannah stopped them before they could do anything. She stopped them just in time. Two days later all five of them had been transferred to different units. I don't know how or what happened to them. Hannah never said a word about it to me, but I have a strong suspicion she was behind their transfer. We never talked about it or what happened. I owe her my life. Three times over."

"Three times? What do you mean?"

"On our last tour, we were working at a village together. It was a show of goodwill toward the villagers. We vaccinated kids, treated the elderly, pregnant women, and anyone who needed help. At the end of the day we were packing and about ready to leave when the first shot broke the quiet. Everybody ran for cover, hiding behind trucks and walls. I ducked behind our medic truck and Hannah was across the road. She ran and hid behind a crumbling wall. It was barely big enough to give her cover. It wasn't safe. Nowhere was." I have to stop and take in a few breaths before I allow the barrage of images flooding my mind to come forth.

"Training kicked in and our group assessed the situation from whatever position they were in. We located three shooters on top of a building fifty or so yards away from us. Hannah was in a bad spot and she knew it. We decided to lay down cover fire so she could move to a safer spot. The team started to shoot at them, but when Hannah tried to run across the road, the first bullet hit her."

River gasps at this and reaches out to me, her hand finds mine, our fingers lace and I draw strength from her touch.

"There was a fourth shooter, hiding behind us—we didn't

see him. We were trapped between them. I ran to her and trying to shield her, to get to her before any more shots came. The truck I had been hiding behind exploded. It'd been hit by a grenade. That was the second time Hannah saved me. If I hadn't run to help her, I would've blown up with that truck. I got to her just as the truck exploded and another bullet hit her. I caught her before she hit the ground, but I knew it was too late. As I held her in my arms, her body shielded me from the explosion and took most of the impact, most of the shrapnel. That's how she saved me a third time. We both fell to the ground. I rolled her under me. I refused to believe she was dead. A secondary explosion knocked me unconscious but not before I felt the impact of hot metal hit my back and side."

River's face is washed in tears now. My own vision blurs, my voice trembles.

"When I came to, two of my men were dragging me into a building. I was still holding onto Hannah. The rest of it is fuzzy. I was in and out of consciousness. A backup team arrived soon after. They caught the shooters. All of them. Hannah and I were airlifted to base. The only next-of-kin I had listed in my records was Mary. She was the one they contacted. Mary knew the last thing I wanted was for my parents or Logan to know what happened to me and she kept my secret. I know it cost her, but she did it because I asked her to before I left—if anything happened to me, I didn't want my parents to know—and she promised me she would keep her word. Mary was the only one I communicated with regularly. I called Logan every so often—he sent me a lot of text messages, but I never responded. I think Mary kept him informed too, but she didn't say anything to anyone about me being hurt. She kept her promise."

"They still don't know?"

"No. Logan has no idea. My parents don't even know I'm

back. I told no one. None of this. No one knows what really happened."

She bites her lip and leans into my chest. My arms go around her. I pull her closer to me and we stay like this for a long time. We're both lost in thought. Slowly, her sugar and cinnamon scent replaces the smell of blood in my memories. The heat from her skin warms the cold in my soul. Her touch heals my pain. Her presence chases away ghosts. Like always, when she's near me, there isn't room for anything else. She fills all my dark and empty spaces until there's nothing left, but I need to pull her closer to me still. I tighten my grip on her—a drowning man holding on to the last source of air.

# CHAPTER TWENTY-NINE

## River

We stay in that position for a long time. Me, between his legs, Liam holding me and letting go of his memories. His body relaxes into mine with each passing minute and I wonder why me? Why of all the people in his life, he chose me to talk to? Then I remember why we're here. For a few blessed moments, Liam's pain made me forget mine. His sharing strengthened me. I understand what he's doing. What he's doing for me. In confessing his darkest secret, in trusting me with this, he's letting me know I'm not alone. He's letting me know he's here for me and that I can trust him too. He's sharing his pain and in doing so, making my own pain lessen somehow.

His vulnerability and openness make it possible for me to be honest with myself. When his words break the silence, they are soft, just above a whisper, but the weight of them nearly crumbles me.

"He raped you."

I suck in a breath and nod. Liam is not asking, he's making an assertion.

"He drugged you and you had no idea who it was until now."

Again, I just nod.

"Tell me what happened, River."

I move away from his lap then, needing to put some distance between us for this. I sit with my legs crossed and face him. But Liam doesn't let me go far. Mimicking my position, he pulls me back until our knees touch. It strikes me then that he'll be the first person to know what happened that night. That he'll be the first person I'll talk to about it. Not my sister, not Becca or any of my friends. Not my mother or my father and not the police. But this man, this man who spends most of our time together teasing me and challenging me. This man with eyes that search my face and see into my soul. He knew it the moment I figured it out myself. I saw the look on his face and he knew it. Logan didn't pick it up. Skye is utterly oblivious, but Liam realized Jon had raped me at the same time I found out myself.

I let my eyes drop to my lap and close them, allowing the few memories I have to float back in. I've spent the better part of a year trying to forget them. Probably not in the best way to deal with them and now I'm inviting them back in. Liam's patient. He doesn't push or ask again but waits for me to be ready.

"It happened about a year ago. I was at a frat party with my friend Becca. We hadn't been there for an hour when Becca told me she was leaving for some guy she met. I drank nothing besides a soda. The guy Becca left with had a car and she gave me her keys so I could drive myself home. I thought one beer wouldn't hurt me and I could go back to water or soda after. I wasn't planning on staying late because I had a paper to finish. The party had been Becca's idea. After that things get fuzzy. I remember seeing Jon outside, but I ignored him and didn't think he had seen me. I walked to the keg and got a cup and filled it myself. It wasn't even filled to the top. I went back to the living room and sat with some people I knew from sophomore year."

I concentrate, trying to recall anything I might have overlooked before, now that I know it was Jon. And it comes to me. I look up with a sharp inhale of breath as a sliver of memory fights through the haze of that night.

Liam picks up on my reaction. "You remembered something right now, didn't you?"

"Yes."

I look at him, willing the bits and pieces to fit together. "There was this one thing that always bothered me, but it was just outside my grasp."

"What is it? Do you remember?"

"Yes, I think I do."

I take a deep breath. "I'm always careful with my drinks whenever I go out. I've never trusted anyone to get me anything. I'm not stupid. I know shit like this happens." I laugh a humorless laugh. "I never expected it to happen to me."

"No one does." Liam waits for me to gather my thoughts.

"It always bugged me that I couldn't figure how I was drugged. But now I think I know."

I shift on the bed and roll my shoulders. Liam reaches with both hands and squeezes them, kneading the tension away. When he drops his hands after a few minutes I continue.

"My phone was buzzing and when I tried to get it out of my pocket someone bumped into me and I instinctively raised my cup hand so it wouldn't spill on me. The person apologized, and we talked for a moment. I remember seeing Jon walking across the room. And now I realize he had been somewhere behind me. I think when that guy bumped into me, Jon put something in my drink."

I close my eyes, letting the images flow back to me. "I remember feeling nauseous and dizzy, and going upstairs to look for a bathroom to splash cold water on my face and escape the smell of cigarettes. I remember getting to the bathroom and waking up hours later but nothing in between."

"What happened when you woke up?"

My lips tremble and the sting of tears follows. That was the worse of my memories. "I was very confused, had no idea where I was or what had happened. I had a horrible headache, and it felt like I was drunk and had a hangover at the same time." My eyes drop to my lap. This was the hardest part, what happened after I got my bearings, what I realized then. "I was lying inside a bathtub and someone had thrown a towel over me. The shower curtain was closed, and the light was on." I squeeze my eyes shut and take three deep breaths. When I look up at Liam, I can feel the tension radiating from him, but he says nothing. He waits for me to be ready to speak again and I'm grateful for that. "I noticed I was missing one of my sandals. And that"—I choke on the next words—"that my underwear was caught around my right ankle. Then the pain hit me. And when I looked down at myself, the skirt of my dress was hiked up around my waist and there was blood smeared on my thighs."

"Jesus! He hurt you so bad he made you bleed?"

I look him in the eyes. "I was a virgin, Liam." I can see the surprise on his face.

"Everyone thinks I was hooking up left and right and I did have my share of boyfriends and dating. But after seeing what Skye went through with her high school boyfriend, I decided I'd have all the fun I could and still keep my V-card until I was one hundred percent sure the guy I was with would not dump me a week later and then tell stories about me." I smile a fake smile and he knows it.

"I guess it's a moot point now. He took that away from me, too."

"I'm so sorry, River. No one should have to go through anything like this and knowing he took that away from you. . ."

He touches my face, wipes away a rogue tear. The gesture so gentle, it's barely there. His eyes search mine, for what I don't know but he must have found whatever he is looking for, because absolute determination takes over him.

"I'm going to kill him."

"If anyone is going to kill him, it will be me."

I steel myself and tell Liam the rest of the story. "After a few minutes I pieced together what happened. I got out of the bathtub and I found my purse on the floor. When I took my phone out, it was off. I know it was fully charged when I left the house and it had been on, so he must have turned it off. When I pressed the power button, and the phone turned on again, it was five twenty-three in the morning. There were several missed text messages and calls from Skye. The house was silent. My legs were very unsteady and I grabbed the sink to pull myself up. I found my other sandal behind the toilet bowl. Then the heaves started, but there was nothing in my stomach to come up. When I looked at myself in the mirror I didn't recognize the face reflected in it. I was so pale and my eyes looked glazed over, dead. I checked my body and found black and blue marks all over. There were purple welts on my upper arms as if someone had grabbed me very hard. I could see clear fingerprints on my right arm."

Liam's hands fist in anger.

"I realized then I'd been raped." The emotions of that day

rush over me and I speak with my eyes closed. I cannot bear to look at Liam and see pity in his eyes.

"My first instinct was to call the police, but fear and shame slammed into me. My legs wobbled and I sat down on the side of the tub, staring at nothing, I don't know for how long. I looked down and saw my panties still twisted around my ankle. I steeled myself and took deep breaths. I thought about what I could say to the cops. What did I have to go on? I was at a party and I drank half a cup of beer. It had to be laced with something because one cup of beer would not have knocked me out. The last thing I remember is getting up to go to the bathroom, but I did it alone. No one helped me up the stairs or down the hall and then … nothing. I don't remember walking into the bathroom or if anyone followed me inside. But someone must have. Even if I remember nothing after that, someone had to have been watching me and waiting for the drugs to take effect. Then he followed me into that bathroom, raped me and left me behind. When I touched myself, the blood was dry, and there was no semen. Whoever it was, he used a condom. Years of psychology classes kicked in then and I instantly compartmentalized whatever I was feeling. I had studied trauma cases in the three years at RU. I knew all the phases I would go through. I couldn't let everything hit me at once. It would crush me. One step at a time, I thought. First, clean myself up. Second, get out of there. Third, figure out what happened. Fourth, come up with an excuse for Skye. If I told her any of it, she would call our parents and next thing I'd know, I would be home listening to crystal singing bowls and receiving Reiki and energy therapy."

"Now that you do know, what are you going to do?"

"I don't know. It will be his word against mine. I can't testify because I don't remember anything. I can't say for sure it was him. All we have is circumstantial evidence."

"I just want to kill the bastard, but Logan will know what to do."

"You can't, Liam. Promise me you won't go after him. Promise me you won't do anything stupid."

The pleading in my eyes can't be denied and he nods.

"That's not enough, Liam, please. I need to hear you say it."

"I won't go after him, I promise."

I looks at him for a long time, trying to assert if I can trust his word. Finally, I find what I'm looking for and my shoulders relax.

"Death is too good a fate for some people. I'd much rather send him to prison where he'll be someone's bitch."

He laughs as a little of my spitfire spirit comes back. It would poetic, wouldn't it? To see a rapist on the opposite end of the equation.

# CHAPTER THIRTY

## River

I FORGET MY OWN PAIN WHEN I LOOK AT LIAM. THE words that came out of his mouth were hard to hear. My heart breaks for him. For all that he endured and for what he's doing for me right now. He knew. I don't know how he knew, but he did. And it's so much worse for him than it is for me. He has memories and nightmares that will haunt him forever while I have the knowledge but no memories. I have been spared that. I'm thankful for it. We all deal with our demons differently. For me it was always the not knowing. The idea that he—the man who attacked me—could be anyone and anywhere. That he could have been a classmate, a friend, or a complete stranger. And not knowing took away control over my emotions and my body. He had that. He had that knowledge, and I didn't.

But now, now that I know who he is, I can take control back. Knowing gives me that. Having a face and a name to go with my attacker heals something in me. I can't change what happened. But I can change how I live from now on. I'm taking charge of my body, my thoughts, and my actions again. I'm no longer driven by a faceless monster. Now I'm driven by the need to make him pay and the need to create new beautiful memories where the blank spaces exist. He took a piece of me. A tiny piece. But he didn't take my worth, or my courage, or my zest for life. He can't have that. I won't allow it.

My monster didn't have a face until today, and now that he has one, now that I know who to be on the lookout for, the need to watch over my shoulder all the time lessens. Going to parties I didn't want to go to try to trigger a memory, socializing with people I didn't want to be around in hopes someone would say something—all that can stop now. I can stop faking it for Skye's benefit. I can trust again. I have a target and I have a goal. Jon will pay. One way or another. He'll pay.

Looking into Liam's eyes, I find that right now they're more blue than gray, as if the storm I so often saw in them is finally gone.

I kiss him. I lean into him and let my lips graze his. I feel his harsh inhale when he takes the breath out of my mouth and into his, and when he exhales, it's my name on his breath over my lips. He doesn't take over as I expect him to—he lets me explore and take control. He gives me power over him.

With a simple kiss Liam makes me whole again.

I change my position, crawling forward until I'm straddling him. I run my fingers through his hair, grasping it at the base of his neck and pull him down to me. His hands resting on my hips flex and his fingers grasp me. "River," he whispers, his eyes searching mine. "What are you doing?"

"Shh," I shush him and lean up, bridging the last few inches between our lips kissing him for real now. More than a graze, I taste him. I let my lips meet his and I nibble his bottom lip. When I hear the groan that escapes him, I smile against his mouth. *I did that.* Then I pull his face closer and open his lips with mine and let my tongue dip into his mouth. I relish him. I savor Liam and he tastes better than I ever imagined. He kisses me back gently, his hands fisting on my hips as if he's trying to exert control. But I don't want control right now. I don't want him to hold back. I want all the promises he made me. I want all the things he said he would do to me if I just asked. And I'm asking right now. Without words, I'm asking, but Liam's still holding back. I deepen the kiss and whimper when he meets my demands and kicks it up a step higher. His hands tremble with exertion on my hips. I tug at his hair and break the kiss, murmuring his name against his lips. He moans against mine, and his hands finally move.

He grabs me harder and shifts my body over his and—oh God, I could die right now. He's so hard under me and I can feel him pressing into me. One of his arms wraps around my waist and the other tangles into my hair, tilting my head, and he finally, finally takes over our kiss. My hips move of their own accord and I'm rocking and pressing into him, into his hardness—I love how good it feels. I curse the clothes on our bodies that keep us apart. He kisses me like he's been waiting his whole life to do it, his tongue on mine. He sucks and nibbles and challenges me to meet his demands.

"Jesus! River—" He pulls his mouth from mine just to return it to my neck. He grazes the skin there and the rough day-old whiskers on his chin make me shiver.

The hand tangled into my hair tugs my head back, not gently but not hard either. His lips trace patterns of his own making on my skin. His tongue darts out and he licks and nibbles at me. He traces the contours of my jaw and nibbles on my ear and then he bites me. He follows the bite with open-mouthed kisses.

*Holy shit, that's hot!* I'm burning. My skin is on fire and he hasn't even touched any of the good parts yet. And then I remember I have hands too and this whole time I'm just holding on to him. I let my hands travel up his arms and I love the feel of the muscles flexing and contracting under my palms. And when he licks the hollow of my throat, I dig my fingers into his shoulders, then move my hands over his chest and lower over his stomach. His abs contract under my fingertips when he sucks in a breath. I let my hands stay there, tracing the ridges and lines as his mouth returns to mine. I want to move my hand lower, but my position on top of him doesn't allow me to and I don't want to stop. No, I can't stop pressing myself into him because it feels so, so good, but I need more and I need more right now.

"Liam," I speak into his mouth, pulling away from him just enough to look into his eyes. They're dark with lust and something else I can't identify. Gray and blue mingle in his irises. A clear day breaking through storm clouds.

"Liam," I say his name again and he looks at me and shakes his head once.

"Not like this, River. Not when we're dealing with so much pain, not right after all we talked about."

"I want new memories, Liam. And I want them with you."

"I want you and I want a thousand memories with you. I will have you and I will give you those memories. I will make you mine, I promise you, but not right now, not today," he says.

Whimpering, I press into him, rocking into his hardness trying to lessen the ache between my legs. I haven't dated anyone or even touched myself in over a year. My body rebels and demands satisfaction.

"I need, I need . . ." I let the unsaid words dangle between us.

He smiles at me with that wicked smile of his. "Okay, there's something I can do."

Before I know it, he's flipped us over on the bed and I'm lying on my back and he's firmly pressed between my legs, rocking into me. He searches my face and finds whatever he's looking for because he leans over and kisses me. I'm so hot with need and frustration I want to cry, but Liam can read me and he reaches around my right thigh, grabs my butt, and pulls me up, changing the angle in which he's grinding into me and just seconds later my whole body seizes and tightens up, I want to scream, but there are no sounds coming from me as my back arches off the bed and I'm coming for seconds and minutes and days. All the anger, frustration, all the pain and shame, all the fear I carried with me for the last year, gone, released. My body completely relaxes for the first time in over a year. Liam gave me that. He freed me. The irony of it hits me. Making out with Liam, this almost sex, took away the ugliness of my rape. As I come down from my high, I realize I've just had the best orgasm of my life and I didn't even take my pants off. A girl could get used to this. When I finally open my eyes and look at Liam, he's smiling at me.

"Better?" he asks and I want to give him a witty and sarcastic answer and punch him at the same time. Old habits die hard. But I can't move, not even to speak. I have no legs or arms. My body is melted into the bed. I'm a puddle. Liam laughs at me and I can still feel his hardness.

"You," I mumble.

"Don't worry about me. I'm going home to shower and think of you."

Then he scoops me up as if I weigh nothing, pulls the covers, and settles me on the bed. He tucks me in.

"I'll be right back."

Liam walks to the door but stops and stays just behind it.

"What are you doing?" I ask.

"I can't go out there like this." He gestures at his groin, the outline of his erection clear for anyone to see.

My eyes drift down and I bite my lip.

"You're not helping, River."

"What did I do?"

"Stop looking at me like that," he says and adjusts himself.

I smile because really, what else could I do? He groans and turns around, resting his forehead on the door.

"I can still feel you looking at me. Turn around and don't look at me. I'll be back in a minute. I just want to get you water and something to eat before I go home."

I turn around, but I'm still smiling.

A minute later I hear the door open and I call out to him with a loud whisper, "Don't impale anyone with that thing."

He stops, the door half open. "Oh fuck, now you did it again."

I'm trying not to laugh, but my whole body is shaking with mirth.

He glances over his shoulder at me. "I will make you pay for this."

"Promise?" I whisper, the laugh no longer in my voice.

Liam says nothing, but his eyes go dark with promise before he leaves my room and quietly closes the door.

## CHAPTER THIRTY-ONE

# Liam

As soon as I step in the hall, Skye and Logan look at me from their spot on the couch.

I walk into the kitchen and grab two water bottles, a couple of cheese sticks, and a bunch or grapes. I set them on the counter and open cabinets until I find what I'm looking for, pulling out a box of crackers. When I turn to Logan and Skye, they're both looking at me expectantly. "She's okay. Or she'll be okay soon enough." I look pointedly at Logan, willing him to read what's in my eyes and he gets it. I can tell by the way his eyes open slightly and the press of his lips.

I look at Skye. "She will talk to you. Just give her a little time." Then I look at Logan again with a warning not to say anything. This silent communication is something we developed as kids so we could make sure our stories matched when we did something that would annoy our father, a way to avoid his fury. And every little thing annoyed him and unleashed his anger on us. We got really good at silent communication.

I return to her room and close the door behind me. River's sleepy eyes are on me. I sit on her bed and brush a lock of hair away from her face, tucking it behind her ear. Her skin is no longer blotchy, but her eyes are still red. A small smile plays on her lips and I place the food on the bed between us. "I come bearing gifts." I grab a water bottle, break the seal, then give it to her. River sits up and takes a long sip from. There's a question in her eyes. "I told them you're okay and to give you time, but you need to talk to your sister."

She takes a deep breath. "I will—I just need time to get my head around it."

"I know you do. But first eat something and then go to sleep. Call me when you wake up or if you need anything, okay?" I open the second water bottle and drink from it as River pops a grape in her mouth. "I'll tell your sister you're sleeping and not to disturb you. Is that okay?"

She nods. I run my knuckles across her cheek, lean in, and kiss her forehead. My lips linger on her skin. I close my eyes, inhaling the scent of her. River smells like something exotic, spicy with a touch of cinnamon. It's heady.

"I want to talk to Logan. See what he can do in a case like this. Is that okay with you?"

She hesitates. "I guess. I-I feel so ashamed. I feel so stupid."

"Look at me, River." When I'm sure her eyes are on me and she's taking in every word, I continue. "Do you think I'm stupid or I should be ashamed for what happened to me?"

"No!" Her reply is fast and angry. "Of course not! None of it was your fault. You had no control over it. You didn't choose it. How can you even ask me such a thing?"

"Exactly! I didn't choose or have control over it any more than you did. You were drugged, and I was overpowered. It wasn't your fault any more than it was mine. We both should have been able to feel safe among friends. If you feel this way about me, then grant yourself the same level of respect and kindness you've shown me. Can you do that?"

"I can. I guess it would be very hypocritical of me to judge my situation any differently than yours."

"That's my girl. Get some sleep. We'll talk in the morning."

"Liam?"

"Yeah?"

"Can you stay with me until I fall sleep?"

I move the food to the nightstand and settle in her bed. She curls into me, her back to my chest. My arms find their way around her waist as if they had done this a thousand times before. Her body melts into mine. Her scent, the way her chest rises and lowers with each breath, it's all so new to me and yet so familiar. Like remembering a dream. Something that has never been real before and yet I've lived it. Memories of a tomorrow I hope for.

# CHAPTER THIRTY-TWO

## Liam

When Logan and I are finally alone at home, I know I can't put it off any longer. Logan won't let me get away with not saying anything.

He locks the door behind us and drops his keys on the table. Then turns to me as he toes his shoes off. He's waiting, his eyes trying to read me and hear what I'm not saying. He's in full cop mode now.

I run my fingers through my too long hair. I'll need to cut it soon.

He walks to the living room, sits, and waits for me. I exhale and sit across from him.

Logan waits. He doesn't say a word. Again, cop tactics. If you wait long enough, the other person eventually speaks to avoid the uncomfortable silence. I'm not uncomfortable about the silence. What bothers me is the fact I have to share a secret River kept for an entire year even if she did give me permission to talk to Logan. I imagine she's talking to Skye now or will talk to her soon. Shame and pride kept her silent long enough. Some people may never understand that kind of silence. That kind of denial, but I do. One would think a victim of such a horrible thing would want to run to the police and demand their attacker be arrested. But I know different. Even with proof and witnesses, such crimes are hard to prove and all too often fall into the hands of overpaid lawyers or dismissive judges. It's not a question of who's the criminal and who's the victim but a question of who has the best lawyer or the most power behind them. It sickens me and my first instinct is to say, *'fuck the law'* and take it into my own hands. I'd love to put my hands around that asshole's neck and watch his eyes dull and roll over as I squeezed the life out of him. After I beat the shit out of him first. But River read my intent all too well and made me promise I wouldn't do such a stupid thing. Killing him or even hurting him is not worth me going to jail, and Karma will take care of him one way or another. Well, fuck if I don't want to change my name to Karma.

I look down at my hands and realize I've been fisting one hand into the other and cracking my knuckles. My hands itch to cause damage, to break bones. I can barely contain myself. I feel like a caged animal and my own memories come back. I gave River the cliff notes version of it, but there was so much more. Yeah, the five bastards who attacked me beat me pretty good even if they were careful not to leave any marks on my face, but they never finished the job they had intended on. The beating was just to let me know they could, that they had overpowered me. They were trying to break me down. My body first, then my spirit. Hannah saved me. She saved me that day, and she continued to save me every day after. Somehow, she got all five of them transferred far away from me. By the end of the week they were gone to separate places. I never heard of them again, so maybe Karma took care of them too. Hannah was more than a friend and a mentor. She was the one spot of light in the darkness that fell over me for months afterward.

Had they'd been successful on their intent, I don't know what I would have done, but I'm pretty sure I would not be here right now. I think—I think I would have killed myself. I would not be able to live with myself if their intent had come to completion. Half of me can't imagine what River is going through and the other half has a very good idea. I think River having no memory of it might be a blessing. God knows I'd love to be able to forget what happened to me and what almost happened. I'll never forgive them and I'll never forget it. Be it in nightmares or flashback, or just random memories hopping into my head, it's always there.

Except when I'm around River. I never think of that day when she's present. I never think about the day Hannah died either. At first, I didn't realize, but after a few chance encounters, it dawned on me that whenever she's near, the random haunting thoughts in my mind take a back seat to her. It made me angry and grateful. Angry I forgot the sacrifice Hannah made for me. She saved my life again, one last time at the cost of her own. I don't want to forget that, not for a day, not for an hour, not for a second. I owe Hannah more than my life. I owe her my sanity. I owe her all the days ahead. Days she will not have. Days her husband and daughter will go through without her. And then I feel gratitude because for those few moments of whatever the hell we have between us—be it a joke, an argument or a lot of teasing and sexual frustration—for those moments, I forget. For those moments, none of the past happened, and I'm just a twenty-three-year-old guy who's acting like a high school kid being a jerk to the girl he's attracted to. And I'm attracted to River. There's no denying it. All sexual innuendos and not-so-subtle sex jokes aside, from that very first day when she dumped her fruity drink on me, I've felt drawn to her. I may have been pissed as hell that spring morning, but my dick was ecstatic. Which pissed me off even more.

I look back at Logan, silently watching me still. Studying all the emotions crossing my face.

I let a heavy breath out, moving my head from one side to the other, trying to shake off the tension of the last few hours, and then I speak.

"She didn't sleep with Jon. But he did see the beauty mark on her body."

Logan narrows his eyes at me, trying to hear what I haven't said and a second later he gets it.

"He raped her." It was not a question. "But she never reported it. Why?"

"She didn't know it was him until Skye asked her about it. The beauty mark comment gave it away."

"She was drugged?" he asks me, but he already knows the answer.

"Yes. She doesn't remember anything other than taking a few sips of a drink and waking up in a bathroom several hours later."

His eyes drift from mine. "Jesus! I've seen this happen so many times, but you never think it can happen to someone you know. Does she want to press charges now?"

"She said yes, but I don't think she's sure. And I'm not sure he'll be served justice either. It's been a year, and all we have is her word against his."

"Yeah, but guys like him, they very rarely do it just once. There has to be other victims. This may be happening to other girls even now."

He looks at me then and sees the intent in my eyes.

"No!" His voice is firm, and it leaves no doubt he'll fight me on this. Logan has had my back my whole life and I his, but we're not in agreement on this one.

"No, you can't do it, Liam. As much as you want to go after this guy and fix this yourself, you can't."

"Why not?" I ask in defiance.

"You know why. You can't be a vigilante. You can't take matters in your own hands and go beat the shit out of him. He'd come back and send your ass to jail for assault."

"Who said I'd let him come back? Scum like him does not deserve to breathe."

"So, you'd turn into a murderer?"

"Not a murderer. I'd just give Karma a little hand. Make things move along a little faster."

"Yeah? And what about when Karma comes after you to fix your wrongdoing?"

I shrug.

"We'll get this guy, I promise you. But let's be smart about it. He has probably done this more than once. Some of the girls might remember something. We can watch him. We can prevent him from doing it again. We can go after him, but we'll only catch him if we're smart about it."

He takes a deep breath. "Promise me, Liam, promise you're not going to go off on your own and do something stupid."

I meet his eyes. "I've already promised River I wouldn't."

"That's good enough for me."

# CHAPTER THIRTY-THREE

## River

Liam shows up minutes after I get home and he has my favorite drink, raspberry lemonade. He must have been watching out for me.

It feels awkward, being with him again after what happened. After all we shared and me begging him to make out with me.

I guess I lost that bet, but he has not brought up any of it.

Going to class today was strange and liberating at the same time. Now that I have a face for my attacker, I feel safer. I've spent months and months wondering if every guy I came across was the one. Had been the one and was just biding his time to do it again.

I rarely come across Jon on campus. It's big enough that one can easily go all four years and never meet another person unless they are in the same majors or buildings. He and I are not. Come to think of it, the only places I saw that asshole after Skye broke up with him was at parties.

I hesitate for a moment before taking the cup from his

hand. I take a sip and my eyes drop to the floor. We're still at the open door. Neither of us has said a word yet. Liam breaks the awkward silence.

"Can I come in?"

I nod, still not saying anything. What can I possibly say to him now? I have no idea what to do when we're not at each other's throats. Well, with exception of yesterday. But now, under the bright afternoon light and being somewhat removed from the initial shock, I don't know who we are to each other anymore. Do we go back to harassing each other and throwing barbs? Are we kind of friends now? Did the kissing and making out mean anything beyond him trying to comfort me because I begged him to? Does he feel sorry for me and that's the only reason it happened? The thought of Liam pitying me fills me with anger. I don't want him to pity me. I don't want him to look at me and see the rape. I want him to see me. Just me. Nothing else.

My feet take me to the living room and I sit on one end of the sofa, legs folded under me. Liam takes a place on the sofa as well, close enough to touch but still giving me space. He seems to know I need some distance between us. He's studying me, trying to read me. I hate that, and I need that. I need someone to see into me and hear the words I can't speak. I'm a fucking mess. Why would anyone want to be near me now? I don't even want to be near myself.

He takes the cup from my hand and puts it on the table but not before picking up a magazine and using it as a coaster. Attention to detail. I guess he figured Skye's pet peeve about wet cups on the table.

"Hey, how are you?" His voice is soft but not tentative.

*How am I? How the fuck am I?* Anger simmers to the surface

and it must have shown in my eyes. Before I have a chance to say a word, his fingertips touch my lips and silence me. The gesture so tender, so filled with care, it calms me down. Anger dissipates like sugar melting in water.

"No, River. No. I don't want a BS answer. I know you're hurting. I know you're angry. That's not what I'm asking. I'm not asking about the consequences of what happened. I'm not asking about the side effects of what you found out yesterday. I want to know about *you.* The you that exists beyond all that. The only *you* that matters. *The real you.* The *you* we shared yesterday. That's the you I'm asking about."

I shake my head as if I have no clue what he's talking about, but I can't lie to him any more than I can lie to myself. He sees me. I wanted to be seen and got that. I have always been an in your face kind of person. Always acting strong and with an I-don't-give-a-fuck-attitude. But there's a part of me that does care. There's a part of me that just wants to have someone to be in charge for once. I'm tired. So tired of keeping my defenses up.

He waits me out.

"I'm tired, so tired, Liam."

My confession escapes my lips against my will and on the same breath I pull my defenses back up.

"No. Don't do that. We're way past that point. Don't go back."

My gaze drops from his. I've lost the courage to look into those gray eyes. If I do, he'll break all the barriers I've built around me. And then what? I don't know. I never allowed anyone to get this close to me. To see this much.

"Let me in, River, and I'll do the same. I've already done it. You know more about me than anyone else does."

My lips part, but no words came out. Again, I wonder, is it

strange that of all the people I could have confided in, Liam is the person I chose to open up to? Not my sister, not my parents, or any of my friends. It's Liam I feel safest with.

"Why is it," I ask, "of all people I could have talked about this with, it was you I chose?" I look at him, shaking my head. "I don't understand it."

He takes my hand in both of his, turns my palm up with one, and traces his fingers in the middle of it with the other.

"There's strength in vulnerability. In opening yourself to someone else and letting them in, in letting them see you as you are without walls or masks or any of the social niceties people seem to be so fond of. And all the crap people use to create barriers where there should be none."

He looks at me, waiting to make sure I get what he's saying.

"Will you let me in, River? Will you keep the walls down and open for me? Not just today, not just right now, but tomorrow and the day after as well?"

My chest fills with a deep breath. We're having a moment here. A moment where we're not trying to lash at each other or provoke a reaction. A moment of openness. I feel vulnerable. I've had my heart on lockdown for so long and Liam got past all those walls and doors and locks without my even realizing.

If I let him in, he'll have the power to break me. To break me even more than Jon did. Can I take the risk? Can I allow myself to fall in love with him? Is this even what he's asking me?

That little nagging voice in my mind speaks, *'You're already half in love with him, you fool.'*

Tears run down my face without my permission and he wipes them away with his fingers, a touch so gentle, if I hadn't watched his hands do it, I might have thought it was my imagination.

"Why am I crying?"

“Sometimes our eyes cry before our hearts and souls know we need to.”

# CHAPTER THIRTY-FOUR

## Liam

I WATCH THE LAST OF HER TEARS DRY ON HER FACE. Liquid pain, expelled from her body. I watch as her walls crumble and fall, one by one, and the River I see inside is brighter than the sun. This River with no barriers or attitude is tender and gentle. I love it. I love the tough and scary River too. I love all of her parts; all of her quirks and I even love that mean streak she has. But right now, none of it is present. Just River, as she once was, long ago before the world touched her and taught her she needed to hide her real self behind an attitude and guard her too kind heart. I wonder when it first happened. When disappointment touched her and left a mark.

What was it that first drove her inside? I might never know. She probably doesn't remember it herself. Do any of us?

Does anyone remember the very first thing that broke their heart?

That hurt so deep, it left a mark? I don't think so. And it's probably a good thing.

I push a lock of hair behind her ear and she turns her face into my hand. This is River giving in.

Opening for me.

Letting me inside.

I will not take this gift for granted. I will not break this trust.

I know there will be no second chances.

# CHAPTER THIRTY-FIVE

## River

He leans in and kisses my forehead, his lips touching my skin for a long time. His hand is gentle on the back of my head. Then he pulls back. He brings me with him and settles me on his lap. He doesn't say anything else or ask questions, just holds me tenderly and nuzzles my head with his lips, kissing my hair every so often. I relax against him, my body molding to the shape of his. I can feel the heat of his skin, smell the scent of him, his chest moving with each breath. There's nothing sexual about it. It's comforting, and it surprises me. My eyes go heavy and close without my permission.

When I come to, the first thing I realize is that I must have fallen asleep. Not unheard of. I've taken a nap or two after classes before. The second thing I realize is that I'm not on my bed. Or the couch. Nope. Memory of what happened before I fell sleep is slow to break through the fog, but when it does, I know it. I'm on Liam's lap still. I have no idea how long I slept. I'm in that haze that follows unexpected naps. When you don't quite know what time it is, or what day it is and did I have lunch yet because I'm hungry.

When I open my eyes, he's watching me. The blue-gray color draws me in. He's so beautiful. He's smiling at me like he can read my mind. My first impulse is to jump out of his lap. As if anticipating it, the hands that up to this point were loose around me, tighten.

"Good evening, sleepyhead. Did you have a good nap?"

"I fell asleep on you? You should have woken me up."

"Why? You looked so comfortable and you needed the rest."

"How long was I out for?"

"A couple of hours."

"All that? You couldn't be comfortable with me on your lap."

"I'm fine and I enjoyed watching you drool." He laughs.

"I didn't drool," I say, but wipe my mouth anyway.

"And you snore too. This low rumble like a cat purring."

"I don't snore either!" I punch him lightly on the shoulder for emphasis.

"Well, if the snore upsets you, guess I shouldn't tell you about the two farts." He's laughing.

I try to punch him again, with a little more conviction this time, but her grabs my hand and brings it to his lips, kissing first the back and then my open palm.

"I'll have you know, girls don't fart."

"No? What do you call that sound coming out of your bottom?"

"We sing. Girls have musical butts. We're composers."

His whole body is shaking with laughter and I join in.

I don't think I have ever had a fart conversation with anyone before and him telling me those things, oddly enough doesn't embarrass me. But I'm a little nervous maybe I did fart in my sleep. Who knows? Is it possible people fart in their sleep?

He's reading my thoughts again. "No, you didn't fart. I might have, though." He's laughing even harder now.

"Ewww." I punch him on the shoulder again.

# CHAPTER THIRTY-SIX

## Liam

I didn't get much sleep last night. Nightmares kept me awake—my attack and River's mingled into the same dream. The images get fuzzier as the light of day pushes away the night. Every once in a while, a fragment pops into my mind and disappears just as fast.

It's been an interesting few days. River and I meet every day. We hang out at Pat's or either of our places. We talk and get to know each other better. She told me about her growing up on a farm with hippie parents, who gave her and Skye all the freedom they wanted but also the responsibility that went along with it.

Her childhood is so different from mine. She grew up loved and confident in that love. Confident in her place in the world, and in the knowledge that her family would always have her back. I, on the other hand, had to watch my back. Mine and Logan's. We watched out for each other. I can't even imagine what it's like to have that. Shaking off the self-pity, I check the time.

My eyes land on the alarm clock: 8:43 a.m. I grab my phone and find River's number.

**Liam: Hey, what time do you have to be in class?**

**River: Not until eleven.**

Her response is fast.

**Liam: Do you want to grab breakfast at Pat's before you go to school?**

**River: Yes, give me 20 minutes. I'll meet you there.**

I roll out of bed, brush my teeth, and take a quick shower before finding a pair of jeans and a soft gray Henley.

I wait until I see her walking to the café before I cross the street. She's wearing skinny jeans and loose white Riggins University T-shirt.

She stops and waits for me when she sees me walking her way. I meet her out front. We hesitate, not quite sure where to go from here. The scent of apples and cinnamon envelops me in the light breeze. Her scent. It makes me hungry and not for food. Getting ahold of myself, I lean into her and kiss her forehead. My lips linger for a few seconds. Her eyes stay closed a moment longer when I pull back. I take her hand and open the door for her. Pat watches us and when we walk to the counter to order, she already has two cups of coffee lined up, two breakfast quiches, and a blueberry muffin, already cut in half and buttered.

"Pay me tomorrow," Pat says and waves us away. It's the same old Pat. I don't know how she stays in business. I drop a twenty in the tip jar when she turns to help another customer. She narrows her eyes at me. Every so often she'll do this. Tell someone to pay her tomorrow. I guess it's her way of paying it forward or giving back.

We're sitting in our favorite corner by the window now. *Our favorite corner.* When did I start thinking of this spot as ours? I don't know. At some point, over the last two months, I started thinking of River and I as *us,* instead of two separate entities.

Between bites, she updates me on her talk to Skye, which went much the same as with me. Tears and questions of why she didn't ask for help or talk to anyone about it.

"As difficult as it was talking about it, opening to Skye and you, I'm glad I did it. I'm glad you overheard that conversation and pushed me to talk. I feel lighter somehow."

"I know what you mean. I feel the same way." I do. And I don't. I feel lighter, but also exposed. I'm not sure how to behave. I want to be sensitive to what happened to her, and I want to throw her against the wall and have my way with her. *I'm an asshole. Fuck!* I was an asshole three-days ago too. Kissing her and making her come. But she asked me to. Should I have said no? Should I have stopped and left? She said she needed new memories. I understand that. I want new memories too. I want them with River. I'm so confused. I don't know what the proper procedure is. Do we keep talking about it? Do I try to make-believe the making out didn't happen? No. Hell no. It happened and it will happen again. If she lets me. But now, knowing what I know, it doesn't feel right pushing her into our stupid bet. *My stupid bet*, I correct myself.

"I need you to give me a ride to school."

"Okay. You have a couple of hours before your test, right?"

"Yes, but I want you to come with me into admissions and talk with an advisor to see what you need to do to enroll in pre-med."

"What?"

"I want you to talk to someone about enrolling. If we move fast, you can take a couple of summer classes."

My ears heard the words, but my brain is not registering them. She wants me to go to Riggins with her and enroll?

"What are you talking about?"

"What's keeping you from going to med school now? You said, you always wanted to go. Well, just so happens, Riggins has one of the best pre-med and medical programs in the country."

"River, I'm too old. I'm years behind everyone else."

"You're not too old. You're twenty-three. And I don't care if you're a hundred. You're never too old to learn something new or follow your dreams."

"I'm too old. I'm twenty-three now. I'd have four years of undergraduate school, followed by four years of medical school and then three-to-eight years of residency programs. And I always wanted to be a trauma surgeon—that puts me on the higher end of those residencies. I would be thirty-nine by then."

"You will be thirty-nine regardless. The question is, do you want to be thirty-nine doing something you love or not?"

I look away. If she only knew how her words touch me, how raw they make me feel. I've wanted this my entire life. And here she is, giving me the hope I dare not have. But this glimmer of hope is terrifying. It paralyzes me and it pushes me forward. It makes me want to believe in something I gave up long ago.

She touches my hand and my eyes meet her again. "No one should need approval to do what they love. Just imagine all the wasted talent out there because someone was too afraid to move forward and follow their dreams or because a person in their lives was critical or because they never had the support they needed," she says and makes sure I'm still with her, before continuing.

"Imagine all the books you'll never read, all the songs you'll never listen to, all the art work no one will ever see because some asshole was too critical and shattered those people's dreams."

"But I'm not an artist or a writer, I wanted to be a doctor. And the marines gave me a taste of it. I loved what I did, even when I hated all that was happening around me that caused it." I look away again.

Her fingers gently brush my cheek and she guides my face back to hers, waiting until our eyes connect. "What about all the lives that won't be saved because you're not there to do it?"

I gasp. I never thought of it this way. What if I am the person who could make a difference? I know my experience in the marines is something most doctors don't encounter in a lifetime of practicing. And I know I had been the only thing between life and death for many marines before. She gets me with that question and then she finishes me with the next words she says.

"Don't be one of the broken dreamers. Collect your pieces, pull yourself together. You don't need anyone's approval or permission to be yourself and live your live to your full potential, to live the life of your choosing, to live your life the way it was intended to be lived, Liam."

*I don't need anyone's permission.* I'm an adult. I have the means to pay for college. I have the will to pursue it and I have the knowledge to be successful at it. What's holding me back? Nothing. Nothing but ideas and words that are not mine. Ideas and words from my father that even now still convinced me I can't do it.

I focus on River again. I can see so much in her eyes. Hope, expectation, and apprehension that her words have not gotten to me. Then she smiles and I smile back at her. I'm going to do this and she knows it.

# CHAPTER THIRTY-SEVEN

## Liam

Well, I'm a college student now. Or at least I'll be in a couple of weeks. After I decided to do it, I went back home and got all the paperwork and transcripts I needed. The advisor told me they have a special program for veterans and because I want to start in the summer, they would expedite my enrollment.

I filled out a bunch of paperwork at Riggins, and I'm bringing more home, but barring anything else, I can start the summer section in two weeks. Right after commencement.

As soon as we step out of the building, I pull River into me and kiss her. It's a no holds barred kiss.

She melts into me like sunshine into water. I kiss her until her legs go weak and I have to hold her up. Not that I'm letting her go, anyway. I kiss her until my lips hurt and I lose my breath.

I feel giddy, like I'm five years old again and it's Christmas morning.

When our lips part, no more than an inch, my forehead to hers. We stay rooted to that spot, our breaths coming in rapid shallow pants, her chest pressed to mine, moving together and slowing down.

After a few minutes the outside world gets ahold of us again, and I'm aware of more than just her and her taste on my lips. I'm back to reality—snippets of conversations reach us in the gentle warm May breeze. The scent of late spring is heavy in the bright late morning light.

A couple of catcalls, followed by a few claps let us know we have an audience.

I laugh then and River laughs with me. We're both a little bewildered in this moment. We're both a little tentative in our newfound . . . connection? Friendship? Relationship?

I don't know what this is, but I want more. I need more. Whatever this is, it's more than lust, of that I'm sure.

I walk River to her building, her hand in mine, our fingers laced. We're silent as we walk the few minutes to where she's taking her finals. When she stops in front of a three-story red brick building, half of it covered in ivy. I know she's reached her destination.

There are people all around us. The campus is busy and abuzz with students running in and out of doors, books in hand, trying to cram in one last minute of studying. This will be me soon enough. This could have been me a year ago if I had come home when I was discharged. But I wasn't ready then. Not ready to face Logan or live among normal people again. I needed that time to heal my wounds. Both the physical and the less visible ones.

She looks at me, a question in her eyes. I have the same question. What now? What is this we have? Where do we go from here?

I answer them.

"I'm not sure, but I want to explore whatever this is we have between us. I like this. I like *us* a lot." I wave the hand that's not holding hers between us.

She nods, still no spoken words.

"Let's take it a day at a time. See where it leads us."

"Okay, I can do that," she says.

"I don't want anything between us, River. No more walls. No more hiding."

"Okay, I can do that." She repeats her previous words, and it makes me smile.

"But no holding back either. I like no-filter River."

"Oh, thank fuck!" She lets out a huge breath and my smile turns into a laugh.

"It won't be us if we're walking on the proverbial eggshells. Let's be honest with each other. Always. Okay?"

She smirks now. "Okay."

I let her hand go and cup her face, leaning into her, and kissing her again. Softer, slower this time. There are a lot of people around and I can feel their eyes on us. Some of them are her friends or classmates for sure.

"What time are you done for the day?"

"Around three-thirty."

"I'll pick you up. Just text me where to meet you."

"You don't have to. I can—"

"I want to. I have to bring paperwork back anyway. I'll pick you up. Let me know where. Heck, I might just stay on campus and get to know it."

She sees the eagerness in me. How badly I want to be in this place and take that first step into my dream. She walks backward toward the building. A girl with black hair comes up to River and stops her a few steps away from me.

"Hey," she calls to River before glancing at me with curiosity.

River notices her. "Becca!"

"Who's your friend?" she asks with interest.

"Claws off, Becca, this one is mine. Go find a freshman to play with."

The girl named Becca pouts, and she's kind of cute in a crazy scary way. This is the girl who let River down and I want to give her a piece of my mind, but River reads my intent and glares at me.

Becca looks back at River. "Do you need a ride home?"

"No," we both say at the same time.

"Oh, he's the one!" Some kind of understanding in her face.

"It's about damned time!" Becca says, tugging on River's arm and heading up the path to the building behind them.

River calls back. "Liam? Whatever you do, if you go to the cafeteria, don't eat the burrito special."

---

I CALL LOGAN.

"Hey, little bro."

I hate when he calls me little brother, but I'm too excited to be bothered by it.

"Hey, big bro," I mimic his salute.

"What's up?"

"I did it."

"You did what?" I can hear the concern in his voice. He probably thinks I killed Jon. I should let him sweat for a little while.

"It's done."

"Liam . . ." His voice is serious now. All the lightness from before, gone.

"It needed doing. River helped me."

"Fuck!"

"It was her idea, actually."

"Don't say anything else over the phone."

"It wasn't nearly as difficult as I thought it would be."

"Liam, I can't know this."

"We pretty much just walked in, talked for about an hour, signed a bunch of papers, and it's mostly done."

"Wait? What?"

"I mean, I still have to get some paperwork over to them, but they told me with my previous record and experience, I shouldn't have any trouble at all."

"What the fuck are you talking about?"

"College." I'm laughing now, no longer able to contain myself.

"Motherfucker! I'm gonna beat the crap out of you when I get home."

"What did you think I was talking about?"

"You little shit. You know exactly what I thought you were talking about. You nearly gave me a heart attack. Good thing I'm parked and not driving."

"I did it," I repeat, letting the emotion take me over for a moment.

"Liam, I'm so happy for you. Riggins?"

"You know it."

"What made you decide?"

"River."

"Ah . . . the power of pussy."

"Watch your mouth!"

He laughs.

"We were talking and what she said made a lot of sense."

"How did you get it done so fast? Didn't they ask you for a ton of paperwork?"

"Before I left for the navy, I packed all my transcripts, SAT scores, the letters of acceptance Dad hid and gave them to Mary to hold for me. A few weeks ago, she shipped all of it to your house—"

"Our house," Logan cuts me off.

"Our house," I repeat after him. "It was her not so subtle nudge for me to get off my ass."

"I guess it worked."

"Yeah, it did. Between all that and all the certifications and letters of recommendation from the marines, I have a pretty solid case. Riggins is fast-tracking it. I start the summer session in two weeks."

"You make me proud, little bro. We have to celebrate. Dinner at home. I'll call Skye and you talk to River. Pizza and beer. The food of choice for college students everywhere."

"It's a plan."

# CHAPTER THIRTY-EIGHT

## River

I TEXT LIAM AS PROMISED, AND HE'S WAITING FOR ME IN front of the building. He's leaning on the closed passenger door of the Escalade, arms crossed at the chest. Camo cargo shorts low on his hips show a sliver of tanned skin. His biceps bulge against the sleeves of his white T-shirt.

When I'm a few feet from him, he pushes away from the truck and in a single move, his left arm wraps around my back while his right-hand tangles into my hair and the back of my head.

He kisses me.

Long and slow, he savors me. His lips on mine, his tongue playing hide and go seek in my mouth. My hands come to his arms automatically and hold on. I can feel the flex of taut muscle under my fingers and my hands are on the move again, up his arms, shoulders, and the back of his head, where they fist into his hair, still damp from a shower. My body pushes into his, looking for more. His arm tightens around me. We kiss for seconds, minutes, years. Everything fades around us. There's only this. His touch, his taste, the heat of his skin, the clean scent of man and need.

He pulls back after a while. But just enough so we can breathe, his lips graze my cheek, then my forehead and he places a lingering kiss on it. Little by little, the outside world makes an appearance. The bright afternoon light filters around his wide shoulders, giving him a halo effect. The sounds of people, cars, birds pour back into the vacuum that kissing Liam creates. Kissing him fills my every sense until there's no space for anything else. The outside world goes unnoticed, absent, until it forces its way back into my reality again.

Reality being that I'm making out with this beautiful man in the middle of campus, in front of a building where hundreds of people just had their finals and they all witnessed my complete oblivion to anything that's not Liam.

It's only been a day since we dropped our walls. Seventy-two hours since that first kiss. We haven't talked about this, about the simmering need between us. We just stepped into it, not a natural progression really. We weren't exactly friends. We didn't flirt. It was more of a stupidly strong sexual attraction disguised as an annoyance contest—since we couldn't get each other off, we pissed each other off instead.

His words brush against my skin. "Hi, baby."

I have always hated that term of endearment. *Baby.* I'm not a baby. I'm a grown woman. I've always thought it a bit condescending, diminishing. I'm wrong. When said by the right lips, with the right tone behind it, this one word—baby—it says so much more than the two syllables can carry. There is tenderness in the word. It's sweet and kind and sexy, all at the same time.

If some other guy had said it to me, I would have ripped him a new one. But in Liam's voice, I want to hear it again.

"Hi." My voice is breathy, a low rumble in my chest.

He smiles at me, a sexy, all too knowing smile that reminds me of the Liam I'm used to. If he says anything about that bet, I'm gonna knee him in the balls. Baby or no baby.

He doesn't. "How did you do? Ace every test?"

"I think my GPA is safe." I can't hold my smile.

He takes a step back and brings me with him, placing a quick kiss on my cheek before opening the door for me. His hands are on my hips as he helps me up into it. The truck is tall and a good step up. I can easily navigate it, but then again, his hands wouldn't be on me if I did and I kind of like his hands on me.

"We're having dinner at my house tonight. The four of us. Pizza and beer. It's Logan's treat."

"You told him?"

"Yeah, he's pretty excited about it, so he's buying."

I love to see the smile on his face. Love how much lighter his whole demeanor is. He looks younger, without the weight of his tours on his shoulders. As I study him, I realize he's studying me. "What?" I ask.

He shakes his head, a wondering look in his eyes.

# CHAPTER THIRTY-NINE

## Liam

Pizza and beer nigh might just be a new tradition in our little family. It's fun hanging out and talking. No pressure of any kind over our heads right now. I like the way this feels. This sense of belonging and being in the right place with the right people.

Logan and I never had this easiness growing up. Our family meals were always a formal affair. Even when we were kids. I can feel Logan's and Skye's curious glances into my direction and River's, sitting caddy corner from me, but we have not said anything about whatever this is we have between us. I like this. I like this a lot. It feels . . . right.

After I picked River up at school, I dropped her off at her house and they—River and Skye—came back at six for dinner. Skye baked a batch of oatmeal chocolate chip cookies. I know I'll have to grab some and hide them from Logan if I want to have any.

We've been stealing touches for the last hour. Little brushes of hands, elbows bumping, knees touching under the table. I want more. I need more. I need to kiss River again. I could get used to this. It feels almost normal. Almost like the version of me before I enlisted and before I knew my father was hiding my college applications. I'm lost in her and don't realize Logan is talking to me until a piece of pizza crust hits me in the chest. I toss it back at him. He catches it midair and drops it to the paper plate in front of him. Between the two of us, we demolished an entire pepperoni pizza and a half of the girls' veggie one.

"Okay, I waited long enough. What's going on with the two of you?" Logan inquires, a smirk on his face.

"What?"

"You two have been in the same room for over an hour and there have been no insults, no fighting, no cursing. So, we're wondering"—he points between Skye and himself—"what's going on with the two of you?"

I look at River. She shrugs.

"We have a . . ."

"Truce." River finishes my words.

His smirk grows. The SOB is enjoying himself. "So, that's what you kids are calling it nowadays."

"What other name do you have for a truce?" River challenges him.

"For that kind of truce?" He points at us. "Sucking face, making out. There could have been some dry humping, but I couldn't quite tell from where I was."

We both throw a piece of pizza crust at him. He blocks mine, but River's hits him right in the forehead. I high five her.

"I saw you two making out in the car when you dropped her off at home."

Skye has a big smile on her face. "Well, it's about time."

River scoffs. "You two should talk. You are in each other's pants 24/7."

Logan grabs Skye's hand and kisses the back of it. "And that's how I like it. I paid, you two kids clean up."

River and I get the paper plates and toss them into the empty pizza box and start cleaning up the table. And again, I'm elated by this mundane act. *How can something so simple have such a huge effect?* I'm craving simple. I'm craving normal, I realize. The last five years of my life have been anything but.

I'm taking the trash out through the back door when the doorbell rings.

River calls out, "I'll get it."

When I get back in the house, the first thing I notice is the silence. There's a different vibe in the air. I step around the kitchen wall and my eyes land on my parents. I need a minute to get my defenses back up so I step back into the kitchen and wash my hands. When I walk back into the room, I lean on the doorjamb and cross my arms. It's been five years since I last saw them. Five years since I heard their voices. Five years and they choose today to show up. My father always did have perfect timing when it comes to fucking me up.

My mother takes a step toward me, but my father's hand on her arm stops her. She pulls away from him. My body stiffens as she comes closer to me. A velvet navy blue box is in her hands. I recognize that box. It explains how they found I'm back but not why they're here. My father turned his back on me when I refused to comply with his orders. Said I was dead to him. Seeing him here actually surprises me.

Mother wraps her arms around me. Her much smaller body is trembling and her eyes fill with tears. "My baby boy. I missed you so much."

I'm at a loss as to what to do. My mother was never affectionate. My father watches us with displeasure. My arms go around her in an awkward embrace, her head barely up to my shoulder. I don't remember her being this small, this frail. She holds on to me tight as if trying to make up for all the times she didn't hug me when I needed her to.

"Enough of this!" My father's voice breaks the moment.

My mother flinches but keeps her arms around me.

He takes a step in our direction and Logan cuts him off. Father had always been a big man, an imposing man. He used his size and ruthless demeanor to intimidate everyone around him. He thrived on it. But we are not little kids anymore and not so easily intimidated now.

Logan and I, we can hold our own. I can look our father in the eye and not flinch, not back off. He's seething at us.

Mother pulls away from me and hands me the box. I open it, finding the medal I don't think I deserve. I didn't save Hannah after all. It doesn't matter if I saved hundreds of others. I didn't keep my promises to Hannah, the promise to keep her safe.

"I'm so proud of you." Mother's voice rescues me from my self-inflicted misery. *I'm so proud of you.* I never heard those words from her before and up to this moment I had no idea how much I craved them. How much I need my mother to be a mother to me.

My father pushes at Logan and Logan stands his ground. He tries again and Logan speaks up for the first time since they got here. "Don't make me hurt you."

Father sneers at him, his eyes vile and filled with disgust.

"The two soldiers who came to our door to deliver that trinket"—he points at the box in my hands—"said you were discharged a year ago and yet, this is the first we hear about it."

I shrug. Still haven't said a word to either of them. Logan looks at me when he hears Father's words. There's hurt in his eyes, but he covers it fast. We learned early on not to show any kind of weakness in front of our father.

"Why?" he asks me.

"Why what, Father?"

"Why didn't you come back home?"

"I did. I'm home."

"This is not your home. Your place is not here. It is back in Connecticut at my side."

"You're mistaken, Father. This is my home now. I have no intention of returning to Connecticut or ever taking a place at your side."

"Nonsense. You are done playing soldier. You are to pack your things and return with me right now."

I look around the room and find River. There's worry and anger in her eyes.

"Listen, boy. I have been too soft with you. You're a man now. Start acting like it. Do what you're told and get in that car. I'll arrange for enrollment at Harvard. You can start right away and work at the company." My father ignores what I said before and tries to bully me into doing his bidding.

"Which part of this aren't you getting? I'm not going anywhere. You couldn't force me six years ago and you can't force me now."

"If you don't get in that car right now, I will disown you and your brother."

"You did that a long time ago when you both forgot we were your children and not a business deal or a project you could manipulate for your own gain."

"How dare you? You will never see a cent of my money. I'll make sure neither of you get anywhere," Father yells.

Mother recoils but does not say anything.

I look back at the both of them. My parents. The people

who should have loved me most. All my physical needs were met. I had a house but never a home. I had meals, but never a family dinner.

"You never loved us. You were never a father to us. Who taught Logan to ride a bike? Our gardener Joe did, and Logan taught me. Whose bed did I run to when I had nightmares and was scared? It was never yours. Never. Yours. It was Mary who took me in and dried my tears when I was three and you told me to tough it out. It was Mary who read me bedtime stories when you both were too busy with your own lives to be bothered. It was Mary who helped Logan and me with homework and it was Mary who kissed the pain away when I fell and scraped my knees. And when you told me to either go to law school or get out, it was Mary who found me on the street and offered to use her life savings to pay for my college. I could not let her do that and I could not let you two bully me into being something I'm not and will never be. That's why I joined the navy and even though you knew where I was, I never received a single letter from you, not a fucking postcard saying, *'Hey, son, hope you stay safe.'* No, neither one of you bothered. But Mary, well, she sent letters every week and care packages. Sometimes it would be months before the letters reached me and I would get a dozen at a time. I wrote her back, and I called her too. Every opportunity I got. She wanted me to call you two and make peace, but I knew better. You never wanted a son. You wanted an extension of yourself. Well, I have news for you because it seems you just don't get it, do you, Father?"

His hands fist at his sides. There's pure hatred in his eyes.

"I am my own person and so is Logan, and we are not extensions of you."

I can see the hurt in my mother's eyes, but I don't know if she's hurt because of my words or because of her actions, or her lack of actions, really. She's a weak woman and never stood a chance against my father. She did what he told her, she went along whatever path he set for her. Her expression changes. My words hurt her, but I can see now that the pain in her eyes is not for herself but for all she allowed to happen to our family.

My father's oblivious. Of everything I said, his only concern is how close I am to Mary, the only mother I had ever known.

"Mary? That old woman has meddled in our family business and filled your head with illusions. I'll fire her as soon as we get back home. Get in the car, Liam!" he ordered. "We are leaving right now."

"Mary won't be back at the house." I refuse to call that place *home*. "I'll have her pack her things and move out as soon as you leave here. You may want to look into hiring a new chef when you get back." I ignore his remarks about me going back.

"I'll have her arrested. I'll call the police as soon as we are back and have her arrested."

"For what? Mary has never broken the law."

"Things go missing. Accusations can be made," he threatens me.

"Yes, you're right. Things go missing all the time. Have you ever told your partners about the missing ten million dollars? Oh, wait. You did, but you said it was an investment that went belly up, right? Yes, I remember that now." I look at Logan. "Do you remember that, Logan?"

Logan smiles. "Yes, I do. And I still have that old laptop he gave me to use for school. Funny thing about deleted files. You can always recover them."

Father blanches but carries on as if nothing was said. "Enough of this rebellious behavior. You played soldier long enough. Time to face reality and take your place in the family business and be a man. Do as you are told."

River steps in and positions herself between me and my father. "Be a man? What the hell do you know about being a man? You can't even drive yourself. You have someone drive you here while you drink bourbon in the back seat. Your head is shoved so far up your ass, all you can see is your own shit. You know nothing about being a man. Liam did not play soldier. Do you know anything about your son? He's a marine. He's a corpsman and saved hundreds of lives. He was in battle dragging people back from the brink of death while *you* played at monopoly. Did you know he almost died? Did you know his body was covered in shrapnel and he was in a hospital in a coma for days?"

The momentary silence that follows her words is filled with gasps all around us, except from my father. He has no reaction. No one knows about me almost dying and being in a coma. Not even Logan. I never told anyone but River. When River realizes what she just said she looks at me apologetically, but I shrug it off. It's time the truth came out.

My father stews in anger. "Flesh wounds, I bet!" he mutters under his breath.

"Flesh wounds?" River goes on. "Are you dense or just so self-centered you can't see past your own needs?" She pauses for effect and then looks around the room. "Wait? Is there a difference? In your case I think not. People don't go into a coma because of flesh wounds, you moron!"

My father advances on her. "You little bitch! How dare you speak to me like that?"

Both Logan and I jump in, ready to take our father down, when we all stop in our tracks.

"Enough!"

I look over at my mother. I had forgotten she was here for a moment. She is on her knees, tears running down her face. The face that's always composed and perfect is now marred by black lines from ruined makeup. She gets up now and comes to me and she holds me. I hesitate for just a moment before my arms go around her. Then she lets go of me and does the same to Logan. When she lets go of him, she walks up to Dad and stands right in front of him. She pulls her shoulders back and looks him in the eyes, tears still streaming down her face. Not a sound can be heard. We're all in shock. Mother has never raised her voice. Not once had I ever seen her being anything less than perfect.

Then the most amazing thing happens. She slaps him. He looks at her in absolute shock and she slaps him again.

"You will leave here and you will never, ever address my children in such a disrespectful way again. I will return to the house tomorrow to collect my things. Make sure not to be there. I will have my lawyer deliver the divorce papers by the end of the week."

"Olivia? Are you insane? Have you lost your mind? Don't forget your place—"

Mother slaps him again.

Father is furious. Coldness like I had never seen washes over his face. "You cannot divorce me. I own you. Even if you could there is no way you'd have divorce papers ready by the end of the week."

"The divorce papers have been ready for years now. All I need to do is add a few amendments and have it delivered. I suggest you sign it as is," Mother counters. "Like Logan and Liam, I have collected some interesting information over the years. I'm sure the media would be very interested in your escapades into sex clubs and your many mistresses, not to mention the money you have been sending offshore."

"Holy shit!" I hear myself say and look at Logan. His face tells me he already knew about it.

"You will regret this," Father threatens Mother.

I step behind her and put a hand on her shoulder and Logan does the same on her other side.

"No, you will, if you ever threaten any of us again."

He leaves after that and Mother's shoulder's sag. I pull her into a hug and Logan joins me and we both hug her.

"I have to find a hotel to spend the night," she speaks.

"Mother, you can stay with us. We have the room."

She sobs and looks at me and then at Logan. "Call me Mom, please."

I look at Logan and my eyes water. His are a mirror of mine. We were never allowed to call her Mom. Our Father demanded that we call her Mother. Even as toddlers.

"You can stay with us, Mom."

She sighs. I look at River over Mom's shoulder, and she's smiling between her tears. She wipes them with the hem of her shirt and gives me a glimpse of her flat, tanned belly.

Mom disengages from Logan and me and turns to River. Then she walks to her and gives her a hug.

"Thank you for standing up for my son and doing what I should have done long ago."

# CHAPTER FORTY

## Liam

MOTHER—MOM—GOES BACK HOME. I WANTED TO GO with her and make sure my father would not be there or if he was, he would not turn on her, but she wouldn't allow it.

"It's time for me to fight my own battles," she says.

"Your father is not a fool. He knows what he's facing. Self-preservation will win. Besides, I have Hugo." Hugo being the driver who had come back this morning to pick up my mother.

Logan and I hug her and let her go. It's a strange feeling hugging my mother and watching her leave.

Logan's been looking preoccupied all morning, checking his phone on and off and leaving when someone called. Something is up and as soon as Mother leaves, I'm on him.

"What's going on?"

"Nothing, why?"

"Bullshit and you know it."

"I have no idea what you're talking about," he says, glancing at his phone one more time before putting it in his pocket.

"Logan, don't lie to me. I'm not a little kid you have to protect anymore. I'm a grown man and I have seen more shit in one day than you ever will in your whole life. Cut the crap and tell what's going on?"

He sighs, his shoulders sagging. "I had a friend check into local rape by roofie cases."

I'm in his space in two steps.

"And?"

"There are several reported cases of girls waking up and not remembering what happened. There was no DNA evidence, which indicates the rapist used a condom each time. All the girls are between eighteen and twenty-one and either attended Riggins or were friends with someone who did. All the rapes happened at a party. Three of the girls swear they had nothing or very little to drink. The other four could not remember how much they drank. There are enough similarities between these cases and River's to think that maybe Jon was the person behind them, but no physical evidence of any kind to link him to any of the victims."

I'm already shaking my head, my hands fisting with the need to punch something. To hurt something, to draw blood.

"Can they bring him in? Question him?"

"No. We have no reason to do it. No evidence of—"

"But, what about River? We know he did it. He as much as confessed. We heard him!"

"It would be looked at as hearsay. And our word against his. I did some background checking on him. He comes from money. His father is a big shot attorney in New York. We wouldn't have a chance if we bring him in, and then he'd be careful and cover his tracks."

"What then? He walks away to rape someone else?"

"We watch. The only way to get him behind bars is to catch him in the act or to have someone actually come forward and say he did it and odds are no one is coming forward."

My head is spinning. I'm so angry I can't think straight and then I have an idea. And that idea starts to take shape. I look at Logan and he knows.

"What? What are you thinking?"

"If no one will come forward and the only way to get him is to actually catch him, then we set up a trap."

"A trap? What kind of trap?"

"We bait him."

"Bait him how?"

"With something he can't resist. A beautiful girl who refuses him."

Logan rubs his eyes. "Liam, I get what you are saying, but the department will not go for it. And he could claim entrapment."

"Who said anything about involving the department? This is between you and me."

"Whoa, whoa, whoa. Back up a little. You want to use a girl to get him to drug her and then when he's in the middle of raping her, bust in and catch him?"

"Yes. That's exactly what I want to do."

"You're talking about letting him try to rape someone so you can catch him? Who will volunteer for that? And there's like one week left of school. He's graduating and then he'll be gone. How are you going to pull it off?"

"Oh, we are having a party."

# CHAPTER FORTY-ONE

## River

Logan's text message to Skye had us running over here. He didn't give any explanations. Just said we had to come over ASAP. After making sure they both looked unhurt and had all visible parts attached, I can breathe a little easier. This better not be some kind of joke or those previously unseen parts will be forcibly removed. They scared the crap out of me and Skye.

"What's going on?" I ask Logan since he's the one who sent the text.

He points back at his brother. "It's his idea."

"What?" My voice is a few decibels louder.

Skye reaches for me and tugs my arm in the direction of the big chocolate brown sofa parked in front of the even bigger flat screen TV.

"Let's just sit down and I'm sure we'll find out soon enough what the reason of this is . . ." Skye trails off.

She sits down and I drop next to her. "What is this exactly?" She's always so calm. Her calmness makes me even more agitated. I hate not knowing. It doesn't matter what it is. That feeling of not knowing something makes me crazy.

Logan and Liam sit opposite to us. The dark wood coffee table in between. That might be a good thing. If someone doesn't start explaining what's happening right now, my jumping over that table will give them an extra second to try to escape.

Liam takes the lead. His excitement mutes when he looks at me and his voice softens.

"Logan's been investigating sexual assault reports in the area."

He's paying close attention to me, gauging my reaction. I stay cool, trying to not show anything. He goes on. "They have several reports that have a lot in common with—"

He doesn't finish, but we all know what the next word would be. Asserting I'm still okay, Liam speaks again.

"Unfortunately, none of the girls who came forward had any kind of information that could help us. But they were all attacked at a party, either on campus or nearby. None of them remember anything and in each attack, a condom was used."

"How does this help me?"

"It doesn't and the cops can't do anything about it." Liam glances at his brother. "Sorry, Logan."

"It's true. We don't have enough evidence to go on. Even if you were to report what we overheard, it would be our word against his and then he'd get spooked and that would be the end of it. But Liam has this crazy idea and it just might work."

"Okay, go on." I'm nervous. My heart is racing and my hands are shaky now. I sit on them and lean forward.

"We're going to throw a party on Saturday. A last chance to get together before graduation next week and we are going to invite Jon. We will provide the place"—he gestures around the room—"and the beer."

"How do we know we can get Jon here?"

"That's where you two come in. We don't know the asshole, but you two do. What would get him here? And what would tempt him enough him to try to get one last girl?" Logan asks.

"Me." Skye speaks for the first time.

We all look at her.

Logan is on his feet. "No! Absolutely not. I'm not letting that asshole anywhere near you."

Skye just looks at him, calm as ever. "There is only one thing that will get him here for sure and that's me. He knows this will be his last chance to get me. Like Liam said, graduation is in one week. If he thinks he can get to me, he'll come. I'm the one who got away, and in his sick mind, no one says no to him."

I look at my sister. "Skye? I don't know about this . . ."

She interrupts me. "River, I have to do this. I can't forgive myself for what happened to you. I feel it's my fault. If I had never gotten involved with him in the first place, this would've never happened."

I'm shaking my head the whole time she's talking to me. "No, there's no way you could have anticipated this. No way. It's not your fault. It's not my fault. There's only one person at fault and it's Jon."

Skye pulls my left hand from under me and squeezes it. She looks at Logan.

"I have to do this. Him knowing I will be here? That's too much temptation for him. He knows I don't go to parties. I went to one with him. Probably the only reason he didn't do the same to me is because he never had the opportunity, but if he thinks he can get to me and get away with it, he will. I'm the perfect bait."

"You're not bait, Skye." His voice is low, sad. Logan doesn't like it any more that I do, but I can tell by the look in his eyes, he knows what she's saying is true. Jon would see this as the perfect opportunity to get to Skye.

"So, what do you have in mind?" My sister might be the quiet one, but when she gets something in her mind, you may as well give up.

"We are going to rig the house with wireless hidden cameras. One in the kitchen, a couple in the living room. And a couple in the guest bedroom upstairs."

"The bedroom?" I ask.

Liam explains, "Yeah, I figure, we can lock both my room and Logan's from the inside. You should not be at the party. If he sees you, he might scare off. We need you to be upstairs in my bedroom where we will set up the monitors for the cameras. I already checked and we can rent cameras with a remote control so we can follow his every move and he won't know. The feed gets stored into a hard drive."

"And then what?"

"And then we wait for him to make his move."

"Wow, wait! You're not letting him drug Skye and take her upstairs, are you?"

"No." Logan takes over. "The original plan was watch who he was going after and intercept him before he did anything but with enough evidence of him trying to drug someone to get him arrested."

"But now that I'm doing it, I can fake being drugged. Get even more evidence," Skye says.

I look at my sister. "Do you think this can work?"

"I do. We have to try."

"How do we get him here?" Liam asks.

I smile for the first time. "Oh, that's the easy part. I can arrange to have him hear about this awesome party my sister is going to but I can't make because I have to go home for something. I know people who can make sure he knows about the party."

# CHAPTER FORTY-TWO

## Liam

Everything is pretty much in place. I look around the living room. "Cold" by Crossfade is playing in the background, loud enough to make the windows rattle. I haven't listened to music this loud in a while. Not since moving in with Logan. No. That's not true. I listened to music as loud as the speakers would go the first two days I was here. I haven't since the day after River dumped her fruity drink on me.

For a whole year the only way I could drown out the phantom sounds of bullets and explosions out of my head was to listen to music. Loud enough to do damage to my ears. For a while I hoped if I went deaf, I'd stop hearing the sounds inside my head. Futile, I know. The sounds were inside of me. They pounded in my veins, in the beat of my heart, and they'd wake me up drenched in sweat in the quiet of the night.

The nightmares, more real than the facts I remember. I'd wake up with the taste of blood in my mouth. The sting of burning metal cutting my flesh. The pain, so intense and so real, it left me paralyzed for minutes at a time. Then the fear would hit me and keep me trapped inside my mind, inside the nightmare, even when my eyes were open and I was awake. My breath caught in my chest and burned until I could finally breathe again, sucking air and life into my lungs. In those moments I understood why we lost so many vets after the war. After they came home. You may leave the war behind. But the war never leaves you. You may think coming home will erase the nightmares, but it doesn't.

You're no longer the person you were before. You become a version of yourself you don't recognize at times. Anger is real and close to the surface, and it doesn't take much for it to explode.

When I left the hospital, I knew I couldn't go back home in that state. Logan and Mary were the only two people I cared about, or at least that's what I told myself. I didn't want my parents to see me like that and I certainly didn't want Logan and Mary to look at me and . . . and what? I had no idea. I didn't like the person I had become and I didn't want anyone else to have to deal with it. Deal with me. I made the choice to enlist alone, I'd fix myself alone as well. Stupid, I know. But my state of mind back then was not something anyone could call stable.

I spent a year traveling all over Europe. Working odd jobs, sleeping on the street sometimes. I could have gone into my bank account. I could have used the money I had there and stayed in hotels, but I didn't feel I deserved any kind of comfort. Any kind of joy or forgiveness. It has taken well over a year to get to this point . . . and River, for me to see there was nothing I could have done differently. Hannah's death was not my fault, but the guilt still eats at me. More so because I never went back to see her family. I have a few things of hers. Letters she wrote to her husband and daughter and the promise to hand deliver it to them if anything ever happened to her. I have a necklace she bought from a street vendor, a gift for her daughter. I don't know why she had me holding onto it. I told her she would have to deliver it herself, but she made me promise her I would keep those things for her. So, I did. I kept the small package she gave me, exactly the way she gave it to me. Inside the plastic bag still. It's in the bottom of the backpack I traveled thousands of miles with, now sitting on the back of my closet.

Another way I have failed her. I haven't delivered those letters to her family.

I shake my head, trying to get rid of the thoughts and tell myself I'll deliver the letters when we finish this thing with the asshole. I'll wait until the girls graduate and then make the trip to Texas. I feel like a coward. I don't want to face her husband and daughter. I wasn't ready to see them before. There was just too much damage. I'm ready now. I have to do this.

I'm lost in thought. Lost in the past. My eyes looking around me but unseeing. When the gentle touch brushes my back, I jump. I'm ready to fight. Training taking over, instinct overriding everything else, until my mind focuses again and I'm back in the house. Back in the present. It takes me a second to recognize that the person standing in front of me is River. To realize that the hand on my back means no harm. I try to shake the feeling off. I blink a few times. I want to smile at her. I want to assure her I'm okay, but my lips have forgotten how. She doesn't say anything. She doesn't look scared. Maybe she should. But no. None of that happens. Instead, she steps closer to me and her arms wrap around my middle and her head rests on my chest. I heave a deep breath in and her scent grounds me first. It centers me before my body realizes hers is wrapped around mine. My body remembers and my arms come up to pull her closer to me. No words are said. The music is still too loud for any kind of vocal communication, but River doesn't need words to speak to me. To quiet my mind, to fill my dark spaces with light. We stay like this for a while, in each other's arms. Me, feeding off her touch, smell, and strength and her eating away at my darkness.

My lips find her forehead and I let them linger in a kiss I don't want to end. There is nothing sexual in this moment. Just trust, comfort, and . . . and something else I don't dare name just yet.

She pulls away from me and steps up to the docking station where my iPhone is hooked to. The sudden silence is louder than the music playing.

There's this whole silent conversation that passes between us, before words are spoken.

"Are you okay?"

"I am now."

"Where did you go?"

"A place I never want to go back to again."

"Then don't."

"I don't know how to do that just yet but having you near me helps. You ground me."

"We ground each other."

This makes me smile. I want her. And it's not just sex. It's not just the fact I haven't gotten laid in almost two years and she's pretty much the only girl I've talked to since coming back stateside.

She smiles back. "I knocked, but I don't think you would've been able to hear a stampede of T-rexes coming through the door."

The visual makes me laugh.

"I let myself in. I wanted to know if you need any help here. Skye and Logan went to get food and drinks."

She's looking around the room. I removed any identifying

objects, like pictures and anything of value that could be broken or stolen and took it upstairs. We moved the furniture around so people will be able to move more freely. The cameras have been installed and the computer in my room is set up to get a live feed.

"Everything is pretty much done. Can you find the cameras?"

She looks about the place, checking the corners of the room and up the walls. She turns in a small circle and my eyes go straight to her ass. And she catches me. A smirk on her face.

"I can't find them. Where are they?"

I point the cameras to her. One on the ceiling fan right above the middle of the room. One more on a wall disguised as a thermostat and another two on top of the bookcase in the far wall. They are hard to see even if one knows they are there.

"Wow, they're so small."

"Yeah, we got two more in the kitchen, one on the stairs, and a few others in the hall, watching the bathroom door, and one in the guest bedroom upstairs. A dozen, all together."

I step closer to her and take her hand. "Let me show you where you'll be."

We go up to the second floor and into my room, which is clean. I didn't have to pick up because she was coming over. All those years in the service have trained me well and I'm neat by nature. I point at the desk I set up against the wall. On it, a laptop and three large monitors where she will be able to see split video feed from all of the cameras and a large hard drive hooked up to the laptop, which will collect the videos. It cost me some money to rent all of it, but it's money well spent. We're gonna get the asshole one way or another.

She is looking around my room, taking in everything. My bed is made. A deep blue blanket over it. Pillows are fluffed, and I changed the bedding as well, in case she gets tired and needs to rest.

I wait until her eyes are back on me to show her the equipment. "This is like command central."

She looks intimidated by all the hardware on the desk.

I laugh. "It is very simple, actually."

She looks doubtful.

"You really don't have to do anything. Right now, the cameras are on, but not recording. When the party starts, I'll come up and get everything going. You'll know it is recording because each of the images will show a red blinking light in the corner." I point at one of the split screens. "See the number on this screen?"

She nods.

"It corresponds to one of the cameras. This way you know which camera is controlling the feed. All you have to do is watch. The screens are touchscreen and you can zoom in and out with this." I tap on one of the still images and it fills the screen. I tap again and it goes back to the previous size. "I'll come up to check on you often and we can keep in touch via text."

"Yeah, sounds good. I think I can handle it." Her hands are in her jeans pockets. She wears a loose blue T-shirt. I want my hands under it.

"I'll stock you up with some drinks and food so you don't starve, and through that door"—I point at the door on the other side of the bed—"is a bathroom. You don't have to leave the room and risk getting caught by anyone."

She nods. Her eyes meet mine. "Do you think this will work?"

"If we can get him here, yes. I think it will. Guys like him, ones driven by ego, think they're above everyone else and will never get caught. He won't miss this chance."

"Becca talked to a few people who are friends with his friends and someone said he was coming. I hate to say this but using Skye as bait is the only thing that'll get him here. He'll try to get to Skye and . . ."

Her voice cracks and she stops, before saying the word. Before saying that horrible word. I take two steps toward her and pull her into my arms, trapping the hands in her pockets still, between our bodies. "We will get him. One way or another. I promise you."

"Liam . . ." Her voice is muffled against my chest. She pulls back a little, frees her hands, and they come to rest on my waist. Her fingers hook on the belt loops in my jeans. I love this, intimate way her hands rest on my body.

"Liam, you can't promise me that. As much as I want him to pay for what he did to me and God knows how many more girls, you have no control over the outcome of this. We don't even know for sure if he will show up."

Her head is tilted back and the tips of her hair brush my arms around her back.

"We'll get him."

She tries to protest again, but I silence her with my lips. I kiss her gently. I have no intention of taking this further than a silencing kiss, but River has a different idea, and she takes the kiss a step up. Who am I to complain? We kiss and kiss.

# CHAPTER FORTY-THREE

## River

I HAVE AN EAGLE'S EYE VIEW OF EVERYTHING. THE TWELVE camera feeds are split among the three screens in front of me. One for the living room, one for the kitchen and one for the hall and the guest bedroom.

People are mingling around, but he's not here yet. I can see Logan and Liam talking to people, and the beer is flowing as the number of red cups in people's hands indicates there's free alcohol in the place. I can see Skye in the kitchen, a red cup in her hand, but I know there's no alcohol in it. There have to be about thirty people around the house. The stairs going up to the second floor have been closed off with 'do not cross' tape. Logan says it can be bought in any novelty store or online, so it will not raise any suspicions, but it's a clever way to keep people downstairs for now. I know it won't stop Jon if he shows up. I'm watching Logan and Liam when they both rub their necks.

We have a set of agreed upon hand gestures. If either Logan or Liam rub the back of their necks, this means Jon is here. I find him a moment later. He's standing by the front door. My insides contract and my stomach drops. It feels like I'm on a never- ending roller coaster, but I know it's only the shock of seeing him for the first time after knowing what he did to me. I shake off the feeling and tell myself to stop it. He can't hurt me anymore. I zoom in on his face. For anyone else, it may just look like he's casually looking around. But I can tell his eyes are searching. I watch on the next monitor as Skye leaves the kitchen and walks into the living room. Logan must have texted her. That's another thing we are doing. Texting each other, keeping everyone in the loop. My phone vibrates.

**Liam: Are you okay?**

**Me: Yes. I'm good. Let's get the bastard.**

**Liam: We will.**

As I watch, Jon takes a few steps into the room and starts talking to people. He makes his way to the kitchen and gets a cup but does not fill it to the top. He is keeping his wits about him. He's watching Skye. He is not approaching her as I expected him to. He's keeping his distance and watching her from afar.

And for over an hour that's all he does. Skye has made several trips to the kitchen, and every time she comes back with what he thinks is a new beer cup he smirks a little and it dawns on me what his MO is. If he never approaches his victims until the last moment, no one in the party will be able to say he was with them. And by the time he does approach them, most people are drunk or at the very least buzzed and not able to recall Jon ever being near his victims.

Skye is tittering a little to the side. She fake trips on someone and hands come up to steady her, holding both her arms. Jon's hands. He wormed his way next to her and he's talking to her now. Skye's head tilts to the side, and she looks like she's trying to concentrate on what he's saying. Somebody give my sister an Oscar right now. If I didn't know for a fact she hasn't actually consumed any real alcohol, I would swear she's drunk.

I can see Liam a couple of feet behind them. He's keeping track of the cup in Skye's hand. If we are right about this, Jon will try to sneak something into it soon.

He talks to her for a couple of minutes. I zoom the camera on them, I'm trying to read his lips, but I can't. His right hand goes to his jeans pocket and a moment later, it's out and he's holding it at his side. Something is in his hand. He leans into Skye and whispers something in her ear, which makes her turn and lower her head. His hand comes up to the cup and drops something in it. Bingo!

The next moment, Liam bumps into Jon's back and he turns to Liam. Skye dumps the contents of the cup on a potted plant behind her. When Jon turns back, Skye's tilting the cup up as if she just finished her drink, and I can see Jon's satisfied smile. After about ten or fifteen minutes, she starts leaning to the side —this timing is important. We researched this and for most cases, the effects start to show in twenty to thirty minutes after ingesting the roofies, which was the drug found in the girls we believe are Jon's victims. Jon puts an arm around her waist and starts guiding her to the back of the room and toward the stairs. I can see Logan tense and start to follow them. Liam steps in front of him and whispers something in Logan's ear. Whatever Liam said stops Logan from screwing up our plan. We need more than drugs in a cup. We need him to try to hurt Skye, so we can get it on video. We need intent.

Watching it all unfold through the camera lenses is surreal. Jon worms his way to the back of the room while keeping a firm hold on Skye at his side. She's still holding the now empty cup, and he takes it from her hand and chucks it into the trash bin Liam set up by the kitchen. He looks around over her head, but no one is watching him. People are drinking, making out, dancing to the loud music I can hear filtering up to the second floor. He makes his way to the stairs and removes the tape from one side of the wall before taking the first step and then placing the 'do not cross' police tape back in place. I lose them for a few seconds until they show up on the camera in the hallway again.

I know the door is locked, but my heart still speeds up when I hear him trying the door for the room I'm in. All doors are locked, except for the guest bedroom we set up with the cameras, but this time those cameras will also have a sound feed, so we can hear anything he says.

I watch as he tries both the bathroom and Logan's door and then the last door in the hall. The smile on his face when it eases open is sickening. A moment later, there's a knock on my door. I get up to let Logan and Liam in and we rush to the desk to watch the monitors. I realize I'm shaking when Liam's hands cover mine and his arms go around me. He kisses me on the forehead and pulls me close to him. Tension radiates from Logan in waves. He's a tsunami in the making.

Jon wastes no time dragging Skye to the bed. Logan's fists ball next to me and Liam takes one hand off me and squeezes Logan's shoulder.

"We need him to try to do something. Just hold on one more minute."

"I know, but this isn't fucking easy."

Sweat beads on Logan's creased brow, despite the chilled air-conditioned room. Sounds come through the computer and we can hear Jon speaking.

"I almost wish you could remember this tomorrow. But you

won't. Your sister didn't either. She never knew what hit her. Feisty little bitch she was. Even half unconscious she put up a fight. But my special mix guaranties that no one remembers what happens. Not before, not after, and especially not during it. None of them remember and I've done this dozens of times."

He goes up on the mattress and pulls Skye to the middle of the queen-sized bed.

"What? What are you talking about? What mix?" Skye's voice is drowsy, her words slurred.

"You switched the cups, right?" I ask Logan even though I saw him do it on the video.

"Yes. She's acting."

"She's doing one hell of a job," Liam says.

"Oh, I have my own little recipe. Rohypnol, and a few other drugs. They work together quite nicely. And the beauty of all this is that you won't remember a fucking thing. Nothing at all." He laughs.

Shoes off, he starts to unzip his jeans and looks at her, taking in what she's wearing for the first time. This is something we planned. Having Skye wear clothes that would be difficult to remove. She's wearing skin-tight jeans, a tucked in T-shirt, and chocolate brown knee-high boots. The boots are riding boots, with a stretch band on the inside and no zippers. And they are a pain to put on and take off.

"Why are you always so difficult? Couldn't you just wear a skirt like River did? Make my job easier? Now I have to rip these boots and jeans off you before I can get my dick in that cunt of yours. And that pisses me off. I was going to be nice to you for old times' sake, but I'm not going to be nice anymore. I'm going to make you bleed like I did your bitchy little sister. I'm going to leave my mark on you."

Jon's jeans come off, but his underwear is still on and thankfully for us, he loves to hear himself talk.

"I couldn't believe my luck when I heard about this party. My last week on campus and my last chance to get you. Make you pay for all the times you turned me down. I couldn't have thought of a more perfect send-off if I had planned it myself."

Logan's back is so rigid, it's about to snap.

He starts to tug her right boot off and only succeeds in bringing Skye down the bed with it.

"You are really pissing me off now, you know. If I had a knife, I'd just slice this shit off you and I'd make sure to leave a few cuts behind for you to remember me by. Oh, wait? You won't remember a thing."

He removes the first boot. Skye tries to scramble up the bed to get away from him. He follows her.

"No, you don't. We didn't even start to have fun yet."

"What are you doing?" Skye's movements are feeble. The blond hair covers her face, and we can't see her expression.

"What am I doing? Isn't it clear by now, sweet Skye?"

The second boot comes off.

"I'm going to fuck you. And when I'm done. I'm gonna fuck you again. And after that, I think I'll fuck you in the ass. You always did have a nice ass. River got the tits, but you have the ass."

Skye kicks at him, evading his hands, but Jon finds her ankles and pins her legs down to the bed while straddling her knees. His hands go to her jeans' button.

"No, no, please, no."

"Looks like you're going to put up as much of a fight as your sister did. That's okay. I like it when they fight. Makes it all the more fun for me."

"Please, no." There's real fear in Skye's voice. She's no longer acting.

"Beg all you want but be assured there's only one outcome for you tonight. I'm going to rape you. Yes, rape. And you can't stop me. The beauty of it is that you won't remember a thing and no one will be able to help you. No one will know anything. No one was paying any attention to you. It's just you and me."

Her zipper undone, he starts to pull Skye's pants down.

"We got him," I hear myself say and before the words are completely out of my mouth, Logan is out the door with Liam behind him. They told me to stay in this room, don't let Jon see me, to keep him from accusing me—us of a setup. He will have money and his last name in his corner. We need to minimize his chances.

I run after Liam and close the door with me on the inside. One of the hardest things I ever had to do. I want to be near Skye. I need to comfort my sister. Thank her for what she just did for me. I don't have time to dwell on it as Logan and Liam break through the guest bedroom door. They also rigged the door so it could not be locked from the inside even though it looked as such.

I watch as Logan pulls Jon off Skye and Liam checks on her. Logan has Jon pinned on the floor, his hands trapped behind his back so fast I barely registered what happened.

Jon is squirming under him, trying to fight Logan off. I see Liam reach for zip ties in his pocket and hand them to Logan. A second later, Jon's hands are firmly locked behind his back. Liam makes the call to 911.

Jon is screaming and cursing them both. "Get the fuck off me. What the fuck do you think you're doing?"

"I think I'm stopping a rape."

"There's no rape. She's my girlfriend. Ask anyone."

Fucking liar.

Skye is visibly shaking. "No, I'm not. You brought me here, and you said you were going to rape me."

"It was a joke. We're role-playing. She likes when we do it. Let me go!"

Logan's hands are opening and closing and I know it's taking everything he has not to beat the crap out of Jon. This is something we talked about. For the plan to work, the arrest has to be textbook perfect. There can be no reasons for anyone to have any doubts over what happened.

I can hear the sirens. The cops will be here any minute now. I can also hear the commotion of people trying to leave in a hurry downstairs. Liam goes down to meet the police officers, and the house goes suddenly quiet when the music is turned off. The only audible sound is the rapid beating of my heart reverberating in my ears.

I watch everything through the monitors. Cops stop people from leaving the house. There are several of them and they line up people against the wall. The ones who didn't move fast enough and escaped, that is. It is organized chaos. They are checking IDs and asking questions although I can't hear anything because the cameras downstairs have no sound feed.

Liam appears on the monitor, walking toward the last room, followed by two cops. The monitor switches to the bedroom and I can see and hear them. One of the cops nods at Logan, who's still kneeling on Jon's back and keeping him immobile, but Jon's thrashing. When he sees the cops, he starts screaming for help, like he's the victim. *What a fucking asshole!*

"Help. Oh, thank God you guys are here. Get this lunatic off my back. He just attacked me and he's holding me against my will."

It's like he was coached before. He is saying all the right words to make it look and sound like he's the victim.

Logan lets go of him and the two officers pull Jon up by the elbows, hands still zip tied behind his back. Is he going to fucking cry? He's making a sad face at the cops.

One of the cops picks up Jon's pants off the floor with gloved hands.

The other asks, " Are these yours?"

"Yes, can I put them on, please? This is embarrassing. I was just here trying to have some alone time with my girlfriend when these two crazy guys barged in and attacked me."

"Did they hit you?"

"No, but—"

"Did they have any weapons on them?"

"No—"

"Did they hurt you in any way? Are there any marks on your body?"

"No, they just pushed me to the floor and zip-tied my hands together."

"There was no attack then, wouldn't you agree?"

The officer doesn't wait for an answer and looks at his partner, who's going thru the jeans' pockets. He pulls out a wallet from the back pocket and opens it, reading the driver's license. "Is this yours?" he asks, showing Jon his ID.

"Yes. Can you untie me now?" An edge of irritation coats Jon's voice. He's still thinking he can get away with this.

Out of the other back pocket comes a three-pack of condoms. I shudder and Skye, now behind Liam, visibly shakes. I notice for the first time a female officer next to Skye. I'm so enthralled with what's happening with Jon, I never even noticed the addition of the she-cop.

Everything coming out of Jon's pants goes into a brown paper bag.

The cop moves to the front pocket and Jon visibly blanches and tries to lunge at him, but both Logan and cop number one stop him. Cop number one yanks him back a lot harder. I catch the worry on Logan's face before it goes blank again. I know he's dying to get to Skye because his eyes go to her every few seconds and when they do, the expression on his face betrays him. It's pain and love and regret. Hers is fear and determination. I'm so proud of Skye. She has always been one to avoid any kind of confrontation, always the peacemaker. But not today. Today she's a fucking tigress.

Out of the pocket comes a little bag with a whitish powder. And then, another. And another. Three bags total. I'm betting that's what he put in Skye's drink. Jon's little special formula. Jackpot! That seems to be enough for the cops. Cop number two puts the three little bags in another brown bag and Jon's pants and shoes in yet another bigger bag. Then, they start to read him his rights.

"You have the right to remain silent and refuse to answer questions. Anything you say may be used against you in a court of law. You have the right to consult an attorney before speaking to the police and to have an attorney present during questioning now or in the future—"

Jon is putting up a fight now. He's calling to Skye and trying to get her to tell the police he's innocent.

The two male cops leave the room, dragging Jon with them and a moment later, I can hear Jon's shouts and the cop who's still reading him his rights as they walk past Liam's bedroom door.

My eyes go back to the monitor.

Logan steps closer to Skye, but the female cop puts a hand up to stop him. She looks at Skye, a clear question in her face.

"Is this okay?"

Skye nods and goes to Logan and as soon as his arms are around her, she falls apart. Tears come in waves, sobs following soon after. Logan pulls her into him tight, his arms on her back and tangled in her hair and even though he's whispering, in the silence of the room I can hear him repeat again and again. "I'm sorry. I'm so sorry. I'm sorry."

# CHAPTER FORTY-FOUR

## Liam

I STEP OUTSIDE THE ROOM WITH THE FEMALE COP TO GIVE Logan and Skye some privacy. A part of me is happy this is done and we got him. But another regrets putting Skye through this ordeal. Even if she knew she was safe the whole time, I can't imagine what it was like to be in her shoes. There must have been a moment when she thought he was going to get to her. I feel indebted to her, and I am filled with gratitude. Our methods may not have been one 100 percent legal, but the police got enough evidence to lock him up for a while. At least until his father shows up with a bunch of lawyers.

I want to go to River and check on her, but I'm not sure what to do, now that they took Jon. He's in the back of a squad car screaming his head off and threatening to sue us and telling the cops they don't know who they are dealing with. I don't think he's going to make any friends in county jail with that attitude. And tomorrow is Sunday, which means he'll be held at least until Monday before his father can get a judge to set bail. He probably has a clean record, and his rich daddy will push his weight around for sure.

One of the cops comes back and nods at the lady cop next to me. He steps into the room and a moment later, Logan follows him back out. The lady cop goes in and asks Skye if she can ask her some questions.

Logan disappears down the stairs with the cop, which I think is a friend because of the way they're talking. This might be the guy who was digging around for Logan and I wonder if this will help or hinder our plan. Not knowing what to do, I go back to my room and knock on the door for River to let me in.

The door opens suddenly and she nearly knocks me over when she barrels into me. Her face buried in my chest, I can feel the wetness through my T-shirt. She's been crying too.

Fuck! In the middle of all this I didn't think of how watching her sister would affect her. I feel ten kinds of stupid right now. I nudge her back into the room and lock the door behind me. Her arms are tight around my waist. I hug her back and pull her into me, even more. After a moment, her body relaxes into mine. But her silent tears run for a few more minutes. When she looks at me, her lashes are wet and darker, her cheeks are flushed red, and there's a look of desperation in her eyes. I kiss her forehead before wiping what's left of her tears off her face.

"We got him."

"Do you think it will stick?"

"I think we have a very good chance it will. It's out of our hands now. We did all we could. The police will have to take over from here, but with Logan on our side and the attack being on a cop's girlfriend, I think we have a very good chance he'll end up in jail. The police tend to take it personally when someone goes after one of their own."

"I hope you're right."

"Me too, River, me too."

I pull her into me again and breathe her in, filling my lungs with her smell.

"I'm sorry," I speak into her hair.

"What for?"

"For putting you through this. For letting Skye be a part of it. For you having to watch all of it. For a moment when I first had this idea, I thought we could leave the two of you out, do it behind your back, but it would be hard to explain all the cars on the street and a party you two were not invited to. I had visions of you breaking into the party and skewering both my balls."

She laughs. "Nah, just one. I'd rather have you with functioning body parts."

At the mention of said body part, it decides it's a good time to make an appearance. Hard-ons show up at the most inconvenient of times.

*Now is not the time, dude!*

I send a mental note to my dick, but he's having none of it. I know River can feel it, but far from pulling away as I thought she'd do in a moment like this, she actually pushes into me and grinds into my groin.

I moan.

Out loud.

She giggles. I'm glad for the little bit of levity in this moment. And for the fact all of this doesn't seem to be getting between us, between what we built over the last week. It's so new and tender still. I fear something will change and send us back to ground zero. I just can't let that happen. Over the last few months, River found her way into my life and under my skin. And I like it like that. As irritating as she can be, I miss her when she's not around and my thoughts always drift back to her.

A knock on the door has us both jumping. I push her behind me before opening it a crack. Logan. I open the door wider and the other cop is with him. They both walk in and Logan pushes the door closed.

A whistle leaves the cop's lips. "This is it? The whole setup?"

"Yes. We have everything you need right here." Logan points at the hard drive on the desk.

"So, do you think it will fly? Can we claim we had security cameras to make sure no one stole anything?"

"Yes. I believe you can. Lots of people have security cameras, both outside and inside their homes."

River, whom I was still hiding behind my back, steps around me, her hand extended to the cop.

"Officer . . ."

He smiles at her. "I'm sorry, didn't see you there." He takes her hand. "Officer Levy, but you can call me Steven."

I have the urge to punch him in the face as he smiles at River. Primal, caveman jealousy squeezes my chest and I wonder how much time I would get for sucker-punching a cop.

*What the fuck?*

# CHAPTER FORTY-FIVE

## River

It's Mother's Day and I know Mom will be at the very least wondering why we're driving up today and not on Friday afternoon like we usually do when we go home.

We discussed this at length. We know we have to tell our parents the truth, but we don't want to do it now. Not on Mother's Day. And next week is graduation. Not then either. We decided we would tell them after. A few days after when we go home over summer break. I'm going back to Riggins for a couple of summer classes for my masters and I'm still working at the clinic. Skye has a new editing job and her masters in English, which is a blend of online and once a month all-day Saturday classes. This will allow her to stay closer to Logan as well, and Liam and I will be in school at the same time.

This arrangement works for everyone. Except our parents. I know they're looking forward to having us home for the summer, but I also know they will support us in whatever decision we make. Plus, we need to stay close by in case the police need to speak to any of us.

We talked for hours last night and we're exhausted. But the

police gave us a break today and we will pick up wherever they need on Monday. Logan's friend, Steven Levy, is making sure to clean up all the loose ends. Skye declined a blood test, but between the drugs they found on Jon and the video where he talks about raping her and me, they have enough to hold him. Now we hope the other girls and the investigation show enough cause to charge him.

THERE's a knock on the door. It's 8:00 a.m. and we have a couple hours ride ahead of us. The boys are here to pick us up. Despite the changes in their relationship with their mother, in light of everything that happened, they decided to come with us instead of going back to Connecticut to see their mom. They talked to her—that much I know. It's a step in the right direction, but it will take time to heal their relationship. They can't undo twenty-plus years of neglect over a few days. But there's less tension for both of them when they talk about their mom. The father is another story. They haven't mentioned him at all. As if by mutual agreement, no one has. The man simply no longer exists. It's sad, but some people are toxic and they're better off not having that kind of toxic relationship with their father.

Skye makes it to the door and as soon as she opens it, her feet are off the floor and Logan has her in a bear hug. A smile makes its presence known on my face as I watch them and then turns into a full grin when Liam steps around Logan and makes his way to me. His hands cup my face, his touch gentle. His lips meet mine in a chaste kiss. I think I whimper in disappointment and Liam chuckles into my mouth before parting my lips with his and giving me what I want. He reads me so well.

I don't know who breaks the kissing first, us or Skye and

Logan, but when we look at each other, there's an awkward moment before we all laugh. I like this. I need this. We all do. We need this moment of levity. Last night was way more difficult than we had bargained for. Even though the plan worked, I'm worried about the price we had to pay to get him. To get Jon.

The boys walked us back home at three a.m. and went back to their house to wrap things with the cops. Skye slept in my bed. We hadn't done this since we were little kids and were scared after watching a horror movie.

---

"READY?" Logan asks.

"We are." I grab the bag of gifts Skye and I wrapped a couple of days ago. Liam takes it from me and laces his fingers through mine. After one last look around to make sure we didn't forget anything we are on our way.

The two-hour trip home is mostly quiet and all of us take naps in the truck. Logan and Liam insisted on driving and switched mid-way. When they switched, so did Skye and I. I sit on one end of the back seat, against the door, and Liam's head is on my lap. I run my fingers through his hair and he's having a hard time keeping his eyes open. I move my hands over his eyes gently and he flutters them closed. He's sleeping seconds later. I can't even imagine what we all will look like when we get home. A rag-tag team of tired people. I know my parents will notice right away. Mom, especially. She misses nothing. We told them we were at a graduation party and that's the reason for not going home earlier. It is the truth. Sort of.

But will she buy that's all there was to it? We all look weary and every time our eyes meet, there's a whole lot going back and forth between us. A whole silent communication. We may not be putting words to it, but there's a lot being said. Worry, expectations, waiting.

Now, we wait.

And hope.

# CHAPTER FORTY-SIX

## Liam

IT WAS ABOUT NINE WHEN WE GOT HOME LAST NIGHT. WE dropped the girls off and made sure they were okay and then went home. Logan has an early shift today. I feel for him. He didn't get much sleep over the last few days. Neither did I, but I insisted on driving all the way back home, so he could nap in the back seat.

Dinner at the farm was good but awkward. I give Serena and David a lot of credit for giving the girls and us the space we needed. I know my father would not have given a flying fuck about hurting my feelings and demanding to know what was happening. Either that or he'd ignore us completely. Concern for his children was not something he prioritized.

It's nearly noon now. I asked River to text me when she wakes up. This is graduation week and there are no classes. They've finished their finals. The girls don't have to worry about moving out of campus housing since they have their own place. I have to go in and finalize a couple of things, get books and so on. If River is up, maybe she'll go with me. I sit up to grab my phone from the night table and see if any messages came in when it rings in my hand. Logan.

"Hey."

"They got him," Logan says.

"For real?"

"Yes. Between the drugs they found in his pocket, the videos, and Skye's testimony , along with ours, the judge denied bail."

"So, what does that mean?"

"That means he stays in jail until either a trial date is set or the charges are dropped and we have too much evidence for him to get the charges dropped. They're comparing the drugs they found on him to the toxicology test done on the girls who came forward right away. We're sure they will be a match. We're also reaching out to the girls who reported their rapes and showing them his picture to see if they can identify him as being in the same place they were. If any of them recognizes Jon, it ties him to a crime scene."

"Holy shit!"

"It's happening, little brother."

I run my fingers through my too long hair and drop back on the bed, not even bothered by the little brother comment. "I can't believe it."

"Believe it. We have enough evidence to put him away for a while. But now, the lawyer games begin."

"Did you tell the girls yet?"

"Not yet, I'll call them now. Wanted to let you know first."

"Thanks, Bro."

"No, thank you. It was your idea."

TEN MINUTES later my phone rings again. It's River this time.

"Can you believe it?" she asks even before I have a chance to say hello.

"It's great news. Logan is confident he'll get some jail time."

"Thank you. Thank you for doing this, for having my six and giving me my life back."

I smile at her use of the military term. "I'll always have your six. But I also want your twelve, your three, your nine . . ."

She groans and I don't have to see her to know she's rolling her eyes.

# CHAPTER FORTY-SEVEN

## River

When I walked into the kitchen this morning, in my purple undies with the unicorn on the front and a matching tank top, the last person I expected to see lying on my couch was Liam. In fact, I didn't see him at all.

"I used your toothbrush. Hope you don't mind."

A little scream leaves my lips as I jump and turn around, my hand holding my chest where my heart is running a marathon. "Liam! You scared the hell out of me."

A slow smile curves his lips and he stretches on the couch, his arms reaching over his head, his back arching, and then one arm folds under his head while his other hand scratches the five o'clock shadow on his face before it lowers into his bare chest and rests there. My eyes are transfixed on his body, and my mouth goes dry and then waters like I'm looking at the most delicious feast and somewhere in the back of my mind that annoying voice tells me I am. This time, I don't tell it to shut up.

"How do you know it's my toothbrush and not Skye's?"

"Because I heard Skye tell Logan your favorite color is

purple and since you were kids, you would only brush your teeth if you had a purple toothbrush."

He smiles and that hand on his chest lowers a few more inches, stopping just above his belly button. He has an innie, I notice.

"And by what I can see right now, it is true," he says. His eyes travel down my body and lazily came back up again until he meets my eyes.

I remember what I'm wearing but refuse to feel self-conscious about it. I already know he's attracted to me and we haven't lashed out at each other since the day we both broke down and made our confessions. And made out. And kissed. We still tease each other. It wouldn't be us if we didn't, but it no longer holds the edge of anger it once did.

And right now, I'm grateful for three things.

One, that I brushed my teeth before going in search of coffee.

Two, the fact I'd actually closed the bathroom door before going pee because the last thing I need is for Liam to see me sitting on the potty since it looks like he slept here last night.

And three, holy mother of all that is hot! Apparently, Liam likes to sleep in his boxer briefs and it's morning. Have I mentioned that it's morning? Yep, it's morning, and he's wearing tight black boxer briefs or maybe they're tight because it's morning and I'm also very grateful for six packs.

And morning wood.

My eyes keep jumping between his six pack and the tightness in his underwear and all that before I've had my coffee. That's my excuse for why my eyes are stuck in the space between his stomach and his thighs. And also, why I forgot I'm nearly as undressed as he is.

"What are you doing here?" I ask.

"They were making too much noise."

"What do you mean?"

"Your sister, my dear, is a screamer. I got tired of hearing them going at it, took her keys and came over late last night while you were sleeping. I spent the night on the couch."

"Who knew Skye was a screamer? I would've never guessed. She must have been holding back when Logan is over here." I muse.

"With the right guy, every woman is a screamer."

My mouth opens and closes, but nothing comes out for a few seconds. Hell! Why is it everything he says sounds so sexy?

"I'll take your word for it."

"Ah, but we both know you'll take so much more than my word, don't we?"

Annnd I'm speechless again, but my eyes keep doing their thing, feasting on Liam's body.

"Eyes up here, River." He catches me and it takes me a few seconds to register what he's saying and why he's saying it.

When my eyes meet his, they're dark with desire and my skin heats under his stare. I have such a girl boner for him and I don't want to wait another minute. Not when I've fought this for months and denied myself for so long, and not when he's nearly naked and those boxer briefs do nothing to hide the fact he's just as aroused as I am, and especially not when every cell in my body is screaming with lust and they're all yelling his name.

"River." His voice is husky, sensual, and it vibrates in my core.

His chest rises and fills up with air, then releases, once, twice, three times. His strong legs move off the couch and his bare feet hit the hardwood floor. He stands with the grace of a cat—*no. Not a cat.* A cat is cute and cuddly—he makes me think of a panther. All danger and contained power. He takes a step toward me and then another. I bite my lip, anticipating the taste of his mouth on mine. I want to meet him halfway but instead hold my ground as he stalks his way to me.

When he's close enough, both of his hands grasp my hips. He pulls me to him as he takes the last step and dissolves the space between us. His fingers dig onto my hips and then go around my ass and cup me as he pulls me into his body, pressing himself against me. I feel his hardness on my belly and whimper.

My hands wrap around his forearms and move up until they grab the back of his neck, fisting his hair while tugging his face down to mine.

His face inches away, his eyes searching mine and asking for permission. I answer the unspoken question with a kiss. I brush my lips over his and then go on my tiptoes so I can get closer to him. I press my body into Liam's, seeking relief for the ache building between my thighs. His lips part on a moan and my tongue darts into his mouth and stays there. He tastes like my minty toothpaste and Liam. His tongue is hot against mine. We let our lips play. And they play so nice together. My hips push into Liam's and I find myself rocking against him, but I can't quite align myself with what I'm looking for. He groans into my mouth and his hands on my ass lift me a little. He gives me a taste of what I want and it's my turn to groan. Oh God, Liam is far from the first guy I ever made out with, but it never felt like this, this hot, this good. It's so good, it hurts.

Liam keeps kissing me and walks me backward until I'm pressed against the kitchen counter. His hands on my ass come around to my hips and he easily lifts me onto it, pushing himself between my open legs, his mouth never leaving mine. When he's settled between my thighs, his hands on my hips pull me closer to him until I'm sitting on the edge of the counter and my center is aligned with his dick. He pulls his lips from mine and his mouth travels down my jaw and neck. He licks his away around my throat and nibbles on my chin. His breath is warm on my skin and my nipples are painfully hard. I push into him and the moment my breasts touch his chest I hear a hiss come from Liam.

His hands drift up my waist until he grazes the sides of my breasts with his knuckles and then his fingertips. His mouth is at my ear and bites my lobe, his lips caressing me as he pushes his groin into my core. He's so hard and so hot. Or maybe I'm the one who's so hot. I can't tell anymore.

"This counter is the perfect height, River," he whispers. "I can feel you, all of you. Your nipples on my chest, your pussy on my dick. You're so wet, I can feel it through your panties. Is all that for me?"

I have no words left in me. I'm a puddle of need in his hands, so instead of saying anything, I move my legs around his thighs and pull him even harder into me. My body wants to move, but my position on the counter does not give me the room to do what I want. I whimper in frustration and I can hear Liam's low, sultry laugh in between bites and kisses on my neck. He is fucking my neck with his mouth and I want that mouth somewhere else on my body. Liam's hands finally take pity on my poor aching breasts and come around to the front to cup me. He is gentle and firm at the same time, his thumbs grazing my nipples, and I swear by the end of this there will be two nipple-sized holes in my tank top. His mouth finds mine again and he teases me with his lips. He sucks my bottom lip into his mouth and then the top, then he bites me. His tongue comes out to play and licks the spot his teeth were just on. His mouth on mine again, he is kissing me with such desperation, I know he's feeling the same way I am.

After what seems like a lifetime, he pulls away and rests his forehead on mine. His eyes are closed, both of our breaths coming out in fast, shallow pants. His hands on my breasts still squeeze harder and he pinches my nipples. A small gasp leaves me and I feel that pinch to my core. Liam drops his head to the hollow in my throat and kisses me there.

"I love this little spot"—he kisses it again—"right over here. Don't ask me why. I have no idea. I just do." His tongue darts out and he licks it and then his lips trail down my chest until his face presses into the swell of my breasts. He rubs his cheek on one side and then the other. The day-old beard is rough on my skin and I love it. I love the way it feels. My hands run through his hair. It's even longer now. He has not cut it since the first time I saw him and I like it. I like the way his hair grazes the top of his shoulders and how I can grasp fistfuls of it and guide his head where I want it. I tug his hair now and arch my back into his face. He groans into my cleavage. I tug his hair again and I get the same response. Liam likes it when I pull at his hair.

"River." My name leaves his lips in a whisper just before he closes those same lips around a nipple and sucks on it through my tank top. His mouth opens wider and he takes as much of me as he can. And I know I could come, just like this, his dick grinding into my pussy and his mouth sucking on my tits. I think he can tell how close I am. His mouth switches to my other breast, trading places with his hand, and I can feel the fingers on my nipple even more now that the fabric of my tank top is wet. He's shaking, his body trembling against mine. He pulls his mouth from my aching nipple with one last lick and rests his forehead on my chest, and I can tell he's trying to gain some control. My arms go around his shoulders and I can feel the tension in them. Digging my fingers into the tense muscles,

I knead them. After a few moments he relaxes a bit, but he is still so hard against me and I am still aching to have him inside me.

Liam lifts his head from my chest and looks me in the eyes, and I can see his desire. I can see his want and the struggle to hold himself back right now.

"Tell me what you want, River. You have to tell me what you want. I won't go any further if you don't say it."

For a moment I wonder if he is doing this to tease me—if this is one of his games again. We've been playing at it for so long, maybe he's falling back into old habits, but when I look into his eyes, I understand. This is not a game for him. This is serious. He is taking this very seriously, and he wants me to be clear about what I want. He's giving me all the power. The power I need to make the choices I want. And what I want is Liam. I want all of him and I want him right now. I'm not shy and I don't hesitate when I tell him exactly what I need.

"I want you, Liam. I want your hands on my body. I want you to touch every inch of my skin and when your fingers are done, I want you to follow with your tongue and your lips. I want your fingers inside me and I want to taste myself in your mouth when you kiss me. And I want to do the exact same things to you. And when neither one of us can take it any longer, I want you inside me, and I want you to fill me up so completely that we change the laws of physics and two bodies can actually occupy the same space at the same time. That is what I want, Liam. Can you give me that?"

He releases a breath. "Thought you'd never ask."

His hands go around my face and he kisses me gently and then looks into my eyes. "If you want me to stop at any time, you'll tell me, okay?" He waits for my response and I nod. "No, River, I want to hear you say it. You will stop me if you change your mind. You have the right to stop me, do you understand it?"

"Yes, I do."

"And you will tell me if I do anything you don't want me to, okay?"

"Liam?"

"Yes?"

"Shut up and kiss me."

He laughs. "Now, there's the bossy River I know and love."

*Did he just say he loves me? No, that's just an expression, he does not mean it.*

"Liam, put that mouth of yours to better use." I challenge him and his eyes go darker, and knowing I'm the reason for it turns me on even more.

He gives me a wicked smile and that mouth of his promises to do wicked things to me.

# CHAPTER FORTY-EIGHT

## Liam

THIS GIRL IS GOING TO BE THE END OF ME. YES, IT HAS been a long time since I got laid, but it has nothing to do with the way I feel every time I see her. From that first encounter when she dumped her fruity girly drink on me to this very moment, River has inhabited just about every thought that's been in my mind. It's either me being pissed off at something she says or does or me being amused by the stuff that comes out of her mouth, and as of late, it's me being jealous of every guy who looks her way.

My hands go around her hips and I pull her up and off the counter as her legs wrap around me and lock on my hips. Her arms are around my neck and I hold her to me as I make my way to her bedroom when it hits me. I don't have any condoms.

"Please tell me you have condoms."

"No, I don't. But Skye might have some in her room."

"Let's find out."

I walk to her sister's room with River wrapped around me. She leans down to open the door because I'm not letting her go.

"Her nightstand," River says and I bring her to it and sit on the bed so she can open and look through.

"Bingo!" River grabs a box, opens it and starts to take one condom out.

"No." I shake my head. "Take the box."

She raises an eyebrow at me.

"Okay, leave one for my brother."

River takes two condoms out of the box and puts them in the drawer, keeping the box. "Based on what my sister said, Logan is not a one-timer."

I smile then. "Neither am I."

We make our way to her bedroom and she closes the door and locks it. I bring her to the edge of the still unmade bed and let her legs slide off me as I let go of her. She kneels on the bed, moving back into the middle, and I follow her, sitting back on my heels so we are the same height. She leans over and puts the box on her nightstand.

It's early and her curtains are closed, but the morning light filters through the gauzy material, giving the room an ethereal quality. Or maybe it's just the knowledge that I'll soon have River that makes it feel that way.

I search her face to make sure there's no doubt in her mind. That there's no fear. I find none. Then, I kiss her again. I start it gently, tasting her, letting my lips graze hers and brush over her face. I kiss the tip of her nose and the corners of her mouth. I kiss her temples and her closed eyes. I brush her hair back, away from her beautiful face and tug the chestnut locks until she tilts her head back, giving me access to her neck. I kiss, lick, and nibble every inch of her neck before I move down into her collarbone and trace it with my tongue.

My arms wrap around her back, keeping her from falling

back on the bed. Soon but just not yet, I tell myself. She is trembling in my arms and her hands grasp at my shoulders and when I lower my head and lick the space between her breasts, her nails dig in. I gasp at the momentary pain, but in an instant, it turns into pleasure. I pull my face away and smile at the twin wet spots I left on her tank top. She looks at me and her hands are moving over my chest and her mouth meets mine for a brief kiss before moving down to my chin and following the contour of my jaw. River suckles at my neck and it's my turn to shiver. She nibbles at my ear and licks a path from my neck to my shoulder where the tattoo starts. She traces the wing tip design with her tongue. As she touches the colors embedded into my skin, I know she can feel the raised ridges of my many scars, but she does not avoid them or pull away. She traces each with her fingertips and then she licks them and kisses away the tainted memories that made me get the tattoo in the first place. With each touch to the scars on my chest, River kisses away all the pain and the sorrows associated with them until there is nothing left but beautiful artwork. She moves around me and to my back and does the same to the dragon and the eagle. I close my eyes and just feel. She finds each individual scar and kisses it, and with each kiss I heal. With each kiss, I let go. With each kiss, I forgive. With each kiss, I am myself again.

My eyes are still closed when I feel River move around and kneel in front of me again. I'm overcome with emotion, with lust, with gratitude, and with love. When did this happen? When did I fall for this girl? Every time she pushed me, every time she made me angry, every time she made me laugh, and every time she made me want her, she gave me a piece of my life back. I don't trust myself to speak right now, so I do the next best thing. I make love to her. This may have started as just sex and lust, but at some point, without my ever being aware, it turned into something else, but I don't think River is ready to hear the words yet. She has her own demons to conquer, so I will tell her I love her the only way I can. With my body and with my actions.

When I open my eyes River in kneeling between my legs and I can feel the heat of her body, I can smell her sweet and spicy scent, and I can see the desire in her eyes. I reach for her and she comes to me willingly. I brush the edge of her tank top and let my fingers go under it. She sucks in a breath at the contact with her skin and I slide my hands up and under her top, dragging the fabric as I go. My eyes follow my hands as I see each little bit of skin exposed. When my thumbs caress the underside of her breasts my eyes go back to hers and she leans into my hands, seeking fuller contact. I don't deny her. My hands cup her breasts and I feel their fullness, and I love the weight of them in my hands. Her top is bunched just above the swell of her breasts and I push it up as she helps me by pulling it over her head and dropping it to the bed.

I take her in, her beautiful tanned skin and the lighter color where the sun never touches her. I trace a finger over the tan lines, one side and then the other. I'm taking my time with River and holding back is killing me. She moves up on her knees and brings her chest level with my face. I smile at her. Apparently, I'm not moving fast enough for her.

"Impatient?" I ask.

She answers me by grabbing the hairs on the back of my neck and tugging my face into her, and I gladly oblige. My lips latch on a nipple and I tease it with my tongue and teeth while my hand works on the other and then I switch, giving attention to each beautiful round swell in turn. I lick the top of her breasts and the space in between before returning to her nipples.

"Do you like this, River?" I murmur against her skin.

She moans.

"Should I keep going?" I tease with a lick of my tongue.

She tugs at my hair harder.

"I will take that as a yes."

I come up on my knees now and push her back into the mattress, covering her body with mine. We both still have our underwear on and I reach to my hips and pull mine off before settling myself to her side. I let my hands move down her stomach and hips slowly before I follow their path with my mouth. I kiss and nibble my way down her belly. I move over to one hip and lick it, then trail my lips low on her belly and lick the other hip.

River is breathing in rapid, shallow gasps and she's rubbing her thighs onto each other. Her eyes are closed and I can see the shivers on her skin.

I lick down a trail from her belly button to the edge of her purple panties and when I hover over them, I shift my weight to one side so my hand is free. I trace the unicorn picture on the front. "Is this unicorn for me? Did you buy these panties because they made you think of me?" I say remembering the time she asked me if unicorns jump out of my dick when I come.

"Hmm," she moans as my finger traces the outline of the unicorn. "I will never tell."

I kiss her over the design on her panties. "I will also take that as a yes."

Her hips jerk up.

"I'm going to take these off now. Tell me if you want me to stop."

She gasps. "Don't stop."

I hook my fingers on both sides of her hips. She lifts her bottom and I pull her panties down her long legs, tossing them over my shoulder. Then I pull back and feast my eyes on her naked body.

"You are so beautiful." She is absolute perfection. Her full breasts more than fill my large hands and her waist is small. I can almost put my hands around it. Round hips and long tanned legs that I will soon have wrapped around my back as I pound into her.

With gentle hands I move her knees. "Open up for me, River."

She does it with no hesitation and I move in between her legs. I hover over her on my hands and knees and bring my face to hers.

She looks at me. I need to make sure she knows what I'm going to do, and she is okay with it.

"I'm going to taste you now, babe."

River writhes under me as I kiss my way down her body until I find the place I'm looking for.

I let my chin graze the curve of her thigh where it meets her core. I settle myself between her legs and push them open with my shoulders. Her curls are short and neatly trimmed and I move my nose into them. I inhale her deeply and I'm dizzy with her scent.

"You smell so good." I inhale her again. I can't wait a moment longer to taste her.

So, I don't. I let my lips touch her and drop tiny, gentle kisses over her mound then trace her contours with my tongue.

I'm a greedy bastard because all thoughts of moving slow, of letting her get used to my mouth on her evaporate the moment I get that first taste of her pussy.

"Holy fuck! You taste like heaven."

My mouth drops to her again and I devour her. My tongue can't get enough of her taste and I swear I could come just on the taste of her alone. I trace her folds with my tongue and then suck on her clit. She bucks under me and I pull back and gentle my mouth. I'm going out of my mind with need. I wrap my arm under her left thigh and move lower. My tongue finds her wetness and licks at it. She's moaning and her hands are fisting the sheets as her hips move up to meet my mouth. I tongue fuck her pussy over and over again until her hands come to my hair and pull me even closer into her. I move my free hand between her legs and replace my tongue with a finger while my mouth finds her clit, so I nibble and lick it while my finger moves inside. She is so wet and so hot, I know she's ready for me, but I won't move further, not until she comes on my face and fingers. I pull my hand away, then go back in with two fingers and it's a tight fit. She's so close I can feel it in the way her body is moving, in the rapid sounds of her breaths. I search for and find that magical spot inside her and press on it while sucking on her clit and then River breaks apart. Her body tenses up and her hips shoot off the bed. I hold on, never stopping what I'm doing.

The sounds coming out of her are the most beautiful I have ever heard. And still I hold on. I'm not stopping or letting go. I can get more out of her and just when her orgasm hits its plateau, I move my fingers and press that spot again while flicking her clit with my tongue and she rolls into another orgasm. Her whole body is spasming and she screams my name. I gentle my fingers and my mouth and let her come down from it. Her body is limp, her eyes are closed, the only movement the rapid rise and fall of her chest. I watch her—she is the most exquisite thing I have ever seen. Like this, completely spent and coming down from her orgasmic high, her face flushed pink and her lips swollen from my kisses. I climb my way back up her and kiss her. She parts for me and my tongue dips inside her mouth. I kiss her, letting her taste herself.

"River?"

"Hmm, yes," she answers, her eyes still closed.

"Do you taste yourself?"

"I do."

"You taste lick-a-licious."

She opens her eyes now, and the gold mingles with the green. "Lick-a-licious? Is that a word?"

"It is now."

She pulls me to her and kisses me. I brace myself with my arms on either side of her and she brings her legs up and presses her knees to my hips. Her hands reach between us and her palms smooth over my stomach, her fingers tracing the ridges of my six pack. I moan into her mouth. I haven't given her a chance to touch me yet, I was so intent on having her and touching her. She reaches lower and grasps me, closing her hand around the head of my dick and trying to move up and down on my length, but her arms can't quite reach me.

She tries to push me up and over, and I know what she wants to do, but I can't wait any longer to be inside her, I pull her hand away from me.

"Later. Right now, I need to be inside you if you'll have me." I make sure her eyes are on mine. "Do you still want me?"

"God, yes, I do. More than anything I have ever wanted before," she says.

"Are you sure? We can stop right here, right now. We don't have to go any further."

"Liam?"

"Yes?"

She reaches over and fumbles with the box, taking a gold square from it. "Shut up and fuck me."

I take the foil from her and rip it with my teeth, pulling the condom from it. I hold it, making sure I have it the right way, and unroll it over me. River watches my every move, and she licks her lips when I hold myself. And I have a feeling she likes watching me.

I lean over her and let my body lower onto hers until we touch. I move my hand between us and touch her to make sure she's still wet, and she does not disappoint. Then I guide myself into her opening and push in. She is so tight, I find a bit of resistance and stop. Even though I know she's technically not a virgin, this is actually her first time. The one she will remember. I want to make it a good memory.

"I don't want to hurt you," I say, "but I have to push in. I'll go slow and let you get used to me."

Her hips move up to meet me when I push inside her a bit further and I hold off on to the need to just plunge into her.

She moans. "More, Liam. More."

I chuckle and push in another inch. "What if I don't have any more?"

"You promised me eight inches, you better deliver it."

I do. I push myself in the rest of the way until I'm completely buried inside her. She gasps and her hands go down my back and grab my ass. She pulls me to her and her legs wrap around my thighs, locking behind my knees.

"Heaven, River, your body is pure heaven. You are so hot and so tight all around me. It's never felt this good."

She contracts her pelvic muscles and squeezes me inside her.

"Fuck! Oh fuck! You're killing me, babe."

A wicked smile plays on her lips. "Are you inside yet? I can't tell." She laughs when my mouth drops open. She wiggles under me. "Move, Liam, I want you to move."

"Just for that, I should stay here and not move at all."

She squeezes me again, and a hiss escapes my lips, and I move because there's no way I can hold back now. I try to go slow, to let her get used to me being inside her, get used to my size, but she is having none of it. River grabs my ass and using her legs for leverage, she's moving right along with me and pushing me to go faster.

"Harder, Liam, harder."

"I don't. Want"—my voice is strained with lust and pleasure —"to hurt you."

"You won't!"

Her hands grab my ass tighter as I plunge into her. I pull nearly all the way out and then ram into her again hard, but nowhere near as hard as I could go. I'm still holding back. She moans, and she moves under me, meeting each thrust in perfect sync. I brace myself with my elbows on either side of her head, my hands in her hair. My eyes roam everywhere, taking everything in. Her flushed face and her parted lips. Her eyes are closed and her face is washed in rapture. Her breasts move when we move and her hard nipples brush against my chest. I'm overwhelmed by the feeling of her all around me, her tight fit, her smell, her taste. I can feel how close she is and I know I won't last much longer. My lips find her throat and I suck and lick and kiss my way up to her mouth and then plunge into her mouth with the same intensity as I fuck her.

I take and take and take and she gives and gives and gives.

She comes then, moaning into my mouth, and I pull my lips from hers because I want to watch her face as she breaks apart in my arms and around my dick. When I feel the waves of her orgasm lessen, I reach a hand between our bodies, rub her clit, and thrust into her harder and faster, and her ebbing orgasm kicks into another one. She's coming again, screaming my name. I have never seen or heard anything more beautiful. I let go then and join her, letting mine wash over me, and can already tell this is the best I've ever had and it can only get better.

# CHAPTER FORTY-NINE

## River

Bliss.

If I had to describe how I feel right now, the word would be bliss. I'm in a boneless bliss. My whole body is still tingling with the force of the orgasms Liam gave me. I'm completely spent and I don't think I can move. There is nothing left in me. Liam took everything, and I greedily gave it to him. He promised multiples, and he delivered them.

Liam's still inside me, still hard. His breath comes out in hash pants on my neck, his face buried in my hair. He's leaning on his side, holding most of his weight off me, his free hand on my hip. I move my head a bit so I can face him and smooth my hand over his cheek. His eyes are still closed and he turns into my palm and kisses it. His eyes open then and a smile plays on his lips.

"Hi," he says, and it comes out breathy. He's still panting. My own breath is closer to normal now.

"Hi," I say back with a smile myself. "I want to feel your weight on me." I try to pull him down.

"I'll crush you."

"No, I'm not that breakable."

He does it then. He lets me feel his weight on me and a gush of air leaves my lungs at the pressure of his chest on mine. He pulls back immediately, but I wrap my hands around his back and keep him.

"Shh, just for a moment, let me feel all of you."

He does. It's hard to breathe with all of his weight on me, but I love the feeling of his hard muscles pressing into my body and that he's still hard inside me. I squeeze him and he groans and pulls his weight off me, bracing himself on his arms.

I smile. "I think you appreciate all the Kegel exercises I do."

His mouth drops open and I laugh at the expression on his face and then I squeeze him again.

"Isn't he ready for a nap after all the play time he had?" I ask, referring to his dick.

"No, he wants to play more, but he needs to get cleaned up first." He pulls out of me then, slow, and I feel the loss. I want him right back in. How is it possible that I want him again just minutes after sex and after all the orgasms he gave me? I've never felt so fulfilled before.

"I have to clean up." He walks to my door and opens it a couple of inches and then listens. "I don't think Skye is back yet." He looks over his shoulder and when he sees me, on my bed naked, as I did not bother to cover myself with the sheets, he inhales fast. His eyes heat again as they travel over me and I can see his semi getting hard again. "Jesus, River! Cover yourself, will you?"

I giggle but do not reach for the sheet. "Go clean up and hurry back."

He shakes his head at me and goes. I can hear his footsteps on the hardwood floors and the water running in the bathroom. Then I hear him going into the kitchen and when he comes back, he has two water bottles in one hand and his clothes that he must have gotten from the living room in the other, and he is still naked.

*Yum. He is so yummy.*

He drops his clothes on the chair near the desk I use to do my schoolwork and locks the door again. Then he walks back to me and gets on the bed, standing on his knees. His erection proudly displayed between us. I sit up so I can get the water bottle he is holding for me, but Liam has something else in mind. He puts one of the water bottles on the nightstand next to the box of condoms and opens the other, tossing the cap over his shoulder. He holds it just out of my reach. "Come and get it." His smile is devilish.

I get up on my knees and try to reach it, but he raises it over his head, his arm stretched out. I scoot over to him and let my breasts graze his chest and press my belly into his dick as I reach up his arm, sliding my hand over the tattoos. But of course, he's much taller and his arms are much longer and I can't reach it. His free hand goes around my waist and he bends his head and nuzzles my neck before kissing me. He pulls back, putting a few inches between our bodies.

"Open up, River," he says as he starts to tilt the water bottle, a smug smile on his face, and I realize what he is going to do. I try to get away, but his arm has me locked in place, so I have no choice but to open my mouth and hope his aim is true.

He tilts the bottle slowly, looking between my face and the open end, and I feel silly like this looking up with my mouth open, then I remember what we just did and silly is no longer what I feel. The thin stream of water hits my tongue and I swallow as he pours it into my mouth, but then I feel him shift and he moves the bottle over and the water is now coming down my chin and neck and spilling over my breasts, icy cold. I squeal with surprise when the water hits my skin. His mouth follows the water and drinks it off my skin, licking down my neck and my chest. He leans into me, making me lie back down as he pours the icy water over my breasts and his greedy mouth traces the rivulets, licking and sucking. He nibbles at me and sucks on one nipple and then the other. He pours some more between my breasts and the water runs down onto my belly with his mouth right behind it. He pours the water into my belly button and then he slurps from it, making me moan and giggle at the same time. He moves between my legs, spreading them, and more water comes pouring over my right knee and down my inner thigh and he licks his way down until his face hovers over my center and then he looks up at me with a shit-eating grin on his face, or should I say a pussy- eating grin on his face? He pours the icy cold water on my pussy and I gasp as he drinks from me.

*Damn! A girl could get used to this.*

# CHAPTER FIFTY

## Liam

It's mid-morning now and River is sleeping in my arms, her sweet bottom nestled against me. After we made love for the second time, she was so spent, she fell asleep almost as soon as I pulled out of her. She didn't hear me when I went to the bathroom to get cleaned up or when I went into the kitchen and set the coffeemaker to start in a couple of hours. She didn't hear me when I came back into the room and locked the door again but not before taping a sign to it with the words.

DO NOT DISTURB. NO ONE IS HERE. GO AWAY.

I have no idea what her handwriting looks like and just hand-printed words I thought would sound like River. I hope Skye will take the hint and not knock or try to get into the bedroom. When I got back in the bed with her, I pulled her tired body into mine and she curled against me and let out a contented moan. I almost woke her up again. Almost, but she needs rest, and she has to be sore from all the sex we had.

I pull the covers over us and spoon with her. I realize I'm

thinking of this as making love and not sex or fucking. There's a difference. Most people just have sex, some get to make love. I have always enjoyed a good fuck, but sex was basically something I did to scratch an itch.

I have never, until this moment, thought of it as making love. And it had been so good, so fucking good, I know I'll never forget her taste, her smell, and the images in my mind. And I don't want to.

I kiss her head and make myself more comfortable around her and then close my eyes and allow myself to fall sleep.

The smell of coffee wakes me up and I'm starving. I haven't eaten since last night, well, at least nothing with calories, and I guess based on the amount of light coming into the room it has to be past noon. I nuzzle River's hair and inhale her spicy scent. She is fast asleep still and I watch her, unguarded. I take in her peaceful face as she sleeps. Her lips are swollen still from our kisses, her lashes are long and naturally curved. The swell of her breasts rise and fall steadily with each breath. I want her again. I'll never get enough of this girl, but I'm not sure of what we have here. What does she want? Is this just a hookup for her? Friends with benefits? I want more than that, but I'm not sure how to make it clear. I don't want to scare her off. There is so much happening. We still have to figure the issue with Jon. Hell, if both River and Logan hadn't made me promise I wouldn't kill the bastard, he'd be dead by now.

I shake those thoughts away. I don't want to think of that asshole while I'm here with River. I want to enjoy this moment and go back to watching her, and then my lips find the curve of her shoulder and kiss all the exposed skin I can find. Her back, her neck, her shoulder with barely there kisses.

She whimpers and shifts a little and her ass pushes into me.

"Hmm, you're poking me, Liam," she murmurs, and her sleepy voice sounds like an invitation to me, but I hold back.

She turns in my arms and her head rests on my chest. "What time is it?"

I look back over my shoulder at the alarm clock. "One-eleven."

"Hmm, *ones* follow me everywhere. I'm always seeing *ones.* Mom says it's a message from angels."

"It could be, but the only angel I see here is you."

She giggles. "Don't tell me you're also a poet, Liam."

"Sure, I am. Would you like to hear one of my poems?"

She looks at me now, her eyes bright and a smile on her lips. "Let's hear it."

I clear my throat as if I'm about to make an important announcement.

"Roses are red. Violets are blue. I love your pussy and I want inside of you."

She's laughing so hard; her whole body is shaking. "You're a terrible poet."

"What? You think you can do better?"

"Of course!"

"Let's hear it." I toss her words back to her.

"Roses are red. Violets are blue. Your cock is beautiful, can I please suck you?"

I groan and she is getting a big kick out of it. "You're killing me."

"Why? You don't like my poem?" She fake pouts.

"It's the most beautiful thing I've ever heard. If there's an award for poets, you should get it. Heck, I will buy you a trophy myself."

# CHAPTER FIFTY-ONE

## Liam

My hands are shaking and I feel cold despite the early Texas heat. There's a car in the driveway. I assume it's Hannah's husband's.

I glance at the closed door again and for a moment, I don't know if I can do this. River laces her fingers with mine and squeezes. She nods at me. A silent confirmation that I can do it. I watch my free hand rise in slow motion and my finger touches the doorbell. It's shaking so much, I miss the first try. River's hand squeezes mine again. Tears burn my eyes, but I hold them in.

The door opens, and the air trapped in my lungs gets expelled all at once. I suck in another breath. The man on the other side of the door is Michael Russo. I recognize him from the many pictures Hannah showed me and from the few times I saw him while she talked to him via Skype.

His eyes fill with water the moment he recognizes me. I didn't know what would happen but being pulled against his chest in a hug was not it. I expected him to be angry with me.

To punch me. To hate me for not saving his wife, but I never expected this.

River lets go of my hand. And my arms wrap around him. This man I never met before but feel like I know because Hannah told me so much about him. Sweethearts from the first day of high school, she told me. They were together since they were both fourteen. Two people who were meant to be, broken apart by a stupid tragedy.

In this moment, as we hold each other, there's so much shared. The pain, the love, and also the guilt. Hannah told me many times if anything happened to her, her husband would never forgive himself for not keeping her from going to Afghanistan. Her reason to go, a tragedy in itself. She lost her only brother to an IED. The closest unit with a medic was a hundred miles away. She was a doctor and she couldn't save her brother because she was nowhere near him. Hannah wanted to make a difference, and she enlisted. Just one tour, she said. But saving lives is addictive and one tour turned into three. It was supposed to be her last. And it was, just not in the way she imagined it would be.

When he pulls away, both our faces are awash in tears and there's no shame in it. I can hear River sniffling beside me and I know she's crying as well.

"Dad?"

A voice comes from inside the house and when he steps aside, I can see a young girl coming down the stairs. She stops mid-step, and it's like seeing a ghost. She looks exactly like her mother. A younger version of Hannah, a face not marred by the sights of war, and I imagine this is what Hannah looked like before she enlisted. I can see the confusion in her light blue eyes, the same color as her mother's. There's sadness in them but also hope.

"Dad?" Her voice is hesitant now. It cracks on the one syllable word.

"Sweetheart, this is Liam. He was your mother's best friend in the marines."

One of her hands covers her mouth as the other clasps her chest. Tears swim in her eyes. And I don't know if I can do this. River must anticipate what's going through my head because her hand touches my back, so softly it's barely a touch. Just a reminder that she's here with me. For me. Michael steps back into the house, a silent invitation for us to follow. We do.

The entryway is painted in a warm creamy yellow color. I know Hannah painted it herself because she told me. We talked a lot during the many hours we worked together. There are pictures on the walls, mostly of her daughter but a few of she and Michael as well. He waits for me by the opening that leads into their living room. This room too is warm and inviting. Light-colored furniture, splashes of red in pillows, and a blanket over one end of a lazy chair. It makes me want to smile. I know Hannah hated that chair, but it's her husband's favorite.

He gestures for us to sit and we do. River's beside me. He's on his favorite chair, his daughter perched on the side of it.

The silence that follows is heavy with unsaid words but not uncomfortable. There's closeness in this moment, brought by our shared love for the same person. Theirs, the love of a husband and of a daughter, and mine, the love of a friend. He speaks first.

"I hoped you'd come."

"I'm sorry it took me so long."

He shakes his head in denial of my apology. "You can't put a timer on these things. You came when the moment was right. I'm glad you made your way here."

"I wish—" Words vanish. I don't know how to convey to him and his daughter how sorry I am.

"I want to thank you," he goes on as if I hadn't tried to speak, tried to apologize again.

"They told me what happened. They told me about the ambush and how you tried to save my Hannah. How you tried to drag her to safety and shielded her with your body. They told me about the shrapnel you took and the explosion. They told me that…" His voice trembles. He clears his throat. "They told me that even after you blacked out, you had your arms and hands so tightly wrapped around her, trying to protect her still, that it took two men to pry your fingers from her and while you were in and out of consciousness, all you kept saying was, 'Save Hannah, need to save Hannah,' and for that I'm grateful.

"You tried, and she didn't die alone. You had her. And she loved you like a son. If I couldn't be there to spend her last breath with her, I'm grateful you were. I know she would have wanted that."

Tears prick at my eyes. I didn't know this. I didn't know what happened when I blacked out. No one told me.

"Sir, she saved me. But I failed to save her. If I hadn't run to get to her, the explosion that followed would have killed me. I didn't save her, but she saved me."

He nods in understanding. "We could spend hours, days talking about guilt. I feel that if I had asked her to stay, not to go back, she would be here now but then you might have died. I could have prevented her leaving, but I know this is something she had to do. Her brother was the only family she had left. They were very close. She felt the need to do something in honor of his memory. She did what she thought was best. We all did. We can't blame ourselves for it."

We talk for a couple of hours more. The rest of the conversation lighter, humorous even as we trade funny stories about Hannah and how caring and loving she was and how she loved practical jokes and played tricks on me all the time. I don't know if Michael knows what Hannah did for me when I was a green pup still, but I suspect he does.

Before we say our goodbyes, I ask River for the package and she gets it out of her bag. I hand him the package, the same as it was handed to me. Inside the plastic bag still. He gives it to his daughter, and she opens it, looking through the envelopes inside and finding the small box too. She looks at her father then and shows him one of the envelopes. He takes it from her and hands it to me. My name is on it. Chills run down my spine. I never opened that bag. I had no idea it was there. Michael can see the surprise on my face.

He smiles. "I guess Hannah played one last trick on you."

*Yeah, I guess she did.*

---

I DON'T READ the letter right away. I can't. Not here. Not while her husband and daughter watch me. We leave after that. I'm still holding it when River's small hand digs into my jeans pocket and takes out the rental car keys.

"I'll drive. You relax."

I'm thankful for that. Our drive back to the hotel is quiet, the car radio off. Just the sounds of the road under the tires—that, and the thundering of my heart.

When we get to the hotel twenty-five minutes later, I follow River into the elevator and then to the room we stopped in before, barely long enough to drop the weekend bags we packed.

I'm glad she insisted on coming with me. If I had done this

alone, I don't know if I would have had the strength to go through with it.

"I'm going to take a shower," she says as she grabs her bag and makes her way to the bathroom. I know what she's doing. She's giving me space so I can read Hannah's letter.

*Dear Liam,*

*If you're reading this, then I'm dead. I never imagined I would write a letter like this.*

*Even though death is a constant shadow over my shoulder, I'm in the business of saving lives.*

*But being a doctor is not the same as being God and we are limited by what our bodies allow us to do.*

*You may think that writing this letter to you is difficult. I thought the same when I came up with this idea, but it's not.*

*It's freeing actually knowing that my words will be read and taken to heart. That there will be nothing left unsaid from me to you.*

*I'm so proud of you. So, so proud of you. When we first met you were just a kid. A kid who thought he was tough, but nothing in your life could have prepared you for this place and the horrors you saw and will see. I don't think anyone is ever prepared to deal with this. The human mind, the human soul is far too delicate for war. At least the good ones are.*

*And you, Liam, you have a good heart and a good soul. I know your reasons for being here, but don't stay too long. Make sure you leave before it's too late. Before you're too broken to fix. Don't allow my death to turn you into a statistic. I know you will blame yourself for not saving me. For not being able to stop whatever is it that's going to kill me.*

*It is not your fault. I chose to be here, just like you did. We chose it for different reasons, but it was our free will that brought us here. And it will be God's will that will end it.*

*Don't blame God either. It's not God's job to prevent bad things from happening. It's our job. Each of us have responsibility over our actions or lack of action. And we live or die by the consequences of those actions.*

*Please find comfort in knowing I will be happy to see my little brother again. I have missed him more than words can tell.*

*It will hurt me to leave Michael and Cassie behind, but I know I will see them again. I trust in this.*

*One day I will be a distant memory and the war will fade away. But you, you'll go on. You go on living. Leave your mark in the world. Go back to school and finish back home what you started here. You have valuable skills but more than that. You have a heart that's true and pure. You are meant to save lives. Don't throw that away.*

*Go home, leave all this behind, find someone to love. Find someone who understands you. Find someone who cares and be happy.*

*You are a great friend to me and I love you.*

*Now go on. Live!*

*Love,*

*Hannah*

# CHAPTER FIFTY-TWO

## River

It's graduation day. Commencement starts in two hours. I'm so excited, I have to pee every five minutes. I feel like one of those teacup dogs rich girls carry around in a purse—all excitement and pee puddles. Mom and Dad drove up earlier this morning and I can hear them talking in the living room. I took a shower and dried my hair. Now I just have to get dressed and put some makeup on. I don't remember being this happy, ever. I know part of it is because of Liam. Part of it is because of graduation and part is because Logan got great news last night. Five of the girls they reached recognized and identified Jon from the multiple pictures the police showed them. And two of those girls had DNA evidence on them from the time of their own attack. One had skin cells removed from her fingernails and the other had saliva from bite marks on her body. They will be running those tests and they're sure it will be a match. The more counts of rape we can prove against Jon, the greater our chances of getting him behind bars will be. Logan says that once we get confirmation and press more changes against him, other girls are likely to come forward.

There's a knock on the door and it cracks open a few inches. "Can I come in?"

Liam's voice reaches me and causes an immediate tingle in my belly.

I close the purple silk robe around me, tying the knot at my waist.

"Yeah, you can come in." The door opens wide, and he steps in. A moment later the click lets me know he locked it.

I can't help the smile that takes over my lips. We've been together several times in the last few days. Each time is better than the previous one. I can't quite believe this is real. His eyes take me in, traveling all over my body before settling on my face. I don't know what this is we have between us. We haven't put words to it, but every time he's near me, I'm happy and when he's not, I miss him. Even when we're talking on the phone or texting, I still miss him.

"You know, I never thought purple would be my favorite color, but it's growing on me." He's in my space in a few short steps. His hands come up to my face and he tilts it up to him. I don't resist. I gladly give into his touch. I crave it. His lips come to mine in a gentle kiss.

"Are you ready?"

I look down at myself. "No, not unless you want me to flash everyone if the wind blows during graduation."

He groans. "Does that mean you have nothing under this robe?" His fingers trace the edge of the fabric where it overlaps at my waist.

"Why don't you check and find out?"

His hand drops to the hem of my robe and his fingers trace my thigh, bringing the fabric up with them, until he gets to the spot where he should be touching my panties. If I had any on, that is. He groans louder.

"Fuck, River! Your parents are out there. Logan and Skye are out there and all I can think about is burying my face and my dick between your legs," he whispers.

It's my turn to moan. His fingers come around the front and find me already wet for him. I moan louder. He drops to his knees. His lips are on me a second later. I grab onto his shoulders, holding myself up. There's urgency in the way he licks at me. Liam likes to take his time with me, to build me up, and he's a master at delayed gratification, but not right now. He's devouring me and less than two minutes later, I'm coming. I bite my lip so I don't make any noises. I can't believe we're doing this when everyone is just on the other side of the wall and a few feet down the hall. His mouth gentles on me as I come down from my high. He drops little kisses onto me. That's something I have come to expect and love.

Mom's voice comes through the walls. "Breakfast is ready, kids! Come and get it!"

Liam's head touches my belly, and he sucks in a breath. "I forgot they were here. I can't believe I forgot they're all here. I just said they were out there and forgot all about them the moment I got a taste of you. What are you doing to me?" He looks at me then.

"I don't know, but whatever this is, it's mutual. I forgot all about them too."

A huge smile spreads over his face. He kisses my belly, fixes my robe, and gets up. His hands cup my face again and he kisses me, my taste on his lips. "I'll let you finish getting dressed. Don't take too long. I'll wait for you to eat."

He walks to the door and turns just before opening it and looks at me with an intensity that makes my heart speed up.

We may not have put a name to this thing between us yet, but I'm pretty sure I know what it is.

# CHAPTER FIFTY-THREE

## River

GRADUATION IS OVER. OUR NAMES WERE CALLED. WE walked the path—didn't trip—and got our fake diplomas. The real ones will come in the mail in a few weeks.

Bruno, Pat, and to everyone's surprise, Olivia, the boys' mother came. I know it's an olive branch gesture and a small step in the right direction, but Logan and Liam are still a long way from forgiving everything their mother allowed to happen. But they talk often and their parents' divorce is expected to be finalized in the next three or four months. Their father has not tried to contact either of them since the day the boys confronted him. They both say it's better off this way, but my heart hurts for them. I have always taken my loving parents for granted.

Isn't it what parents are supposed to do? Love their kids unconditionally? I never questioned their love. They never questioned my trust in them. It just was. Some of our friends would say we were lucky to have the parents we had, but I never really paid much attention to it until I met Liam's parents. What a couple of fucked up people. Talk about priorities being mixed up. I feel lucky. I feel blessed. I should let Mom and Dad know.

We had a late lunch at a fancy restaurant. But besides the happy celebration atmosphere, Mom kept glancing at me and Skye. I'm not surprised. She always knew when something was up. Since we were kids, we couldn't get away with anything. Ever! Mom's sixth sense has a sixth sense. And right now, I can see and hear the alarm bells going off in her head. But she's biding her time until we get to our place. The six of us are sharing the space in Logan's SUV. It's big enough to fit all of us comfortably. I know my parents are not going back home without us talking first.

As soon as the door to our apartment clicks closed, it happens.

"All right, I have been patient enough. Someone tell me what's going on."

Logan and Liam look at each other and then at Mom, like the proverbial deer in the headlight.

"What do you mean?" Logan tries to deflect.

Skye just shakes her head at him and waves her hand. She looks at me for permission and I nod.

I take over from there. "We may as well sit. This is not the kind of talk one has standing up."

Dad, as always, is completely oblivious to everything, but he has been with Mom long enough not to doubt or question any of her weirdness, and I swear it's exactly that—her weirdness—what he loves most about her. Or as he likes to put it, Mom's woo-woo ways.

The boys look at me and Skye and hesitate, then each takes a seat next to us. Mom and Dad sit across from us, the coffee table marking neutral ground.

"Something happened. Something I didn't tell you or Skye

or anyone for that matter. I should have, but at the time, I was confused, angry at myself, and ashamed."

I take a deep breath and both Liam's and Skye's hands reach out at the same time to take one of my hands in theirs. They smile at each other and lend me the support and strength I need to go on.

"Mom, Dad." My lungs fill with air and expel it, one last attempt at delaying the pain my words will cause them. "I was raped."

Mom's gasp fills the silence, instant tears swimming in her eyes. Liam's fingers squeeze one of my hands, as Skye holds the other to her chest. Dad's always smiling face darkens. I rush to fill the empty space those three words I spoke created.

"I don't remember anything. I was drugged and up until about a week ago, I had no idea who did it."

"When?" Dad asks the one-word question.

"Nearly a year ago. I'm sorry it took this long to tell you, to tell anyone, but it has taken me this long to come to terms with it."

"Who?"

The silence falls heavy between us. I know as soon as I say his name my parents will recognize it. They know Skye dated him for a few weeks. They know how much I despise him. I feel like a coward all over again because his name refuses to leave my lips.

Skye takes the weight of those words away from me and I'm grateful for her stepping in.

"It was Jon, Dad."

My parents met Jon once when they came up to visit us. Mom didn't like him much either, but she never did interfere with our lives. She voices her feelings, gives advice when we ask for, but always allows us to make our own decisions.

Mom hasn't said a word. It's so unlike her to not say anything, but the silent tears streaming down her face, a face so much like my own, say it all. She's hurting for me.

I don't cry. I don't have any tears left in me and I'm done hurting over what he did to me. I'm taking my life back.

"Son." Dad looks at Logan. "You may not want to hear what I have to say next, being that you're the law and all, but I must say I have a lot of land and some machines that can dig very deep holes." He looks back at me. "Where can I find this piece of shit, River?"

Dad never curses. Never. He's completely in control, and cold rage along with the single curse word scare me more than words can say. I know Dad means everything he's saying. If he gets a hold of Jon, he will kill him and bury him somewhere no one can find him.

Logan steps in. "He's under arrest, sir. His bail has been denied. River was not the only one he hurt. There are several others. He's going away for a long time."

"My way is more permanent, son."

A corner of Liam's lip tips up at Dad's words.. Dad winks at him. Not a fun, amused wink. It's more of an 'I've got your back' wink. Dad frightens me a bit just then.

Mom finds her voice. "What can we do to help?"

I look at Skye and the boys. "There's nothing else to do but wait. We have a few girls who came forward and tied him to the place and time of their attack. We have video evidence as well. We think we may have some DNA evidence, but he was careful to cover his tracks. There are no witnesses."

"How did you find out?" Mom asks me.

Liam speaks for the first time. "We overheard a conversation. Something he said to someone."

Liam can feel my discomfort. "Maybe I can tell you what he said another time."

Dad nods at Liam. He can feel my discomfort as well.

"Logan, I don't know if either of my daughters ever told you this, but I was a lawyer a long time ago, before I got bewitched by this lovely lady sitting next to me and decided to be a farmer." This makes me smile. Dad sometimes calls Mom a witch, but it's always in the most loving of ways, his special nickname for her.

"Now, if I remember well, this boy"—venom drips at the word boy. Dad is refusing to address Jon by his name—"has a rich father and friends in high places."

"That's true, sir, but we hope the DNA evidence is a match and it will be enough to get him behind bars for a long time and—"

Dad interrupts Logan. "You know, on my first day of college, I was a very green eighteen-year-old. On that day I met my roommate, and we went on being roommates for the next four years and then another four when we went to law school together. That man would turn into a best friend of over thirty years."

I'm wondering where Dad is going with this.

"You know the name of that man, son?"

Logan looks confused. "I don't think so . . ."

"I bet you do. His name is George Lafayette."

Logan smiles. Mom smiles. I look at Liam and Skye, and they are just as confused as I am.

"Dad? What about Uncle George? What does he have to do with anything?"

"Oh, nothing much," Dad says. "Except that George is a state's attorney."

"Is that like a district attorney?" Skye asks.

"Yep."

"River, did you know that?"

"No. I haven't seen Uncle George since we started college."

"Does this mean what I think it means?" It's Liam turn to speak.

Logan's smile is even bigger now.

"River, if there's one other person, besides your boyfriend here, who would help me dig that hole, no questions asked, it's your uncle George."

"I'm feeling really dumb right now and maybe I should have paid more attention in Social Studies class or watched more CSI, but what can Uncle George do to help us?"

"Oh, he can bring in the heavy guns, so to speak, make sure we have the best prosecutors, put a lot of pressure on whoever takes up that piece of shit's defense, make him pay for everything he did to you, those other girls, and more."

# CHAPTER FIFTY-FOUR

## River

After we explained all the details on how we got Jon to my parents, and they went back home, exhaustion hit me. All the excitement and tension of the day finally caught up with me. We said our goodbyes, Mom's and Dad's hugs were extra tight and extra- long. A lot was said in those hugs and in the way they both looked at Liam and Logan. Their gratitude is palpable. Knowing all the boys did to right this wrong and how much Logan is risking to get Jon behind bars—he's putting his job at stake. What they did, what we did, isn't exactly legal. But it served a purpose.

When we come back into the house, the air is heavy with silence as we look at each other. This has been a day of celebration but also of confessions and pain. We didn't intend to say anything to Mom and Dad today, but there's only so much we can keep from my mother. Sooner or later, she figures things out. Had she been around from the beginning, she would have known months ago. Of that I'm sure.

Logan puts as an arm around Skye's shoulders and walks her to the door.

"See you tomorrow," he calls out before closing the door behind them. As if by some kind of mutual agreement, Skye leaves with Logan, but Liam stays with me. He looks at me, uncertainty in his demeanor. I extend my hand to him and he comes to me in an instant, pulling me into his chest and dropping his head to the curve of my neck.

"I'm so tired," I say.

He kisses my forehead. "Come, I'll help you get ready for bed."

"I'm sure you will," I joke.

"Nah, I think you could use a hot shower to relax you and then a long night of sleep."

"It sounds good to me. Now I just need to find the energy to do all that."

"I'll take care of you."

Before I can reply, my feet are off the floor and he's carrying me like a baby. He walks to the bathroom and stands me up. Unzipping my dress, he guides the sleeves down my arms. When I step out of it, Liam folds the dress and lays it on the side of the bathtub, then unhooks and removes my bra. I'm barefoot as my shoes came off as soon as we walked through the front door.

"You won't need these either." His gentle thumbs hook in my panties and he brushes his fingers all the way down my legs as my panties go with them. I step to the side and he tosses the panties in the hamper and then reaches around me to turn the shower on. Grabbing a hair tie, he makes a high ponytail on top of my head and turns it into a bun.

My back is still turned to him, I can hear as his shoes and clothes come off and land on the side of the tub next to my dress. One thing I always loved about this bathroom was that it has a separate tub and shower. Skye loves baths. I'm more of a shower kind of girl. We can share the bathroom and neither of us gets mad about the other taking too long. It works perfectly.

Liam's hands on my hips bring me back to reality and he walks me into the shower, then adjusts the water spray so it points down and doesn't get my hair wet. I step under the stream of hot water and moan. I'm a firm believer that a long hot shower cures most things. Liam's hands find my shoulders and start kneading. The combination of heat and touch undoes the tension that has been building up all day. He reaches for the soap and starts to wash me. His big hands cover way more skin than mine do. I let him. I stand there and let him wash me. His hands everywhere. It's not sexual, but it's sensual. After several minutes of his hands touching, massaging, and soaping me, he guides the spray along my body. He presses his chest to my back and I can feel how hard he is. My eyes have been closed this whole time, but as I turn around, I open them. A dripping wet and hard Liam is an image to behold. All my tiredness evaporates and I feel a surge of energy.

"Take me to bed, Liam."

The water turns off. A towel wraps around me. His hands are gentle when he dries away the drops on my skin, patting here and there, the movements a caress. He dries himself quickly and with way less gentleness that he dried me.

"Take me to bed, Liam," I say it again.

"Are you sure? This was a hard day for you."

"Every time you kiss me, every time you touch me, every time you make love to me, you chip away at all that hurt me before and you give me new, beautiful memories to hold onto."

His mouth is on mine in an instant. He tastes like forgiveness, like sunshine and happy days ahead. I thrive on his kisses.

As I LIE on my stomach, naked still, the sheet down to my hips, Liam brushes my hair off my shoulders and over to the side. His fingers trace random designs on my back, light as butterfly kisses. I relax even more and close my eyes, enjoying how gentle he can be considering the almost violent intensity with which he'd just taken me and I start to drift to sleep as his fingers continue to play on my back.

I realize the touch is not random at all and he's tracing letters on my skin. And just before sleep claims me, I make out the words . . . I LOVE YOU.

# CHAPTER FIFTY-FIVE

## River

WELL, HAVING AN UNCLE WHO IS THE DA REALLY DOES come in handy. Even if Uncle George is not really my uncle by blood since both my parents are only children, I grew up with him around. We saw him often. He was like a brother to Dad and it made him a part of our family. He doesn't have any kids and kind of adopted us as his own by proxy.

It's been three days since the trial that put an end to Jon Asshole's raping spree. He thought he could get away with what he did, but there were enough witnesses and enough corroborating evidence to put him at the scene of all the rapes. And the DNA came through. It was a match. Add to that the testimony and video we had of his attempt on Skye, thanks to Uncle George for making sure it was admissible in court, the drugs they found on him, and the prosecutors were able to prove intent as well.

With Uncle George's weight behind the prosecution and the media circus talking about putting an end to rape culture and rich boys' privilege, the judge felt the pressure. Especially after that case with the swimmer guy who raped an unconscious woman. Jon was found guilty for each count of rape the prosecution brought against him and got between four and ten years for each of those cases for a grand total of thirty-seven years in prison. He will be nearly sixty years old by the time he sees freedom again. My only regret is not having said anything sooner. Maybe I could have prevented it from happening to someone else, but then again, if I had, he would not have been caught. I'm sure of that. Jon is smart. If he thought anyone had any suspicion or started talking about it, he would just lie low for a long while or go prey somewhere far away from campus.

This is the thing I'll never understand. Even though he is an asshole, Jon could be charming. He is good-looking and has money. There were always willing girls he could have hooked up with, but he chose not to do that. That was just not good enough for him. He needed the thrill of dominance and he likes it with a fight. He's a sick bastard.

For the most part, I'm myself again. I have learned to let go of the blame and shame. Every once in a while, it pops back up, but I think that's normal. And with time it will happen less and less frequently. I'm keeping busy with classes and my job at the clinic, and whatever free time I have is filled with Liam. If anyone had told me on that first day—the day I dumped my raspberry lemonade on him—that just a few months later I would be completely in love with Liam, I would have told them they were crazy. Insane. Loony. Nutty as a fruitcake. But look at me now. The thought makes me laugh.

I feel movement behind me. An arm hooks around my waist and pulls me back until my whole body is enveloped in Liam's.

"What are you laughing about?"

He nuzzles into my hair and speaks into my neck. His voice is rough and low with sleep, the heat from his bare skin warming mine. I love the feel of him all around me. Love the way his arm pulls me into his chest and how I can feel his hardness nestled onto my bottom. Gosh, I could wake up like this every day and be happy. Also save a ton on pajamas since the first thing Liam does when he comes to my bed is to strip me naked. He says he never wants to have anything between us again. Not even clothes.

"Nothing really, I was just thinking about that first day we met and how far from that day we've come."

He manages to nuzzle even deeper into my back and hold me tighter.

"I wanted to kiss you so bad that day."

"What?" I push away so I can turn and face him. "What do you mean you wanted to kiss me? You were so angry, I thought you were going to hit me."

"I'd never hit you and I was angry, but not at you. I was mad at myself because you took me by surprise and when I saw you, all I wanted to do was taste on your mouth whatever that drink was that you dumped on me."

"You did?" Wow. I can't believe this. Would've never guessed. Not in a million years.

"So, so much. And when my brother put his arm around you, I thought you were his girlfriend and I got even more pissed off because then you'd be off-limits and, in my mind, I already had you bent over the hood of that truck."

"Hmm . . . I don't think you can bend me over the hood of the truck. It's pretty high. It could never happen."

"Oh, I can make it happen, believe me."

"I'm not so sure. Maybe you need to give me some visuals."

Yeah, he does give me some visuals. And I believe him.

# CHAPTER FIFTY-SIX

## Liam

The bastard kicked me out of the house. Like for good. I don't mean for just the day or the weekend or a week. I mean, this morning Logan suggested that maybe I want to sleep in the dorms and get the full college experience and I replied, "Why would I want to give up my comfortable home and share a room barely bigger than a prison cell with a complete stranger?"

He has a good reason why I need to get out of the house. Great even, and he wants me to do it soon. Heck, I don't blame him. If it were me in his place, I would probably do the same.

Then I imagine me in his place and find myself smiling. *Lucky bastard.* He's sure she's going to agree with him, but I figure I'll wait to hear the actual words. Maybe I can do the same.

Well, not exactly the same. I don't think River and I are quite there yet, but I know we will be. I don't want to freak her out. Baby steps. We can probably just start with a simple swap. Because I'll need a place to stay and there's no way I'm staying in a dorm.

Maybe when I was eighteen, but not at twenty-four. I imagine sharing a room with an eighteen-year-old kid and shudder. I've seen too much, lived too much to be able to try to fit in with the kids around me. I have made some new friends in my classes, but for the most part it's superficial. I seem to intimidate other guys. The girls, on the other hand, they don't get intimidated at all.

Until they see River, that is. One glare from her and they all scurry away. Yesterday she told me I'm too hot for my own good. Best compliment ever.

Part of me can't believe Logan is popping the question to Skye and part of me can't believe it took this long. He's crazy about her. Spends every free minute with her and schedules his shifts around her work and classes. Skye is doing great at the newspaper and going for her master's at the same time.

River is going for her master's in Psychology and I'm in my second semester of pre-med, thanks to all the summer classes I took. I love it. But not enough to get a dorm on campus.

If River says no to what I have in mind, I'll have to scramble to find a place fast.

## CHAPTER FIFTY-SEVEN

# River

"What do you mean you're moving out?" My voice rises up a few decibels.

One might expect her twin sister not to be so giddy when giving the news that she's moving out. Out of the place we've shared for over four years.

We have never lived apart. Never.

Don't get me wrong. I'm all for Skye finding her own way, standing on her own two feet and all that, but I never saw this coming. Skye was always the one who wanted to do everything together. The one who kind of depended on me. She may be older by three minutes, but I was always the leader and Skye the follower. I always imagined it would be me first venturing into the world alone.

And it always worried me I would break her heart a little by leaving her alone. Why is it then my heart feels a little broken right now?

"I'm moving out, River. I need to pack and get rid of my dingy stay-in clothes and buy some casual clothes and new underwear. You have to go shopping with me and force me to buy the racy stuff I know I won't buy if I go alone."

She's so excited, her voice comes out in spurts between breaths and giggles. I think my sister is high.

"Are you high? Did you smoke some pot? No, that would make you mellow," I answer myself. "Are you on crack or something?"

That seems to get her back down from the cloud nine she's been floating on.

"What? No! Of course not. You know I don't do drugs. I don't even like to take an aspirin."

I know this, my twin, the goody-goody girl who never goes over the speed limit, much less ventures into illegal drugs. I've never been into any of that stuff either. Okay, I tried pot once in high school. Skye was too chicken to even go near it and made sure to stay downwind. God forbid she accidentally inhaled it.

"Skye, you are freaking me out over here. I don't understand what you are saying. I hear the words and it sounds like you said you are moving out and I will have this place all to myself, but it doesn't make any sense."

She takes a deep breath and settles as her body relaxes into the sofa we're both sitting on. Then, she shows me her left hand. And I see it. A beautiful white gold ring. A diamond encircled in topaz stones, the blue color nearly identical to her eyes.

I hold her hand in mine and look between her and the ring a few times.

"Is this what I think it is?"

"Yes!"

My free hand covers my mouth, holding in the gasp and surprise. My eyes start to mist and before I know it, we have our arms wrapped around each other.

"Oh my God, Skye," I speak into her hair. "He proposed? Logan proposed? How? When? How? Tell me everything." I demand, pulling away from her so I can see her face.

She grabs the baby blue pillow behind her and hugs it to her chest.

"It was just so sweet and so romantic. I feel like I'm in a dream still." Her eyes drift upward in thought.

"You're killing me with the suspense. Tell me already."

She giggles.

"You know how he's been trying to teach me to ice skate for weeks now?"

"Yes, I saw the big purple mark on your ass from the last time you went."

"Well, he took me to the rink last night after closing time. We had the whole place to ourselves. It was dark, except for the lights right over the ice. And there were all these songs playing that they usually don't play at the rink. They were slow and sweet and all the lyrics were about loving someone. A Thousand Years by Christina Perri—"

"I love that song!" I interrupt her.

"I know, I do too. All my favorite love songs were playing. 'I'm Falling Even More in Love With You' by Lifehouse, 'Truly, Madly, Deeply' by Savage Garden, but I still didn't think much of it. I was concentrating too hard on not falling on my ass."

She stops, a dreamy look on her face.

"Tell me, woman! What happens next?"

"We're skating—or rather, he's skating. I'm wobbling around like a drunk duck—and then all the lights go off. It's pitch-black dark. He tells me to stay where I am. Not to move. He's going to check out what happened with the lights. I stand there for a few seconds. I'm afraid to move and then 'Marry Me' by Train starts playing. And I think it's weird that the music is playing when the place is completely dark because I thought it was a power outage. When the song gets to that part that says marry me, a single spotlight comes on, right where I am, and he's kneeling before me, holding the ring in his hand."

My mouth drops open. That's just about the most romantic thing I ever heard. I squeal. Skye squeals and then we're hugging again and I'm crying.

Fuck this shit! I do not cry. Not for this girly stuff. I'm not a crybaby, except that right now I am. I'm so happy for Skye. She is such a pure-hearted person. She deserves this. She deserves her little piece of heaven. And Logan is just the guy to give it to her.

"Oh my God, Skye. That is so sweet. And then what?"

"I said yes, of course." She giggles some more, happy tears still streaming down her face. She's glowing with happiness. "I was so surprised. I had no idea he was planning on asking me. No clue at all."

I huff at that. "Please. He's crazy about you. Anyone with eyes can see it."

"I know he loves me. He tells me he does often enough, but after the fiasco with his ex, and his own parents' messed-up marriage, I thought that maybe he would be like one of those guys who never makes the jump."

"Okay, so what happened next?"

"He put the ring on my finger, kissed me and said he loved me, and said the most beautiful things. We went back to his place, and he made love to me with such adoration, River. It was magical. I mean, it's always good, but last night it was special. It had more meaning somehow. He had to go to work this morning and just dropped me off. Saying goodbye, even if for just a few hours, is so hard. I don't think my feet have touched the ground yet."

"I'm so happy for you, Skye."

We hug again.

"Thank you, River. Gah! I think I'm gonna cry again."

I laugh. She hasn't stopped crying since she showed me the ring. Which reminds me of my original question.

"Okay, I get you two are getting married, but it is not happening right away, right? What is this talk about moving?"

"Logan wants me to move in with him. And I said yes. I practically spend more time there than here anyway." She squeezes my hand in hers.

"I want this, River. I want to be with him. I want to live with him and wake up next to him every morning and have breakfast together, fall asleep with him. I want it so bad."

I nod at my sister. I understand. What they have is rare and special. They don't want to waste any time apart.

"I hope you're not mad at me for just leaving without talking to you first."

"I'm not," I'm quick to assure her. "But what about Liam? Won't it be weird living with the two of them? You won't have a lot of privacy."

"Well . . ." She hedges, her eyes shifting.

"What? What aren't you telling me?"

"Logan asked Liam to move out. He asked him to move into the dorms."

I snort at that. Liam, living in the dorms? Sharing the small space with some freshman guy? Then I remember that the undergrad buildings are all coed and it does not sit well with me. Not at all. *Jealous much, River?*

"There's no way Liam will agree to moving to the dorms. No way."

"Well . . ." Skye repeats herself.

"Spit it out, Skye."

"You're right. Logan said he talked to Liam, and he refused to move into the dorms. Liam said he will find a place to rent, but in the meantime, he is staying put."

"Okay, that's not so bad. Liam will find—"

"Then I suggested that since I'm moving there, he could have my room and now he's moving here tomorrow." The last seven words were said in a rush, without any spaces in between them. Andnowheismovingheretomorrow

"What? You kind of mumbled something there at the end that sounded a lot like 'and now he is moving here tomorrow,' but I know that can't be, because my sister would not invite a man to move in with me without first talking to me, would she? Please tell me I didn't hear you right."

"Well . . ." It's the third time she says "well" in as many minutes. I'm starting to fear the word.

"It is not like he's a random man. It's Liam. Your boyfriend. And it's not permanent. Just until he finds a place of his own to rent."

I get up and start moving about the room. I can't just sit there and calmly speak while my insides are twisting around like trapped tornado with nowhere to go.

"Not permanent? A place of his own?" My hands move around like they're having seizures. "You do know this is a college town, right? And that every rental place in a ten-mile radius is either already taken, too expensive, or it sucks. Liam won't find a place close enough to Riggins. Not any time soon. Not until the semester ends and some people graduate and move away."

She opens her mouth.

"Do not say 'well' again, or so help me God . . ." I don't finish. Whatever I was going to say would not have been good and I don't want to put a damper on Skye's joy right now.

My head drops to my chest and I run my fingers through my hair. It's so long now. I haven't cut it in months. My insides churn at the idea of Liam moving in with me. The part of me that's scared about it is pissed at the part of me that's all too happy about the idea of having Liam at my fingertips all the time. Ugh. My hands drop and I sit back on the sofa, facing Skye. Her face is a juxtaposition of emotions. Eagerness, worry, happiness. I heave a heavy breath.

"Okay, I guess it's okay if he takes your room and stays here for a while. But I'm not doing his laundry or picking up after him."

She lunges at me, both of us falling back on the sofa.

"Thank you, thank you, thank you. And you don't have to worry about Liam. He's a neat freak. Logan said he was not like this before going into the marines, but he came back a clean freak and he's always putting stuff away and cleaning things up. You are in luck. It will probably be him doing your laundry and picking up after your sloppy ass."

"Doing my laundry is a plus. And my ass is not sloppy. I have it on good authority that my ass is fantastic. You could bounce a quarter off it."

Skye giggles.

"I want to bounce something off that ass for sure."

Skye and I both jump and turn to see Liam standing just inside the door. *Yeah*. Of course, he had to come in just in time to hear me talking about my quarter-bouncing ass.

And he already has a box in his hand. So much for waiting until tomorrow to move in with me.

If the lust-hungry look on his face is any indication of his thoughts on this idea, I'd have to say Liam is just as happy to be moving in as Skye is to be moving out.

I'm screwed.

# CHAPTER FIFTY-EIGHT

## Liam

"I'll go finish packing," Skye announces before floating down the hall. Yes, floating. I don't think her feet touched the ground. She's high on happiness. My brother is a lucky bastard and so is she. Lucky, that is. Not a bastard. I'd never call a girl a bastard.

I look at River from my spot just inside the front door. I'm trying to gauge how she feels about my moving in. I didn't catch the whole of their conversation. Just the last part. If I were a betting man, I'd bet that the whole convo was about me moving in. Wait? I did have a few bets with River, so I guess it does make me a betting man.

She looks at me with a mixture of apprehension and joy. I know she's happy to see me, but I also know we're kind of early in our relationship if one is counting days and weeks and months, but we've also shared a shitload of stuff that most people never have to deal with, and it has brought us closer somehow.

All of our insecurities and cracked pieces fit together and fill each other's gaps. Our weaknesses together make us stronger.

She watches me in silence as I walk into the room and drop the box I'm carrying on top of the dining table. I walk back to her and sit on the coffee table across from her. She has one leg folded under her, the other on the floor. I reach over to her and grab her hips, pulling her to the edge of the couch. She comes willingly, both of her bare feet on the floor now. I slide my hands up her sides and over her shoulders until I'm cupping her face in my hands and then I kiss her. Just a gentle touch of lips. Just a taste before we talk. I nibble at her lower lip and her mouth parts. The tip of her tongue teases me and that's the end of my good intentions, of just giving her a hello kiss.

This kiss goes from sweet and innocent to R rated in three seconds flat. I pull her closer and she climbs onto my lap, straddling me on the coffee table. My arms wrap around her back, melding her into me. And from then on, all rational thought is lost. There are only sensations and feelings.

Her hard nipples on my chest. Her legs around my hips, the heat of her center on my cock, the taste of her mouth on mine, the silkiness of her hair brushing my arms, the tremble of her skin under my fingertips. The sounds of our shallow breaths filled with little moans and grunts.

It is fierce, it is raw and honest and beautiful. I love this River.

The River who hides nothing, who gives all, who takes all.

She's mine. Mine. Mine. Mine.

The possessiveness surprises me. I have never felt this way before. It overwhelms me and scares me, but I don't pull back. I don't retreat. I push forward past the fear and break through it. More than break through it. I embrace it. I recognized it for what it is. I look it in the eye and man up. There's no going back from here. Realization washes over me. I don't want to anyway.

I love this girl. I love this girl. I love this girl. And this is it.

# CHAPTER FIFTY-NINE

## River

So much for talking and trying to figure out the new living situation. I do have to say I can see some advantages to having Liam here. But part of me is afraid this is too much, too soon. That being thrust together under the same roof, will somehow push us apart. We already live mere yards away from each other. We go to the same college and even share a class. He drives me to and from school. And we have meals together with our siblings a few times a week. He spends half of his nights here. It already feels like we are living together, but now we will actually be under the same roof. *Will it be too much?*

All those thoughts running through my mind are promptly pushed aside as soon as his lips touch mine. Before I know it, I'm on him, straddling his lap, and we are wrapped around each other. His mouth on mine, his tongue explores, and he nibbles as he tastes me.

When his lips part from mine, it's to run alongside my jaw and neck and I can feel him inhaling me as his arms tighten around my back. Shivers run across my skin, leaving a trail of goose bumps behind. He's breathing as hard as I am and I can feel him so hard against me, so hot. I'm about to combust and then it hits me—the irony that the only guy who can set me on fire like this is also the only one who can put it out.

"Liam . . ."

I don't know if I'm asking him to keep going or to stop. I want to finish what we just started, but I also know we need to talk this out and make sure living together will not complicate things. But maybe the talk can wait a little, because his hands are coming to my sides and they brush the side of my breasts and God, he knows how much I like when he does this.

*Later.*

We can talk later. I'm about to rip my own shirt off when a loud noise startles me and I remember we're not alone. Skye is just down the hall, a room away. *Ugh. Get a hold of yourself, River.*

Liam must come to the same conclusion because his head drops to my shoulder and his hands are loose around my hips. His breath comes out shallow and fast. After a moment he gently disengages me from him and sits me back on the couch before taking the other end of it and grabbing a pillow to hide his erection.

And not a moment too soon, as we can hear Skye walking back to the living room.

I can't help my smirk when I glance at the innocent baby blue pillow being violated by Liam in his attempt to hide the effect I have on him. It's a heady feeling knowing I did that. His eyes are dark with lust. They zero in on my breasts. I'm wearing a tank top and no bra. No hiding that my nipples are probably as hard as his dick. He's the one smirking now.

Skye walks in and is completely oblivious to the heated stare between us. I don't know how she can miss it. It feels like it's a thousand degrees here. She's puttering around and drags a suitcase into the room, then goes back down the hall. The front door opens again and Logan comes in. Jesus, no one knows how to knock before they walk in?

"Hey, aren't you supposed to be working?" I ask Logan, who's in uniform.

"I'm on a break." His eyes go from Liam to me and back.

Well, Skye may have been oblivious to the lust hanging in the air between Liam and me, but Logan sure isn't. One look at the both of us and he's the one smirking. I can feel my face flaming. Liam just shrugs. Logan laughs, shakes his head, and walks down the hall. A moment later we hear Skye's squeals and her bedroom door close, followed by the clicking of the lock.

# CHAPTER SIXTY

## Liam

I CAN TELL RIVER IS NERVOUS ABOUT MY MOVING IN. AND I'm not sure myself if it's a good idea. Or how her parents will react to the news. We are too new and too fresh in our relationship and living together could be too much pressure. It can either derail everything or cement our connection.

We've known each other for six months and have been together for a little over four.

We've never discussed the whole dating thing. From that day on, from the day we found out about Jon and opened up to each other, the day we kissed for the first time, there was a mutual understanding, even if we never put words to it.

Maybe it's time we talked about it. But I'm nervous too. What if I say the wrong thing? What if she thinks I don't want to be with her?

"Wanna go for a ride?" I ask.

"Sure, where to?"

"Nowhere. Let's just get in the truck and see where it takes us."

She looks at me for a second longer than it should take to

answer the question, River, too, is trying to read me and figure how this move will affect us.

"Okay," she finally says. "Let me grab my stuff and get my shoes on."

We don't bother telling our siblings we're leaving. Five minutes later we are out the door and walking to my driveway where Grandpa's old truck is parked. I open the door for her and we are gone.

I drive aimlessly for ten minutes, getting away from town. No words are exchanged. The radio is on whatever was the last station Logan listened to. Some kind of rock country song plays softly, and it warms my heart when I remember this was Grandpa's favorite kind of song. He used to say, *"Country with just enough rock so you don't need the cowboy hat or boots to listen to it."* Grandpa had a quirky sense of humor. I pay attention to the words and it's as if this song was written for this specific moment.

*We came together,*
*When I never believed we could.*
*We came together,*
*When all odds were against us.*

*We came together,*
*And here we are at a standing still.*
*Sitting in this old truck*
*As the tires eat the miles on the road.*

*Where will the path take us?*
*Is it too soon to say I love you?*
*Where will the path take us?*

*Is it too soon to say I love you?*

*We came together,*
*When I never believed we could.*
*We came together,*
*When everyone doubted us.*
*We came together,*
*And out of our darkness, light was born.*
*We came together,*
*And took a chance on each other.*

*Where will the path take us?*
*Is it too soon to say I love you?*
*Where will the path take us?*
*Is it too soon to say I love you?*

*Can it ever be too soon to say I love you?*
*I love you.*
*I love you.*
*I love you.*

I glance at River and her eyes are ıxed on the radio. Can she hear the same thing I do? Can she read the meaning behind the words and if so, does she feel the same way I do? Is it too soon to say I love her?

And what if she doesn't feel the same way about me? What if she's just hanging on because of what she went through?

An old memory flickers to life when I see a sign on the side of the road.

Old Mill Lake.

I take the turn as if it had been my intention all along and not a result of my random driving. It's been years since I was last down this road, aptly named after the old mill on the edge of the lake. The stone structure is aged by time and weather. It's part of a nature preserve and the Historical Society keeps it in shape.

When we were kids, this was a favorite hangout for lazy summer afternoons. A bunch of teens would pile up in cars and drive up to the lake for a swim. There's a stone ledge we can climb and jump into the lake from. It's deep enough to be safe.

Today, it's just us driving down the two-lane road winding through the trees. At this time in the morning on a mid-September weekday, most people are either at work or school.

Neither one of us has school or work today. Mondays are a free day for us, handpicked so we could extend the weekend and avoid the most hated day of the week.

I bring the truck closer to the lake, turn it around, and park facing away from the shore.

River raises an eyebrow at me but doesn't say anything. She hops out of the truck and I turn to the back and grab the blankets and overstuffed pillows I know Logan always keeps behind the driver's seat.

I jump on the back of the truck and spread the thick blanket over the truck bed along with the second, lighter blanket and the two overstuffed pillows.

River's eyebrow hikes up a little higher.

"Looks like you have a plan in mind."

"No, no plan. I didn't even think of this place until I saw the sign on the side of the road."

I hop off the truck and take her hand.

"Let's go for a walk."

Her hand feels right in mine. Our fingers lace and fit like pieces of a puzzle.

It's a bright day, not warm or cold. The kind of day that feels good while you're in the sun but gets a little chilly in the shade. We walk along the side of the lake in the direction of the mill. Pebbles and sand crunch under our feet. A soft wind blows and carries the sounds of nature in the breeze. The chirping of birds and insects, the water lapping on the shore, our breaths and all the thoughts in our heads, unspoken but too loud all the same.

"I used to come here when I was a kid and jump off that ledge." I point at the stone ramp coming off the side of the mill.

"It looks like fun. And a little scary. You can never tell what's under the dark water."

Her words make me think of Grandpa again.

"Grandpa used to say people are like water. Some are clear and you can see right into their souls. Kids are like clear waters. Most people are a little muddled. If you wait long enough so what's churning them stops, and the sediment falls to the bottom, they too became clear. And if they allow that sediment to stay down, it will eventually become the foundation of everything they build upon. And some—some are like dark, deep waters. Try as you might you may never see into them."

She stops and looks up at me, deep in thought.

"Which one are you?" she asks.

I think about it. If anyone had asked me this question a few months ago, I would've certainly answered the dark waters. But today I'm not so sure. Today I think I've stopped churning long enough for the sediment to go down. Today I can see all that I've gone through as the foundation on which I can build my life. With River by my side if she'll have me.

# CHAPTER SIXTY-ONE

## River

"I THINK I'M IN THE MIDDLE AND I THINK I HAVE STOPPED churning," he says.

I squeeze his hand. "I think I've stopped churning too."

The rest of the walk is done in silence. We're both in our heads and in each other's minds. I can tell by the way he glances at me, by the way his body brushes against mine, when we get to the mill and walk through the narrow opening into it. There's nothing inside but the stone walls, high wooden beams, and the mill wheel in the center.

We make our way back to the truck and Liam helps me up into the back and onto the blankets.

I lean on a pillow and turn to face him.

"Are we going to talk about it?"

Liam reaches to me and tucks a lock of hair behind my ear.

"I'm a little scared."

Finally. I let out a breath. I'm not alone in this.

"I'm a little scared too."

He smiles then and his smile is all the confirmation I need

that he still wants to be with me even if like me, he thinks that living together might be a mistake.

"We should set some ground rules. Make sure we're not stepping on each other's toes," he says.

"I agree."

"As much as I love sleeping with you, I think we should keep separate bedrooms. It will give us both an extra layer of privacy."

Oh, thank God. I was so worried he'd feel obligated to share a bed every night.

"We'll probably end up in each other's beds anyway, but I agree. There might be times in which we just need some space," I say.

"And I'll pay for half of the rent and expenses. We also have to figure out chores and who does what."

"My parents pay for the rent—"

"River, I'm not taking advantage of your parents like that. Whatever the cost for rent and utilities is, I'll pay for half of it. I have money saved from all the years in service. I never spent much of it. I also have a trust fund I've never touched."

*Sorry subject.* "Okay," I appease him. "You can pay for half of everything. I'm not sure how much that will be. I'll have to ask my parents."

"Sorry," he apologizes.

I smile. "No worries. Now, about meals. Neither one of us can cook. Maybe you can use that rent money for takeout."

He grimaces. "I can't do takeout every day, but maybe we can learn to cook. I saw an ad on a board at Riggins. This chef comes to your house and teaches you how to cook. He teaches you everything, goes to the store with you, tells you what to buy and then how to prepare, cook, and freeze leftovers."

"That sounds cool. I think it would be fun and with a pro there, I'm sure we can have something edible."

"Okay, I'll take care of that and pay for it. It'll count toward my half of the expenses. Now, for the chores, what do you absolutely hate?"

"This is going to take a while."

He laughs. "Okay, how about I take care of all the floors, bathroom, garbage, and my own laundry? And you can do the dusting and cleaning up after meals? And we can adjust as needed."

I think on it. It sounds fair. The apartment is small, and Skye said he's a clean freak, which I can attest to if his bedroom at Logan's is something to go by.

I give him my hand to shake on, but Liam has other ideas. He tucks me under him and with the grace of a panther, he pulls the spare blanket over us.

In the next second he's kissing me and the moment his lips touch mine, all my doubts and fears are forgotten. There's nothing but the heat of his body on mine, the press of his thigh between mine, the hardness of his erection on my hip. His hands pull me closer still. One tangles into my hair and the other curves over my ass, lifting me to him.

He moves completely in between my legs now and presses into my center, grinding into me. His tongue in my mouth mimics the rhythm of his hips.

Glorious sensations wash over me, the layers of fabric not in the least able to stall the orgasm building inside of me, I break the kiss and gasp for air. I open my eyes and see Liam's beautiful face, framed by the bluest of skies, and in his gray eyes, the promise of much more. My whole body shudders under his when I let go of the last of my worries and come undone.

# CHAPTER SIXTY-TWO

## Liam

"I LOVE TO MAKE YOU COME. I LOVE THE SOUNDS YOU make and how your skin heats up under my touch. I love the look of pleasure on your face and how your eyes go darker with lust. But more than anything else, I love that I'm the one doing this to you."

Her lips part, but no words are said. Even without them, I can still read all the questions and doubts in her mind. She's wondering if this thing we have between us is more than lust and like, if it's more than friction and heat, if it's more than either one of us is willing to admit right now.

I won't say the words outright, but I can say everything else and show her. We're not ready for more right now, but I hope we will be soon.

She says nothing still. Instead, her fingers tread through my too long hair and she pulls me to her and kisses me with such tenderness and love, it makes me feel like I can melt into her, like we can fuse together into a single symbiotic being.

We stay in that kiss, in that embrace, in the light touch of lips and mingled breathes until the crunch of tires on gravel tell us we have company. I disengage and lie next to her, a few inches between our bodies now, a wall of modesty for public eyes growing between us.

I cross my arms behind my head and glance at River. She closes her eyes, nestles further into the blanket and pillow, and lifts her face to the sun, drinking in the moment of peace and contentment. I follow her lead and do the same.

A couple of minutes later I hear steps and a gravelly voice.

"Good morning, folks."

I open my eyes and a park ranger stands by the tailgate of the truck, arms crossed over his chest. I come up on my elbows.

"Good morning, Officer."

"What are you kids up to?"

I look at River, who for all accounts looks like is deep into a nap. But I know better. She's letting me take the heat for this one.

"Just enjoying the beautiful day, sir. It's been a long time since I've been here."

He eyes us, making sure nothing nefarious is happening.

"Is she okay?" the park ranger asks.

I nudge River and her eyes flutter and open. She blinks a couple of times. Then casually glances toward the ranger and looks surprised.

"Oh, I guess I fell asleep." She sits up and stretches, pushing her chest out, and bestows the ranger with a smile that could melt the polar caps.

*Jesus!*

I know she's beautiful. I'm not blind to that. But River has never, not once used her looks and that smile on me. She's putting a show for this guy and that tells me how much she's aware of her appearance and how much she goes out of her way to tone it down when most girls would probably be flaunting their looks.

The ranger's cheeks go red and he stammers.

"Ok-okay, folks. Stay safe." He touches his hat and tips it at us, turning away, but not before giving me a look that says, *lucky bastard.* I grin at him like an idiot. Yes, I am.

---

It's been five weeks since we officially moved in together. It's been fine, but it's also been a little odd. River is not herself. I can tell she's holding back and treading carefully, trying to still be with me but at the same time not giving in and completely relaxing into this living arrangement. She's keeping her guard up. I gave her time to get used to the idea of me being here. But I'm afraid she's still worried about what all of this means. I haven't brought up moving out and to be honest I don't want to move out. I like this. I like hanging out with her. I like us driving to school together, watching movies, helping each other study. And I like learning to cook. We both enjoy preparing meals together. We even ventured into trying new recipes and we're getting really good at it.

I don't want to wait any longer. I can't wait any longer.

I glance at River. She's lying on the couch, her feet on my lap, watching a cooking show on the TV. I pick up the remote and pause the show.

She looks at me, an eyebrow raised in question.

I take her in. She's wearing one of my T-shirts and no pants. I love no-pants River. I love all of her versions.

"I want my River back," I say and hold on to her feet in purple socks with unicorns all over them.

"You don't have a River," she challenges me.

"But I do. And she is beautiful and untamed. She is sweet and infuriating. She is completely and utterly inappropriate ninety-five percent of the time and she should come with a warning. Mamas should cover their kids' ears any time she is around, and she is definitely not safe for work."

I move her feet off my lap and kneel on the floor next to her, smile, and graze her bottom lip with my thumb. "But she is mine and I want her back."

Her eyes search mine for the truth in my words.

"She is mine and I love everything about her. I love her lips and the crazy words that come out of them and I especially love when she says dick."

River snickers.

"I love that when she enters a room, she fills it with so much life that there's no possible way I can ignore her. And I tried, girl, I tried." I lean in until my forehead touches hers. I take a deep breath in, inhaling her scent, then I pull back a few inches so I can look her in the eyes.

"I love the way she moves as if she owns the entire world and I love that she does not give a rat's ass what anyone thinks. She's her own woman, and she doesn't need anyone's approval or permission. And I love that one day she told me *'Not one drop of my worth depends on your acceptance of me,'* and those words reminded me that I was the only one blaming myself. That I was the only one unwilling to accept that none of the things that happened to me were in any way my fault or a reflection of my self-worth."

She blinks and all mirth is gone from her face. Her eyes search mine.

"You made me more than I was. You made me a whole person again. You filled all my dark places with light and laugher, and you did it over and over again until there was nothing left but you inside of me. You have filled my heart and soul so completely with joy and love that I learned to forgive myself and I learned to let go of the guilt and pain I carried with me for so many years."

"I did that?" she asks me on a whisper.

"You did more than that, River. You taught me to love and you are teaching me still."

I take a deep breath, filling my lungs with air and River. I want her in every way possible.

"I love you, River. I'm in love with you and I think—I hope—you're a little bit in love with me too."

# CHAPTER SIXTY-THREE

## River

"You love me?" I hear myself ask.

Part of me knows this. Part of me hopes Liam loves me, but I've been afraid to trust myself. Part of me believes I'm tainted goods, not deserving of someone as beautiful inside and out as Liam.

That's the damage rape causes. It's not just the physical. The physical damage is easier to get over. The body heals, cells regenerate, scars fade, but the anguish, the thoughts, the self-recrimination, the what-ifs—those stay far longer than anyone can guess or predict.

I may forget about it for hours and even days, but then something happens, and it comes right back, fresh and intrusive like a paper cut. Invisible to most, but you know it's there, and it hurts.

"I do, I love you," Liam says. "I've been in love with you for a while now. But I've been waiting and biding my time. I don't want to put any pressure on you. I don't want you to feel obligated to say the words back to m—"

"I love you too," I'm quick to reply. I can see the hope in his eyes and also a little bit of fear. Fear that I won't love him back.

His hand goes to my chest and my heart responds by picking up speed. I mimic his gesture and press my palm to his chest too. His heart responds to mine. We stay like this, looking into each other's eyes, feeling each other's hearts under the palms of our hands.

Our hearts have a conversation of their own. Our lips follow their example and communicate without words. The kiss starts slow, teasing, just a touch, a light caress, a taste. Then a nibble, a lick, and the intensity grows. Liam is on the move now. He comes to the couch and settles on top of me, but he holds most of his weight on his hands and knees. He can't touch me, but my hands are free and I make good use of them, tracing every muscle, every dip and ridge I can reach. I start with his biceps, travel up to his shoulders and back, cop a feel of his backside, then trace my fingers alongside the edges of the shorts low on his hips.

Liam moans into my mouth. His arms tremble on either side of my shoulders. Muscles flex when his hands claw at the couch with the effort of holding himself up when I know all he wants to do is to drop his weight. I give him a nudge by wrapping my legs around his thighs and pulling him into me.

I love the feel of his body on top of mine. Love the weight of him and how he fits so perfectly in the space between my open legs. I push my hips up into him, nibble his bottom lip, and break the kiss.

"Liam?"

"Yeah?" His eyes are dark with lust and alight with love.

"You have too many clothes on."

His chuckle reverberates through my entire body.

"What are you going to do about it?"

I show him.

My hands grab at the waistband of his shorts and I push them down his hips as far as I can and use my feet and legs to do the rest. It's awkward and funny and we're both laughing. Next, I pull his T-shirt up. He shifts his weight, and I pull one arm out at a time. He's naked on top of me. The heat of his skin spreads fire on mine.

"Now, who has too many clothes on?"

I shift under him in response and tug my—err . . . his T-shirt off. My bare chest meets his when he lowers his body onto mine again. My nipples press into his hard chest. My stomach clenches in anticipation.

He lifts his body a little and looks into the small space between us. I look too and I'm gifted with a vision I want burned into my mind forever. Ripples of taught muscles and a proud and erect cock rests millimeters above my belly.

Liam leans against the back of the couch. His free hands trace the contours of my waist and hip and hooks on the side of my panties. He works his magic and takes them off me with one hand. I help by lifting my hips and I'm rewarded with the feel of his hardness against me.

We're both naked now. Skin on skin. Heat building between us and we haven't done much more than kiss. The couch doesn't give us much room to move, but our bodies press and push into each other, wanting, seeking, needy.

"Fuck!" he says, frustration clear in his voice.

"What?"

"Condom. It's all the way back in the bedroom."

The bedroom may as well be miles away instead of a few yards. Neither one of us wants to stop.

"Liam?"

"Yeah?" God, he's beautiful.

I hesitate. Look away from him, buying an extra second before I speak.

"I'm on the pill."

His stare is so intense I have to look away. My teeth nibble on my bottom lip, but it's too late to take the words back. What if he doesn't want me like that? Bare? What if the idea disgusts him because of what happened before. What if—

He shuts down the train wreck of thoughts in my mind with a kiss so fierce it bruises my lips. A second later he's sliding inside of me. No hesitation, no pause, no holding back. He fills me up completely and shudders. Our lips part and his forehead touches mine, then drops to my shoulder.

"Oh, God . . ." he moans into my neck.

"I have . . ."

Thrust.

"Never . . ."

Thrust.

"Ever . . ."

Thrust

"Been . . ."

Thrust.

"Bare with anyone else before."

He stills inside of me this time. His hold on me tightens. He's trembling, his skin covered in shivers. I hold Liam to me, wrapping myself around him, arms, legs and soul.

"So good, so good, so good, babe."

His lips find mine, gentle, commanding, giving. He moves again—ripples of pleasure take over me, sail over my skin, roll under my spine, awaken a hunger in my body that demands satisfaction. I move with him, meeting each of his thrusts with one of my own. I lace my fingers into his hair, tugging him to me closer still.

Our bodies move, find a tempo, building, building, building until I'm ready to explode.

Crescendo.

When the orgasm hits us—his and mine in synchronicity —it rips through us both, hot, blissful, a high like no other. It comes at me like a tsunami on a loop. Wave after wave of pleasure ripples over my body. I'm overtaken by a pleasure so intense, it hurts. It hurts in the best of ways. My lungs are robbed of air. My body convulses in sweet agony. It lasts seconds, minutes, days. All of eternity, contained in a moment of pure bliss.

Liam's body, still thrumming with rapid breaths, takes an extra minute to relax into mine. My own breath is shallow and rapid. As each heartbeat slows to normal, the weight of satisfaction settles over me like a warm blanket and I can feel myself drifting to sleep.

I wake up hours later in my own bed with Liam curled around me. Big spoon and little spoon style. The memory of him moving inside of me bare sends tingles over my skin. I don't remember getting to my own bed. Liam must have carried me. I can't believe I slept through it, and it feels like he cleaned me up too. A tinge of embarrassment mingles with a latent desire. Knowing he carried me and cleaned me up touches something inside of me, makes me feel more than loved, makes me feel cherished.

Liam's arm tightens around my waist, and he pulls me even closer to him.

"Hey," he murmurs into my hair. "You passed out on me. Scared me a little."

I turn just enough so I can look at him, the extra inch of space between our bodies already making me miss the touch of his bare skin on mine.

"Knocked out by orgasms." I giggle.

The smile that takes over his face is so full of pride and self-satisfaction, it makes me laugh louder.

"Well, luckily for you, I'm a corpsman and well trained in CPR and mouth-to-mouth."

"Yeah, want to show me some of that technique?"

He does. Again.

# CHAPTER SIXTY-FOUR

## Liam

It's Halloween. There are parties everywhere, but we decided to stay in. Logan and Skye will be stopping by soon to try one of our newly-learned dishes. River and I have become quite proficient at cooking.

Well, we can make about six or seven different meals really well and we rotate them with takeout, pizza, and Chinese. Because on some nights you just need General Tso's Chicken, and our culinary skills haven't expanded past Italy yet. Case in point, we're making pasta primavera tonight.

The doorbell rings again. Kids have been ringing the doorbell for the last hour. It started minutes after school ended for the day.

"I'll get it," River calls out to me.

I glance at her, taking in the sway of her hips as she walks to the door, grabbing a bucket of candy on the way. I sneak after her. She's been running to the door every time the bell rings. She's having as much fun passing out mini chocolate bars as the kids getting them. I watch as she waves to parents waiting by the curb and talks to the kids and jokes with them, making comments about their costumes in between all the "trick or treats" being thrown at her.

A vision of a future where we're the parents waiting at the curb and two little kids—our kids—walking up to someone's door dressed for Halloween swims in my mind. I cuddle the vision, holding it close.

Not yet. But one day, not too far in the future, it will be us. I can see our children. A spitfire little girl, as temperamental as her mother, and a boy with the patience of a saint.

I laugh at the images playing in my head and River hears me. She waves to the departing kids and closes the door.

"What?" she asks me.

I shake my head. I'm not ready to share my vision for our future just yet. "Nothing—just enjoying you enjoying the kids."

She walks up to me and goes on tiptoes to kiss me. The kiss goes from chaste to scorching at lightning speed. All the bumping and rubbing against each other while preparing dinner in the small kitchen tonight has left us on edge. Not that it takes much.

We're still kissing by the open apartment door when Logan and Skye come in from the outside, bringing a gust of cold wind with them. River shivers in my arms, but we both know it has nothing to do with the temporary drop in temperature.

"I could have you two arrested for lewd behavior, you know?"

Skye laughs.

We break apart, and River takes the offense.

"You two should talk. I had to sleep with earbuds on more times than I can count, Mr. and Mrs. ohmygodohmygodohmygod."

Logan laughs and high fives me. Skye being Skye, just blushes.

"Come on, let's eat!"

"You guys are getting really good at this cooking thing," Logan says as he picks up the empty plates and brings them to the kitchen sink. "I must confess, the first time you invited us over and said you were cooking, I was a little scared."

Skye sends a warning glare his way.

I look at River. "They had no faith in our culinary skills, babe."

"I had no faith in our culinary skills either," she says with a laugh. "Who could ever imagine me being all domestic and playing house?"

"I can," I say before I can hold my tongue.

River's focus is on me. Is that . . . hope I see in her eyes?

# EPILOGUE

## River

### Four Years Later

I can't believe we're done with school. Well, I'm done. For a while at least. I'll hold off on getting a PhD for a couple of years. Liam starts the second year of med school in the fall. I'm so proud of him. He finished undergrad in three years all the while holding a perfect 4.0.

I have a job waiting for me in the clinic I have worked in for the past six years and to no one's surprise, Liam never moved out. This roommate thing works well for us. I love waking up with him wrapped around me, especially in winter. The man is like a furnace. Who needs heat when I have Liam?

He's leaving a trail of kisses on my back and shoulders.

"What are thinking about?" he asks.

"About graduation. I can't believe I'm done with college."

"I'm so proud of you. You looked hot in your graduation gown." Liam turns me over, so I'm on my back now. He settles on top of me, his naked skin heating up mine. We're both naked. I don't think I have slept in PJs more than a handful of nights since he moved in. The man likes to sleep naked and demands I do the same. I secretly love it. And he probably knows I do too.

"I kept picturing you naked under that gown and imagining no one but me knew about it." The smile he gives me should be illegal in all fifty states.

"Perv!" I smack his shoulder and run my fingers through his much shorter hair now. I kind of miss the long locks, but Liam cut it shorter when he started med school. He said he needed to look like a doctor and not a hot mess. I told him he was a hot mess I liked to fuck. That bought me another two weeks with the long hair. But I get it, his need to look professional, whatever that means. So, it's short, but not so short I can't still grab it. Liam loves it when I grab at his hair.

"I got a video of you and Skye walking. Well, you walking and Skye wobbling. Logan was freaking out the whole time, afraid she would trip on the stairs and fall."

I giggle. "I know. He begged me to stay close to her and make sure she didn't trip. You'd think she was about to give birth and not three weeks away from her due date."

"She does look like she could tip over any minute with that huge belly. Logan is half terrified and half euphoric about being a dad."

There's a touch of longing in his voice. I pull his face to mine and kiss him. This is one of the things we never talk about. The future. It's always been one day at a time. It works for us, but sometimes I wonder.

All thoughts vanish when Liam deepens the kiss, taking it to another level, letting me know of his intentions for the next hour. His lips whisper silent promises into tiny kisses all over my face, neck, and shoulders. He lowers his head and finds my breasts.

Touching each other, kissing, tasting—this never gets old. Each time is better than the last. Every time he touches me, my skin responds. My body thrums with unreleased energy.

Liam is taking his time with me, but I'm impatient and I want him now. I tug at his hair and pull his head from his favorite place in my body.

"Come up here, Liam. I want you inside of me."

He complies.

"I'm drunk on the taste of you."

He enters me and I can't help the sounds that leave me. I moan.

His lips find mine and he kisses with everything he has. His hips move against mine. Ripples of pleasure dance on my skin. I'm simultaneously aware of every inch of my body and floating in the air, outside of myself.

Liam shifts on top of me and reaches for something on the side of the bed. I open my eyes in question. He moves inside me a few more times and stills.

"You feel so good all around me, River. So hot and soft. I think I could spend the rest of my life inside of you. I want the next one hundred years with your taste in my mouth and my dick in your pussy," he says.

"I love you and I love the way you feel inside me. All eight inches of you, but I don't think it's possible for you to spend the next one hundred years inside me," I joke.

He kisses me and smiles.

"You wanna bet?" he says.

Then he holds up a ring.

"River, I love you. And I want to spend as much time as possible with you just like this. I want to be so deep inside of you, inside of your heart, inside of your mind, inside of your soul, that nothing and no one can ever come between us. Please say yes. Please let me be the one holding you for the rest of our lives."

I glance at the ring and back at Liam and then at the ring again. It's beautiful. A center stone is surrounded by two smaller ones, set in white gold.

"Did you just propose to me? While we're naked and in bed?" I ask, because I have to make sure.

"While we're naked and in bed and fucking," he replies.

"Liam!"

"Is that a yes?"

"What am I going to say to my mother when she asks how you popped the question?"

"You'll say, 'Well, Mom, it was very romantic. Liam was dick deep inside of me and said he wanted to fuck me forever, so I had to say yes, of course, because no better looking or better tasting dick has ever existed and I had to put a ring on it. Not a literal ring on the dick. We don't really need that, but I'm sure Liam would do anything if I asked.'"

He grins at me. I'm silent for all of five seconds before I burst out laughing.

"I would too," he says, a serious tone now. "I'll do anything for you if you ask me. Anything. I love you. I love you more than I ever thought it possible to love someone, and I'm still waiting for that *yes*."

I give him my left hand. "Yes," I say.

He slides the ring on. Then he slides even deeper inside of me.

# EPILOGUE TO THE EPILOGUE

## River

We wake up a few hours later to the buzzing and ringing sounds of both our phones.

Disentangling our limbs, we reach for the phones at the same time.

I blink several times and try to focus on the alarm clock on the night table.

Who's calling at 4:49 am?

Liam reaches over me with his much longer arm and grabs both our phones from the table, hands me mine, and checks his phone while I try to focus on my screen.

We look at each other's phones and scramble out of bed at the same time.

*'I'm a mom'* and *'I'm a dad'* messages shine on the iPhone screens.

My phone rings and we both stop. I answer it.

"Skye?"

Her voice is a little strained, but calm.

"River, you are an auntie."

I squeal. "Oh my God! But, but, but—it's not time yet. You have another three weeks."

Liam jumps over the bed and comes to my side. I'm momentarily distracted by his nakedness.

"I guess babies have their own time schedule," she says.

"I'm an aunt, and you're an uncle." I grin at Liam.

"Are you okay? Is everything good? Did it hurt? And the babies? How's Logan?"

Words come tumbling off my lips and I'm bouncing on my feet. I'm so happy for my sister, my excitement can't be contained.

I hear Skye giggle.

"Everything is perfect."

That one word—perfect—answers all of my questions. Skye found in Logan a man who sees and loves her. She's a mom. I'm an aunt. Liam and I are getting married. Just one word to describe it all—perfect.

Relief and joy swell in my chest and spill out of my eyes. Liam's arms go around me in an instant. He presses my head to his chest, phone in my ear still.

"When can we come in?" I ask.

"Visiting hours start at nine. Logan wanted to wait until morning to call, but I knew you'd kick my ass if I didn't tell you right away. I wanted to call before, but my water broke in the middle of the night and the contractions started so fast, we didn't have time to do anything other than run to the hospital. The doctor was very surprised by how quick the labor developed, especially for being a first-time mother."

"I'm so happy for you."

Liam points at himself and makes the sign of a phone call with his hand.

"Liam says hi, and he's super excited to be an uncle too. Tell Logan to call him."

"I will. His hands are quite full right now, but I'm going to try to nurse and I'll tell him to call Liam."

"Okay, go nurse and rest. I'll see you in a few hours."

"Bye, Sis. I love you."

"Love you too, Skye."

---

LIAM

BEING in a hospital as a med student or as a visitor is quite different from being in a hospital as a patient. For a while I wondered if everything I went through in the service would taint me as a future doctor. But I now know it will give me an edge. I'll be able to relate to my future patients in a deeper level because of everything I experienced. Being in a hospital no longer feels like being in a prison. I'm not trapped by my wounds and scars. They no longer wear me down. I wear them with honor and pride. Every cut to my flesh and soul brought me here, and here is undiluted happiness.

I look at all the faces around me. Everyone has a story to tell and all of them have their dark moments. We all do. The key is not to dwell on those dark moments. The key is to use the dark to find the light. Because in the darkest nights, you can see even the smallest light. And that's all it takes to find your way out. Just follow that one small spark of light. I followed River's spark and I'll keep on following her forever.

I look at my twin nephews. Skye holds one and Logan the other. The tiny babies, wrapped in blue, make happy sounds in their parents' arms. I want this for myself. I want this with River. Her voice brings me back to the room.

"I still think you should name them River Two and River Three." She waves her hand at the babies—her left hand. The ring sparkles under the fluorescent lights above. I watch as Skye's eyes widen when she sees the ring.

"Is that a . . . ?" she asks River but doesn't finish the question.

River glances at me and gives away the answer to the question. I just smile. We decided not to say anything until Skye is back home, but I guess that plan failed.

Serena, the girls' mom, steps closer and takes River's hand. Logan looks at me. He already knows. I told him before I proposed and asked him to keep quiet about it. Skye's surprise is a good indication Logan didn't share my secret.

"When did this happen?" Serena asks River.

River gives me a look that tells me trouble is coming and then smirks.

*Oh, fuck!*

"Well, Mom. It was very romantic . . ."

# #MeToo

# A NOTE FROM THE AUTHOR

Dear reader:

I hope you enjoyed this book. If you did, please consider leaving a brief review.

Reviews are a writer's bread and butter. We need them. They help us evaluate our work, and they help us find other readers.

You can leave a review in one or more of the following:

Amazon
GoodReads
BookBub

# ACKNOWLEDGMENTS

Writing is a solitary endeavor, but that does not mean that we are alone in this author journey. The book you hold in your hands, be it virtual words on a device or a paperback, is just the tip of an iceberg made up of many people. People who stands in the shadows and behind the curtains. But their support and presence is no less important. While I can't name every person whom in one way or another guided and helped me in this journey, my heartfelt thanks travels across the universe to each of them, and each of you.

To my husband—my real life book boyfriend and the inspiration for all the sexy scenes, a man who knows the true meaning of ladies first (yes, I said it)—I'll love you across space and time and multiple life times.

To my two boys, who taught me the meaning of unconditional love. You are as excited as I am about every book. But no, you can't read them until you're at least 30.

Thank you Kristy Stalter deBoer for all the help in reading the final manuscript and your eagle eyes. Thank you Rachelle Westcott for being an awesome ARC reader.

I also want to thank my fellow authors in the Do Not Disturb Book Club. You guys have been a great source of knowledge and support. Dear reader, if you are not in our club, you need to join us. We have loads of fun every day.

And last, but not least, I want to say thanks to you, reading these words right now. Your support allows me to make a reality out of the stories.

Thank you for the kindness, for telling me the words I've written has touched you. You have no idea how meaningful it is to me that something I created has touched you. Because above all, as human beings, what we crave is connection. And words are a beautiful bridge between us.

Much love,
Erica.

## ALSO BY ERICA ALEXANDER

Would you like a signed paperback?
Find them at:
www.authorericaalexander.com/signed-paperbacks

---

### Because of Logan

Book One in the Riggins U Series

All her life *Skye Devereaux* has been content to live in the shadow of her beautiful and vivacious fraternal twin.

But when she meets a sexy and charming police officer, Skye decides she deserves more.

She's worthy of more.

Now she wants to throw off her introvert shell.

She wants to challenge her fears.

And she wants him.

So what if she's scared?

She'll fake it until she makes it.

*Logan Cole* left behind a life he never chose to live.

Being a cop gave him the escape he needed to be on his own.

With a past he'd rather forget, he holds everyone at bay.

But when chance brings him face-to-face with an intriguing and

So what if he's scared?

He just needs to figure out how to let her in while protecting his heart.

## Seventeen Wishes

*If knowing the truth could leave you more broken than believing the lies, would you still want to know it?*

This is a story about a boy and a girl.

About friendship.

Secrets.

Omission.

Fate.

About the lies we tell ourselves so we can hold on to hope.

About the lies we tell those we love to protect them.

About risking it all and the price one pays when choices are made.

But above all, this is a story about wishes, love and the hope we hold on to when there's nothing left to grasp.

There was never a time when Zac and Lilly hadn't been in each other's lives. They are neighbors, playmates, and best friends. But unknown to Lilly, she's also the love of his life.

And the reason for Zac's secrets.

Erica Alexander has been a storyteller her entire life. If she's not writing stories, she's daydreaming them. Which has gotten her in trouble once or twice. She has an inclination to use sarcasm and she can make anything that comes out of her mouth, sound dirty. It's a gift.

Erica's life goals are: to make sure her family is happy and healthy, bring to life all the stories in her head, visit Australia, and jump off a plane. Preferably with a parachute.

Erica has degrees in Communications and Computer Science and she loves history, all things Native American, and anything that's off the beaten path and weird.

You can find Erica at:
**www.authorericaalexander.com**

Join Erica's Reader Group:
**www.facebook.com/groups/EricasHEA/**

Sign up for her newsletter:
**https://tinyurl.com/EricasNL**

And at any of the places below:

facebook.com/AuthorEricaWrites

twitter.com/author_erica

instagram.com/authorericaalexander

pinterest.com/authorerica

tinyurl.com/EricasGR

amazon.com/default/e/B01LRQQG80/

bookbub.com/authors/erica-alexander

tinyurl.com/EricasYouTube